THE DARK ARMY

THE DARK ARMY

JOSEPH DELANEY

GREENWILLOW BOOKS
An Imprint of HarperCollins*Publishers*

The Dark Army
Copyright © 2016 by Joseph Delaney
First published in 2016 in Great Britain by The Bodley Head,
an imprint of Random House Children's Books,
under the title The Starblade Chronicles: The Dark Army.
First published in 2016 in the United States by Greenwillow Books.

The text of this book is set in 12-point Venetian 301 BT.
Book design by Paul Zakris

Library of Congress Control Number: 2016947345

ISBN 978-0-06-233456-5 (hardback)

16 17 18 19 20 PC/RRDH 10 9 8 7 6 5 4 3 2 1

 Greenwillow Books

FOR MARIE

FOR MARY

We face a dark army, but its whole is greater than just the Kobalos' military might, and far larger than the terrible battle entities that they have created.

It includes the gods who support them—deities such as Golgoth, the Lord of Winter, who will blast the green from the earth and create a road of ice along which their warriors may glide to victory.

Grimalkin

PROLOGUE

About an hour after dark, Jenny began to climb the spiral steps that led to the tallest of the high eastern turrets. She was slightly breathless, but it was not just because of the exertion of the steep climb.

She was nervous. Her palms were sweating, and she could feel a weakness in her knees.

The attic she was heading for was haunted.

She was only an apprentice, and it would be many years before she'd become a spook. Was she taking on too much? She wondered.

It was cold, and her breath was steaming from her nostrils. Step after step she forced herself upward.

Jenny was carrying a lantern; one pocket was filled with salt and the other with iron; additionally, she had tied the silver chain around her waist and was also gripping a rowan staff. She was ready for any threat from the dark.

The way to deal with ghosts was to talk to them—to try and persuade them to go to the light—but Jenny wasn't taking any chances. In this cold northern land, so far from the County, who knew what she might encounter? Ghosts might be very different here. She felt better with her pockets full and a weapon in her hand.

She reached the stout wooden attic door and tried one of the eight big keys on the heavy bunch. She was lucky: Although the lock was stiff, the second key turned.

The door creaked open on rusty hinges, the bottom juddering toward her over the flags as she dragged it open. It had swollen with the damp and probably hadn't been opened for many years.

Jenny took a deep breath to steady her nerves and stepped into the room. She was a seventh daughter of a seventh daughter with the gift of sensitivity to the dark; instantly she sensed that something threatening was nearby. She raised the lantern high and examined her surroundings: a small room, the wooden paneling stained with patches of fungus, and a table and two chairs covered in a thick layer of dust. Another door was directly ahead of her, no doubt leading to the main chamber.

She shivered. It was cold enough to make her glad of her sheepskin jacket. But the worst thing was the smell. This was just about one of the stinkiest places she'd ever been in. Back in the County, she'd once walked out onto the Morecambe Bay sands to see what a crowd of people were staring at. There'd been a school of huge fish washed up on the beach. They'd been dead for some time, and they stank. What she smelled now was similar, but there was some kind of living animal smell mixed in. It was a bit like walking into a stable of sweating horses and sodden sawdust. Then there was a third element to the mix—a hint of burning flesh and a taste of sulfur on her tongue.

By the yellow light of the lantern, she saw a big spider high on the wall above the inner door. As she approached, the creature scuttled off toward a huge web in the corner.

There was no lock—just a metal handle. She turned it and tried to open it by pushing it away from her. There was resistance, so she reversed direction, pulling it smoothly outward.

Her sense of a threat from the dark was growing.

The lantern illuminated what had once been someone's opulent living quarters, now ruined by damp and neglect. Three huge fireplaces gaped like monstrous mouths, their rusty metal grates filled with ashes. Water dripped from the ceiling onto a rusty chandelier. There were the remnants of fine carpets on the floor; now they were damp, dirty, and mildewed.

Then something unexpected caught her attention: four couches at the center of the room formed a square, facing in toward something very unusual—a dark circular hole about ten feet in diameter. It was ringed with stones, and someone had left a wineglass precariously balanced there. It looked as if the slightest disturbance would send it plummeting down into the darkness. The stones themselves glistened with water.

Jenny approached the ring of stones and gazed down into the dark hole, holding the lantern over it. It looked like a well. Was there water at the bottom?

Then Jenny realized that there was something impossible about what she was seeing. How could it be a well?

She was standing in an attic right at the top of a turret. There were rooms below and then, directly beneath them, in the palace itself, first a kitchen, and then, on the lowest level, the second-largest throne room, where Prince Stanislaw, the ruler of this land, received petitions, held meetings, and dispensed justice.

She had been given a tour of this part of the castle a day or so earlier. If this dark shaft ran through the turret rooms and then down into the ground, then there would have had to be some sort of circular stone structure, like a chimney, in each of the large rooms near the ground. Surely she would have noticed such a thing?

But for the sound of her muffled footsteps across the damp carpet and the water dripping onto the chandelier, the room was quiet. But Jenny could hear something new—a trickling, as if water was being poured into some small vessel.

She stared at the wineglass. It was slowly filling with red wine. A thin stream was falling into the glass, but there was no visible source for the liquid. Was it being poured by an invisible hand?

A second later, an unmistakable metallic odor told her that she was wrong about the liquid. It wasn't wine. It was blood.

Jenny watched in fearful fascination as the glass slowly filled. The blood reached the brim and then spilled over onto the stone. The droplets began to steam, and the sudden sharp stench made her heave. As she watched, the blood in the glass began to bubble.

Then the vessel wobbled and fell into the dark shaft.

Jenny counted to ten, but there was no splash, no sound at all. The shaft appeared to be bottomless.

The room had been dank and cold, but now it seemed to be growing warmer. Steam began to rise from the circle of wet stones.

Her sense of danger increased. She could feel the hairs on the back of her neck stand up, and her fingertips were tingling. These reactions told her that this attic contained something far worse than a poor soul to be coaxed toward the light. She had hoped to demonstrate her bravery and prove her competence to become a spook. She had to learn to cope alone.

Terror gripped her. She sensed that there was something really bad here . . . something really big and dangerous . . . something that wanted to kill her.

Jenny stepped away from the circle of stones, away from the couches, pressing her back against the wall.

From the depths below, something enormous took a breath. It was so vast that the air it sucked in rushed past her with the force of a gale, slamming the inner door shut with a bang. The blast made Jenny stagger forward onto her knees before it swirled away down the dark shaft, toward an unseen mouth and cavernous lungs.

She dropped the lantern and was plunged into total darkness.

Jenny cried out in terror as a monstrous glowing shape bulged up out of the vast impossible space and hovered in the air above it. Six glowing ruby-red eyes stared toward her, eyes set deep within a bulbous head.

When it exhaled, the breath of this creature—whatever it was—felt hot and putrid. There was a stench of decay, of dead things that still slithered or crawled in a subterranean darkness.

Then tentacles were coiling and writhing, reaching out toward her, intending to twine about her and drag her back down into that dark impossible hole.

She would never live to become a spook now.

She would die here alone in the darkness.

Jenny Calder

I
Like a Puppet

Y<small>ESTERDAY</small> was the worst day of my life.

It was the day that Thomas Ward, the Chipenden Spook, my master, died.

Tom should have been back in the County fighting the dark, dealing with ghosts, ghasts, witches, and boggarts. We should have been visiting places such as Priestown, Caster, Poulton, Burnley, and Blackburn. I should have spent time in the Chipenden library and garden, being trained as a spook's apprentice. I should have been practicing digging boggart pits and improving my skills with a silver chain.

Instead we followed the witch assassin Grimalkin on a long, doomed journey north toward the lands of the Kobalos. They're barbaric nonhuman warriors with a thick hide of fur and faces like wolves. They plan to make war on the human race; they intend to kill all the men and boys and enslave the females.

One of their warriors, a Shaiksa assassin with deadly fighting skills, had been visiting the river, the divide between the territories of men and Kobalos. He'd been issuing challenges, then fighting human opponents in single combat, killing his adversaries with ease. But the holy men of this land, the magowie, had been visited by a winged figure—a figure who had the appearance of an angel and who had made a prophecy:

"One day soon a human will come who will defeat the Kobalos warrior. After his victory, he will lead the combined armies of the principalities to victory!"

Hearing of this prophecy, Grimalkin had formulated a plan. It was a plan that cost Tom his life.

Grimalkin's scheme was for Tom Ward to fight and defeat the warrior and then lead an army into Kobalos lands so that she could learn of their magical and military abilities.

Tom had indeed defeated the warrior, but the Kobalos's dying act had been to pierce Tom's body with his saber.

So Tom Ward had died too.

That was yesterday.

Today we are going to bury him.

✚

Tom's coffin rested on the grass in the open. Prince Stanislaw, who ruled Polyznia, the largest of the principalities bordering Kobalos territory, stood beside it, flanked by two of his guards. He nodded toward Grimalkin and me, and then beckoned four of his men forward. They hefted the coffin up onto their shoulders.

He and this armed escort were with us to do honor to Tom. I wished they didn't have to be here; I wanted to take Tom back to the County, where his old master was buried and his family still lived on their farm.

I glanced sideways at the prince—a big man with short gray hair, a large nose, and close-set eyes. He was in his fifties, I guessed, and hadn't an ounce of fat on his body. His intelligent eyes looked sad now.

He and his warriors had been impressed by Tom's fighting skill. Despite suffering a mortal wound, Tom had slayed the Kobalos warrior, something that the prince's own champions had been unable to do.

As we trudged up toward the place where Tom was to be buried, thunder crashed overhead, and soon torrential rain had soaked us to the skin. Grimalkin gripped my shoulder. I suppose she meant to be comforting—insofar as someone as wild and cruel as a witch assassin can be. But Tom's death had been brought about by her machinations, and anger began to build within me. Her grip was firm to the point of hurting, but I shrugged her off and took a step nearer to the open grave.

I glanced at the headstone and began to read what had been carved upon it.

HERE LIETH PRINCE THOMAS OF CASTER,

A BRAVE WARRIOR

WHO FELL IN COMBAT

BUT TRIUMPHED WHERE OTHERS FAILED

The lie we had created—that Tom was a prince— had gone too far, and now here it was written upon his gravestone. It made my stomach turn. Tom was a young spook who had fought the dark, and this should have been acknowledged. *This shouldn't have happened,* I thought bitterly. He deserved the truth.

But this again had been Grimalkin's doing. Tom had needed to pose as a prince because the armies of the principalities would not follow a commoner.

I watched as a hooded magowie, one of their priests, prayed for Tom, rain dripping from the end of his nose. The smell of wet soil was very strong. Soon it would cover Tom's remains.

Then the prayers were over, and the gravediggers began to shovel wet earth down upon the coffin. I glanced back at Grimalkin and saw that she was grinding her teeth. She seemed more angry than sad, but I was churning with mixed emotions too.

Suddenly the men stopped working and looked up. There was movement and light in the air high above us. I gasped as I spotted a winged figure hovering far above the grave. It glowed with a silver light, its fluttering wings huge.

It was the same angel-like being that had hovered over the hill while the three magowie had made their prophecy, foretelling the coming of a champion to defeat the Shaiksa assassin and lead humans across the river to victory.

Suddenly it folded its white wings and dropped toward us like a stone, coming to a stop less than thirty feet above our heads. Now I could make out a beautiful face that shone with pale light. Everyone was gazing upward now, exclaiming in astonishment.

There was a noise from the grave, but fascinated by the winged figure, I continued to look up. It was only when the sound came again that I glanced down.

At first I thought my eyes were playing tricks on me, but I wasn't the only person staring down into the grave. I saw that the casket was slightly tilted, and the sodden earth that covered it was sliding away to reveal the wet wooden lid.

Grimalkin hissed in anger and stared up at the winged being. I could understand her annoyance at the interference. Couldn't Tom even be left to be buried in peace? But then I saw that the coffin was moving. What could be causing that?

I hardly dared to hope . . . could it be that Tom was alive . . . ?

With a jerk, the coffin rose up into the air above the grave and began to spin, spraying mud and droplets of water in all directions. The corner caught one of the gravediggers and knocked him backward into the waiting mound of earth.

I stared in astonishment as the coffin slowly rose upward. Grimalkin rushed forward, stretching out her arms as if to grab it. But, spinning faster and faster, it eluded her grasp and whirled toward the winged figure. I heard another hiss of anger from Grimalkin—but it was lost in an earsplitting boom of thunder that set my teeth on edge.

Suddenly the heavens were split with intense light— not the sheet lightning we had experienced so far. This was a jagged fork of blue lightning that seemed to come from the winged figure. It struck Tom's coffin with a crack that hurt my ears.

It had to be something supernatural—a wielding of dark magic. Judging by her reactions, it certainly wasn't Grimalkin's doing. But who was responsible?

The coffin immediately disintegrated, splinters of wood falling toward us. I quickly retreated, shielding my head with my arms, bumping into people in my haste to get clear. Some of the pieces splashed into the water at the bottom of the empty grave; others fell around me.

When I looked up again, Tom's corpse was spinning above us, his arms and legs flopping and jerking, his body spiraling down toward the grave again. I stared at him in amazement. The eyes were closed in death; he looked like a puppet dangling from invisible controlling strings. I could hardly bear to watch—that such an indignity should be inflicted upon him!

Suddenly, far above him, the winged creature vanished like a candle flame snuffed out by a giant thumb and forefinger. Sheet lightning flashed, and Tom's corpse fell twenty feet or more into the mound of soil beside the grave.

For a moment there was absolute silence. I held my breath, stunned by what I had just witnessed, a whole range of emotions churning through me.

Then, from the corpse, we heard an unmistakable groan.

2
Lukrasta

GRIMALKIN was the first to reach Tom. She lifted him out of the mud and carried him in her arms like a child, pushing through the crowd and ignoring even the prince. She was hurrying back toward the camp. I ran after her, calling her name, but she never even glanced back.

Soon we were back in the tent where we had washed the corpse—which now seemed very much alive. Grimalkin laid Tom on the pallet and covered him with a blanket. He was breathing and giving the occasional moan, but he didn't open his eyes.

"Tom! Tom!" I cried, kneeling beside him, but Grimalkin pushed me away.

"Leave him, child! He needs to sleep deeply," she commanded, giving me a glimpse of her pointy teeth. She seemed concerned, but angry too. Being a seventh daughter of a seventh daughter, one of my gifts is that of empathy—but it didn't work with the witch assassin. Perhaps she had magical barriers in place.

Soon Prince Stanislaw, escorted by four guards, came to see Tom. He had a brief animated conversation with Grimalkin in the local language, Losta. She didn't bother to translate for me, so I don't know exactly what was said—though sometimes I can read people's thoughts, and the prince's mind was open to me. He was excited and astonished and filled with rapture, believing that he had witnessed a miracle. He was happy for Tom, too, happy that he still lived, and fervently wished for a full recovery. But beneath all these thoughts was calculation: already he was anticipating using Tom as a figurehead to rally more troops and launch an attack upon the Kobalos.

After the departure of the prince, we were left alone in the tent. Grimalkin sat beside Tom, staring down into his face while I paced back and forth in agitation, my mind racing with what I had seen. I longed to ask Grimalkin how he was doing, but her expression was forbidding. At last I blurted out my question.

"Will he get better?" I asked. "Is it possible?"

"Come here, child," Grimalkin told me. "Look at this. . . ."

I approached the low trestle table where Tom lay. She pulled back the sheet and pointed to the place where the

Kobalos's saber had transfixed his body. I had seen scales around Tom's wound before, but now it had closed right up, sealed with scales.

"It's a miracle!" I exclaimed. "The angel has restored him to life!"

Grimalkin shook her head, looking nothing like her usual confident self. "It was not a miracle, and that creature was no angel. In part, the healing came about because of the lamia blood that courses through his veins—something that he inherited from his mother. But he was certainly dead, and restoring him to life required a dark magic so powerful that everyone who witnessed it should be afraid."

Lamia witches were shape-shifters. In their "domestic" form, they had the appearance of human women but for the line of green and yellow scales that ran the length of their spines. In their "feral" shape, they scuttled around on all fours with sharp teeth and talons, crunching bones and drinking the blood of their victims.

I knew that Tom's mam had been a healer and a midwife, but to my astonishment, Grimalkin had revealed that she had also been a lamia. She had passed on to Tom the ability to heal himself. But surviving death was something far beyond that.

"Who used the magic?" I asked.

Grimalkin didn't answer. Was she even listening to me? I wondered. She seemed to have retreated into her own private world. I heard a murmuring outside, and rather than repeating my question, I went over and lifted the tent flap. Scores of warriors stood outside, staring at the tent.

I returned to Tom's makeshift bed. He was breathing slowly, in a deep sleep, but looked as if he might open his eyes at any moment. I wondered fearfully if he could really be himself after such a trauma. He might have been tipped into insanity or have no recollection of his former life.

"There are ranks of warriors outside. What do they want?" I asked Grimalkin.

She sighed, drew back the blanket, and inspected Tom's wound again. She spoke so quietly that I had to lean closer to catch her words. "They want this sleeping prince to lead them across the river and destroy the Kobalos. They have seen Tom defeat the Shaiksa; now they have witnessed his return from the dead, an even greater accomplishment. They want what I wanted. We have reached the position I hoped for all along. But someone else has brought us to this point—someone who had already planted the seeds of this harvest months before we arrived here with Tom. Someone who has seen the larger picture of events and schemed to bring about this very situation."

"Months?" I asked. How could she know this?

"The winged being has been appearing to the magowie for some time. It has been controlled by someone who hides in the shadows so that I cannot see him."

"Do you know who it is?" I asked, suddenly afraid. I had thought Grimalkin was the great schemer, but now, it seemed, there was someone too powerful for even her to detect.

"I know only one person capable of such powerful dark magic," she said. "A human mage I have encountered before. His name is Lukrasta, and he once served the Fiend. His purpose now is to ensure the survival of humanity and the destruction of the Kobalos."

"Tom told me a little of Lukrasta—isn't he the dark mage his friend Alice now works with?"

"Yes, that is the one," the witch assassin admitted, her face grim. Her mouth twitched, and I wondered if she was afraid. . . .

"But don't we all want the same outcome, then?" I asked. Surely this mage Lukrasta would be a valuable ally.

"Lukrasta is indeed fighting on our side against the Kobalos—but sometimes the means he uses are too terrible, and the goal is not worth it," Grimalkin replied, shaking her head. "I watched the final stage of Tom's struggle with the assassin very carefully. He fought perfectly, exactly as I had trained him—but as he delivered the killing blow, he made an elementary mistake. His stance allowed the Shaiksa to deliver the killing thrust."

"But the Kobalos warrior was highly skilled. Are you sure Tom made a mistake? Anybody can make a mistake in the heat of battle, surely?"

"I am *certain*, child," Grimalkin retorted angrily, showing her sharp teeth. "Tom Ward would never have made such an elementary mistake of his own volition. I think his actions were influenced by some magical force. He had to die so that these warriors could witness his resurrection. They are now more likely to follow him into battle obediently and without question. The winged creature and the prophecies made by the magowie . . . it all fits together only too well. We have been used as part of a clever scheme, pawns in a much larger game.

"Think *what* has been done and *how* it has been done!" she spat. "Tom has suffered to meet the needs of this mage. He died a painful death and perhaps an even more painful resurrection. We are all expendable. Tom Ward and Lukrasta are enemies. Last year they fought, and Tom won. There is something cruel and vindictive about what has been done here. I suspect that in hurting Tom, the mage has exacted a painful revenge over his rival."

"How is Lukrasta Tom's rival? Is it because of Alice? Does Tom still care for Alice?" I hoped he didn't—it couldn't be good for a spook to be so close to a witch.

Grimalkin smiled bitterly. "Alice and Tom were very close. He is hurt by her absence. Now she is closer to Lukrasta than she ever was to Tom. Yes, they are truly rivals for the friendship of Alice."

For a while I did not reply. I'd never seen the witch assassin so upset before. I could feel myself wilting under the fierce heat of her anger. Then at last I screwed up my courage and asked the question that had been bothering me.

"How could Tom have been manipulated by a magical force during his battle with the Shaiksa? He was wielding the Starblade that you forged for him. You both thought that made him invulnerable to magic."

"It should have done so. I believed that it would protect against any dark magic intended to harm him—magic wielded by both humans and Kobalos. That is what worries me. The magic used against Tom was more powerful than the blade. I suspect that Lukrasta and Alice combined their magical power to achieve that." Grimalkin's hands were trembling slightly—but was it from fear or anger?

After a while she spoke again, her tone softer and friendlier. "You look tired, girl—you have been through a lot. I will watch over Tom. Go back to our own tent and sleep. I will ask the prince to provide you with an escort through the camp."

I hesitated. I was reluctant to leave Tom. I really wanted to be there if he woke up, but Grimalkin was staring at me, and I was forced to look away from her fierce gaze.

Within the hour I was back at our own little camp, watched over by a couple of the prince's guard. I was tired, but I fed and watered the horses before crawling under my blanket. Almost immediately I fell into a deep, dreamless sleep.

It was late morning when I awoke and went outside. I saw that the guards had gone, as had most of the nearby tents. There was no sign of human activity.

I was puzzled and tempted to investigate further, but the horses badly needed to be exercised, so I put aside my curiosity and dealt with their needs first, riding them along the riverbank. It was a fine bright morning and I enjoyed the gallop. I was so pleased that Tom seemed to have a chance of recovering, but that was balanced by what Grimalkin had told me of Lukrasta and Alice. How could Alice be Tom's friend and yet conspire to cause him such pain?

As I approached the camp again, I saw the witch assassin striding toward me between the remaining tents.

"Where is everyone?" I asked.

"They've set off for a castle belonging to Prince Stanislaw. We are to stay there for a time while we strengthen our forces and prepare to cross the river into the Kobalos lands."

Her words filled me with utter dismay. I couldn't believe that they were still planning the attack. I'd been hoping that Tom would be able to travel back to the County.

"What about Tom? Is he conscious?"

"No, he is still in a very deep sleep. He is being carried there on a cart, watched over by the prince's guard. We need to strike camp and follow."

The journey to the castle took us through a great forest of tall spruce and pine trees. How I longed to be back among the oaks and sycamores of the County! When Tom recovered, he would surely need a period of convalescence. He certainly wouldn't be strong enough to ride at the head of an army. Grimalkin had talked of crossing the river to attack the Kobalos, but perhaps I could persuade him to go home. I would certainly try my best.

Grimalkin was not best pleased when the castle finally came into view. "This is no place to position an armed camp! It will be impossible to defend!" she exclaimed.

Set on high ground, rising out of the haze from hundreds of campfires, the castle was a beautiful and impressive sight, surrounded by pine trees and wild meadows. However, it lacked the moat and high defensive walls of castles that I'd seen back in the County.

"No doubt Prince Stanislaw uses it as a base to hunt boar and deer," she continued. "It's a place to entertain his nobles and other princelings. We should have gone farther south, closer to the capital. Our Kobalos enemies might seize the initiative and attack first."

I had only seen one of the Kobalos so far—the assassin that Tom had defeated in single combat. Yet I knew that many of their warriors dwelled across the river, and that even greater numbers lived in the great Kobalos city called Valkarky. Their intention was to kill all human men and boys and enslave the women. The threat they posed was terrifying.

They had their powerful new god, Talkus, whose birth had encouraged them to invade human territory.

He had also drawn other Old Gods to his side.

The most formidable of these allies was Golgoth, the

Lord of Winter, who shared the Kobalos's love of the frozen wastes; he was a god who threatened to bring ice and snow to the whole world, creating a new age of ice. These gods, the Kobalos, and their battle entities were the dark army that we faced.

When we reached the castle, we were treated with courtesy and our horses were fed and watered. Somehow they found room for them in the crowded stables. The castle was very full as well. The rulers of the other principalities had brought their warriors to join the cause and resist the expected Kobalos attack, and each had been given quarters there. The consequence was that I had to share a small room in the southern turret with Grimalkin.

Still, our room had two narrow beds. I was grateful for that, because in sleep Grimalkin can be terrifying. Sometimes she cries out as if in agony or speaks harsh, angry words in some foreign language. Most scary of all is the way she sometimes grinds her teeth together and growls deep in her throat.

Time passed slowly, and I moped in my room, making notes on what had happened and writing this account in Tom's notebook. Occasionally I broke the tedium with a brisk walk in the cold, pacing back and forth within the courtyard. I really wanted to explore the grounds, but the soldiers camped there were loud and boisterous, and I avoided them.

Grimalkin seemed to spend all her time by Tom's bedside, but when I tried to see him, she wouldn't let me enter the room.

Then, on the third morning, she came and told me that Tom was conscious and wished to speak to me.

So this will be my final entry in his notebook.

I am happy to return it to him, but I wonder what will happen now. Will he want to go home? I really hope so. I am about to find out.

Thomas Ward

3
Farmer Boy

ALICE turned and smiled at me. We'd just cooked two rabbits in the embers of our campfire. Now we were eating them, the tender meat almost melting in our mouths.

I smiled back. She was a really pretty girl with nice brown eyes, dark hair, and high cheekbones. It was easy to forget that she'd been trained in witchcraft by a witch called Bony Lizzie. But we'd just survived a terrible threat from the dark, and Alice had helped me—so rather than imprison her in a pit, the Spook had given her another chance. I was taking her to stay with her aunt at Staumin, to the west of the County.

We finished the rabbits and sat in silence. It was one of those comfortable silences where you didn't need to speak. I felt relaxed and happy; it was good to just sit there next to her, staring into the warm embers of the fire.

But suddenly Alice did something really strange. She reached across and held my hand.

We still didn't speak and stayed like that for a long time, Alice staring into the embers of the fire. I looked up at the stars. I didn't want to break away, but I was all mixed up. My left hand was holding her left hand, and I felt guilty. I felt as if I was holding hands with the dark. I knew the Spook wouldn't like it.

There was no way I could get away from the truth. It was very likely that Alice was going to be a witch one day. It was then that I remembered what Mam had said about her—that she'd always be somewhere in between, neither wholly good nor wholly bad.

But wasn't that true of all of us? Not one of us was perfect.

So I didn't take my hand away. I just sat there, one part of me enjoying holding her hand, which was comforting after all that had happened, while the other part was overcome with guilt. . . .

All at once I found myself lying in my bed. My heart sank like a stone.

It had all been a dream about what had happened years earlier, during the first months of my apprenticeship.

I'd enjoyed those moments with Alice, but now I

remembered more recent events. Our close friendship had lasted years, and I'd truly loved her—it was Alice who had brought it to an end. She'd betrayed me and gone off with the mage Lukrasta. The pain of it was still as fresh now as the moment it had happened.

Alice had become a witch. She had gone to the dark. I had lost her forever.

I looked at the weak sunlight streaming into the room and shivered. They still hadn't returned my clothes, and pulling the heavy woolen gown about me, I left my bed for the first time since regaining consciousness. Once again I remembered the sudden pain as the saber had entered my flesh; I remembered falling into the darkness of death.

There was an ache in my belly, and the floorboards were cold. My knees trembled as I walked unsteadily over to the window seat and peered down.

This castle was the most northerly seat of Prince Stanislaw of Polyznia. Grimalkin had already told me that it could not be defended. She seemed to be finding fault with everything. I had tried to remain calm in her presence, but I felt increasingly bitter at the way she had manipulated me, bringing me to this northern principality without telling me that her intention was for me to fight the Shaiksa assassin. Her scheme had led to my death.

I looked through the window at an army made up of the prince's own blue-jacketed forces and those from the other northern principalities that bordered the Kobalos territory. I could see part of their camp from the window. Their fires had created a brown haze that hung over the meadows between the castle and the forest.

Reinforcements were also joining us from the larger Germanic kingdoms immediately to the south. We would need every man we could get, but there would never be enough of them.

Somewhere across the Shanna River, two hours to the north, were our enemies—the Kobalos army, which was many times the size of our own. They could attack at any time.

They were a fierce race of bestial creatures, and their new god, Talkus, had increased the power of their mages and fueled this war. He might now be the most powerful entity of the dark. That was why I had let Grimalkin persuade me to travel here—to gather information that might help to defeat them long before they fought their way to the sea and threatened the County.

We had destroyed the Fiend, only to find something worse taking his place.

Following the predictions of the magowie, the wise men who served the rulers of the principalities, thousands of men-at-arms had converged on this castle and now, because of my victory over the assassin, I was supposed to lead them. But I was a spook, not a prince. I didn't want to lead them to their deaths.

I sat there with the sun on my face; its rays felt warm through the glass. But I knew that beyond these walls, the air was chilly. Soon it would be winter. I wanted to go home before the weather closed in and made that impossible.

The days were getting shorter, and in just a few hours the sun would set. I didn't welcome the night. Darkness made me uneasy now. The sound of a mouse scratching under the floorboards set my heart racing and my nerves jumping with anxiety. My apprenticeship had gradually allowed me to overcome such fears, but all at once it was as if all my training had been for nothing.

How could I function as a spook in this condition? How long would it be before I returned to full physical and mental health? Had I truly died? Sometimes everything seemed unreal. I had to touch the stone walls and press my fingers against the wooden door in order to convince myself that they were solid. Was I actually back in the world, or really still dead and suffering in the dark?

By an effort of will I forced myself not to dwell on such thoughts. Grimalkin tells me that I was certainly dead—but if so, I could remember nothing of it.

At the moment I struck the blow that gave me victory, I was aware of the Shaiksa assassin's saber thrusting toward my body. I tried to twist away. I could have done it—I should have avoided that fatal counter stroke—but my lower body was seized with a sudden paralysis.

I remember feeling a terrible pain, then looking down and seeing the blade, knowing that I couldn't hope to survive such a wound. I was cold and numb and terribly afraid. I didn't want to die.

Grimalkin believes that dark magic was used against me. She suspects that it was Lukrasta. She also suspects that he orchestrated my return from death—that the winged being that tore me from my coffin was his creature. I felt angry and remembered how I had defeated him in combat but then spared his life. What a fool I'd been to do so! I'd fought Lukrasta in his tower and won. His magic couldn't work against me while I wielded the sword that Grimalkin had forged.

So what had changed?

I'd never seen Grimalkin look so uneasy. It was surely because the Starblade hadn't protected me against dark magic—something she now viewed as her personal failure. She wasn't accustomed to being thwarted, and it disturbed her deeply.

I thought about that failure, and it brought another type of uncertainty and pain to me.

Alice had once been my close friend. How could she have put me through such a terrible experience?

There was a double rap on the door, interrupting my dark thoughts. It opened wide, and a guard briefly stepped forward and bowed before stepping back to allow another to enter.

It was Jenny, my apprentice, and she was carrying my notebook.

I smiled at her reassuringly, attempting to hide my true feelings. She was fifteen, just two years younger than I was—to the day. She looked like a healthy farmer's daughter: She had a bright, cheerful face, mousy hair, and freckles. Her left eye was blue and her right eye brown; that was unusual enough, but there was something about the expression in her eyes that set her apart from other girls. I still couldn't work out what it was, but it was there, all right.

I had already tested her by taking her onto Hangman's Hill near the farm where I was born and brought up. I'd let her face the ghasts, the soul fragments of the soldiers who'd been hanged there generations ago, at the end of the Civil War. She'd shown bravery and sensitivity to their plight. It had been enough for me to take her on as my apprentice.

She was probably the first girl ever to become a spook's apprentice. According to my master, the minimum qualification for the job was to be a seventh son of a seventh son, like me. This meant that you could see and speak to the dead and had some immunity against witchcraft. So far I had been given no proof of what Jenny claimed to be—a seventh daughter of a seventh daughter—because she'd been raised by foster parents who knew nothing of her original family.

But she did have gifts that I had seen in action: She could empathize with people and learn how they felt just by looking at them. It wasn't quite mind-reading, but it was close. She could also make herself very hard to see—not true invisibility, but something very near.

"Sit down," I invited, gesturing to the space on the seat next to me.

She did so and smiled at me. "How are you feeling? You look pale."

"I feel like I've been kicked in the belly by a mule, but apart from that I'm fine!" I forced a smile onto my face, then noticed that Jenny's hands were trembling. "Are you all right?" I asked.

Despite her smile, I could tell that she was upset. "I'm glad you're getting better," she said as a tear trickled down her left cheek. "I hope you don't mind—I've made some entries in your notebook covering the three days that you . . ."

Instead of completing her sentence, she handed over the book. I turned to her first page of notes and began to read. After a few minutes, I closed it and looked at her.

"It's a very detailed account," I said. "As you know, I usually just make brief notes, then write a full version in another book—sometimes weeks later."

I'd spoken without thinking and immediately cursed my stupidity. The girl was upset enough without my being critical and making her feel worse.

"I'm sorry," she said. "I hope you don't mind. Doing that each night helped to ease the memories of what had happened. I wrote it in your book because I believed you were gone forever. I was trying to finish the story of your life." Jenny gave a sob, and both eyes began to leak tears.

I leaned forward and rested my hand briefly on hers. "I don't mind you writing in my book. Don't worry. I'll look at it later," I said. "It'll be good to read another version of what happened after my fight with the assassin. Grimalkin told me some of it, but she didn't go into such detail."

Jenny nodded. "Isn't that an amazing sight?" she said, pointing to the thousands of men below. "They say more are arriving every day."

"Grimalkin isn't impressed," I said. "She says the Kobalos have an army many times larger than ours. They will have savage creatures, battle entities, that are far stronger, larger and more deadly than humans. Remember those terrible creatures called varteki that we killed near Chipenden?"

We had fought young ones back in the County. They were huge, many-legged monsters, able to burrow underground and spit globules of acid that could burn through flesh to the bone in seconds.

"We may face fully grown versions," I told her. "They'll break through our lines in moments. When we flee, the slaughter will begin."

Grimalkin had spent time in the lair of the mage I'd killed. She had grown a number of creatures from the samples she'd found in the tree, hoping to discover their strengths and weaknesses. But two varteki had escaped the pentacle in which she'd contained them. They were burrowers and difficult to catch. We had barely been in time to slay the second one and prevent it from laying waste to the village of Topley, close to the farm where I'd been born and brought up.

"But I thought she *wanted* to cross the river and invade. Wasn't that her plan?"

"She wanted to probe with a much smaller force," I

explained. "She hoped to cross quickly into Kobalos territory, learn what she could, and then get out. What's being planned is more like a full-scale attack, and she feels we're bound to lose."

I shivered, and a sudden pain deep in my belly made me gasp.

Jenny came to her feet, looking concerned. "I'll leave you now. You should rest. Are you hungry?" she asked me. "We're being treated very well. Anything we request, we get. Shall I order something for you? We're like royalty!"

"Don't get above yourself!" I said with a smile. "I'm the prince, and you're just a cheeky servant girl! But the truth is, I don't have much appetite."

It was worse than that. I felt nauseous, and the last thing I felt like doing was eating. But perhaps I'd be better with something inside me.

"Please ask them to send me a little bread and cheese," I said.

Jenny smiled and patted my shoulder, then left me alone with my thoughts.

Within five minutes a servant had brought me a basket containing bread, butter, a wedge of cheese, and a glass of a light ale. I nibbled at the cheese, staring down at the army that encircled the castle. The cheese was hard and bland—nothing like the tangy, crumbly County cheese

I loved. But eating made me feel better, and I began to feel drowsy.

As I was thinking about sleep, the door suddenly opened and Prince Stanislaw strode into the room. I made to rise and greet him, but he gestured that I should remain where I was. He dragged a heavy ornate chair across from the far wall and sat down opposite me.

The prince was not handsome, but there was a dignity about him, and now, when he smiled at me, he exuded warmth. I liked him, and certainly respected him. But now I detected something different in his demeanor—though I couldn't quite put my finger on what it was.

He opened his mouth to speak, and I wondered why Grimalkin was not present to interpret for me. I quickly found out.

"You are feeling better, no?" he asked.

My mouth dropped open in astonishment. "I thought you didn't speak our language," I said.

He shrugged. "I do not speak well, but I can say enough. I understand more what I hear than I am able to reply. To rule, you must learn. I study many languages. You learn more by listening than speaking, no? So that is what I do. I have learned much already by listening to your conversations with the sorceress. I know you false. I know you to be farmer boy, not prince."

4
A Council of War

"WELL is that not so?" he demanded, raising his eyebrows. "You no more a prince than I am wolf!"

One of Prince Stanislaw's many titles was the Wolf of Polyznia.

Grimalkin had pretended that I was a prince. I hadn't liked the deceit, but she'd argued that it was the only way to get Prince Stanislaw to allow me to fight the Kobalos champion.

"Then why did you allow me to fight?" I asked, silently cursing my foolishness in going along with Grimalkin's plan.

"My magowie said you must fight. He said the angelus say that."

"The angelus?"

"The creature which fly. The creature with wings which give you new life."

I nodded. "I'm truly sorry that we deceived you, but we felt it was necessary. You'd never have listened to a commoner. What now?"

The prince shrugged. "Is it true that you just farmer boy? How can that be? If so, how you fight so good like that? Why you come here?"

"I was raised on a farm—so, yes, I am a farmer's lad—but I'm also the seventh son of a seventh son. I can talk to the dead, and I have some protection against dark magic. Because of that, I was trained as what we call a spook. My job is to fight the dark and deal with ghosts and malevolent entities. The Kobalos god Talkus is from the dark as well. His followers threaten the whole of humankind, not just your northern principalities. If they win here, they will advance south and eventually overrun my own land. As for my ability to fight . . . I was trained by Grimalkin, who's just about the greatest warrior I've ever seen. So we came here to help vanquish our common enemies. Despite our deceit, we meant well."

Stanislaw nodded and let out a big sigh. "Then let it be as sorceress plan," he said at last. "We will attack Valkarky. Eat—go strong. Get ready. In two weeks we ride."

✦

Later, I had a third visitor. Grimalkin arrived clutching a long roll of parchment. I gave her an account of what the prince and I had said to each other.

"I cannot believe I did not see that!" she exclaimed, shaking her head. "I should have known that he was just pretending not to understand. How can I have been so blind?"

I could see her agitation. She could usually see through to the truth of people and situations. This was the second thing she'd gotten wrong. First the Starblade had failed to protect me against dark magic, and now this. The witch assassin was not used to making mistakes.

"It's turned out the same in the end," I said. "As the prince said, we'll cross the river in two weeks. I need to get fit. At the moment I can hardly walk. I can't imagine how I'm going to recover sufficiently and be able to ride at the head of an army in such a short time. I'd probably be better off going home back to the County to regain my heath."

"There isn't time for that," Grimalkin said, showing her pointy teeth in displeasure. "You will soon be stronger. But first we must plan and make these princelings bow to our will."

She walked across to the small table, unrolled the parchment, and held it flat on the wooden surface, securing it with four pins. It was an old map, the outlines faded to yellow, but there had been more recent additions in black ink.

"This is the Shanna River," Grimalkin said, tracing it with her forefinger. "Here, to the north, is the Fittzanda Fissure, a region of volcanic instability. It was once the boundary between human and Kobalos territories. And there, far to the north, is the huge city of Valkarky, the heart of the Kobalos's strength. We are not going there. It would be suicide at this stage."

Valkarky was the great city of the Kobalos; they believed it would grow until it covered the entire world.

"So where are we going?" I asked wearily.

She pointed to what was no more than a cross on the map in black ink, a position far to the southwest of Valkarky, not far north of the fissure.

"You have studied Browne's glossary of the Kobalos?" she asked.

It was something that Grimalkin had found on her travels. Browne was an ancient spook who had studied the Kobalos. The glossary was a key list of Kobalos terminology. I'd made a copy and hoped to update it with any new knowledge that we acquired on this expedition.

I nodded.

"Then you know what a kulad is?"

"It's a fortified tower," I said. "Nicholas Browne says they're also used as slave markets."

"That is true," said Grimalkin. "I visited one during my travels last year; it was mostly used to sell and buy slaves. But there are others that Browne was ignorant of. Each of these is ruled by a mage—they are private dwellings, seats of power and repositories of Kobalos mage magic. This one is special!" she exclaimed, jabbing at the cross on the map with her finger.

"It is called Kartuna and is the private kulad of a mage called Lenklewth. He is one of the triumvirate of mages who rule Valkarky—the second most powerful of the three. If we are lucky, he will be in the city and we will not need to face his magic. When we cross the river, we will ride toward Valkarky for a while—to fool the Kobalos scouts who will be observing and recording our movements. But then we will quickly veer westward to attack and hopefully seize Kartuna.

"Give me some time within that tower and I could learn much that might lead to the eventual defeat of our enemies," she said. "So we grab what we can and then retreat back across the river. Then we will ride home to the County as I promised. But we do *not* tell Prince Stanislaw about the retreat, or it will threaten both his ambitions and his pride. He must believe that we are making only a short detour before pressing on to Valkarky. Once he sees what we are up against, he will be only too glad to retreat, believe you me."

I wasn't convinced that Grimalkin was right. "Are you sure about that? He's a brave man and seems very determined to fight."

"Remember the varteki?" she asked.

I nodded.

"Well, the two you encountered were young and small in comparison with the full-grown adult version. The Kobalos may deploy hundreds of such creatures. In the face of that, even the brave prince will retreat!"

"Have you told him about the kulad?"

"Not yet. I will leave that to you. Gather your strength. At the end of the week, we will have a meeting with all the princelings, a council of war. There *you* must be the one to take command. You have returned from the dead and filled them with hope and confidence of certain victory. They'll expect you to be decisive and lead them with confidence. Would you like to practice now what you will say?"

I nodded, and allowed Grimalkin to rehearse me in my manner of delivery and how best to explain our supposed intentions. It would be difficult. My words and manner would have to persuade real princes to do as I ordered.

And the strategy wasn't even mine—it was devised by Grimalkin.

I resented my role in this. I did my best to conceal my feelings from her, but I was becoming more and more angry.

Once more I was being manipulated.

5
The Haunted Attics

I slept a lot, but I had no energy. Despite that, I made it my business to continue Jenny's training as best I could. I felt increasingly guilty about having brought her here; I certainly didn't want her to feel that I was neglecting my duty to train her. I had to make her as good a spook as I possibly could.

Late each afternoon, I gave her a lesson in my room. I talked while she took notes. Toward the end of the third lesson, she suddenly asked me a question.

"Don't you think it's strange having a witch like Grimalkin for an ally?" she wondered.

I'd been teaching her about the dark, explaining the dangers from water witches. In an attempt to make it more interesting and hold her attention, I'd given her an account of my time working with John Gregory in the north of the County and our encounters with Morwena, the most powerful water witch of them all.

"It's true that it isn't in our traditions. My master was against it at first, but after a while even he saw the need for alliances with witches such as Grimalkin. She's saved my life on more than one occasion. I was being hunted by Morwena in the dark. I was alone on the marsh, nothing ahead for me but death, but then Grimalkin came to my aid, and together we defeated the water witch."

Jenny didn't look convinced.

"We've had enough theory for today," I told her suddenly.

"I've had enough to last me a lifetime!" Jenny retorted. She smiled but meant every word.

"That's why we're going to have a bit of a change. Tomorrow we'll do some practical work," I continued. "The prince has told me that in the eastern wing of the palace there are a number of sealed, haunted attics that aren't used. It's time these ghosts were sorted out. So we'll see if you can manage to send a lingerer to the light." Lingerers were souls trapped on earth—often ghosts who didn't even know that they were dead.

The previous evening, thinking of Jenny's training needs, I'd asked Prince Stanislaw if his ancient castle had any ghosts.

He'd smiled with his mouth but not his eyes. "Yes,

we have ghosts. Many ghosts. There are places we cannot go. There is big danger. Many dark rooms. When lit by candles, shadows move strangely and air become very cold. We lock rooms long time. Seal danger inside. Old problem."

"I need to train my apprentice," I told him. "I could clear the ghosts from those rooms for you, and then you'd be able to use them again."

He'd looked at me like I was crazy. "You think you can do this? Many fail. Magowie have tried also many years ago. They try, and die."

I smiled at him. "I'm sure I can help. Will you let me try?"

Ghosts couldn't usually kill people but did sometimes drive them insane. But there were exceptions—for example, there were strangler ghosts back in the County that spooks ranked from one to three. The very strongest, those of the first rank, were extremely rare, but they could asphyxiate their prey. They put their hands around the neck of their victims and squeezed. If they did it to the weak, they could stop their breath.

In my master's Bestiary, his personal compendium of creatures of the dark, there was also an account of something even more dangerous—his own encounter with an exceptionally strong strangler ghost that had killed a number of people. But it hadn't been able to kill John Gregory because of what he was. However, the news of the magowie deaths did make me think. We were far from the County. Perhaps things were different here?

"I'm a seventh son of a seventh son," I told Stanislaw, giving him a confident smile. "Even the strongest ghost can't kill me."

The prince had shrugged. "Then I will give you the keys. So try do it. But flee if danger too great. Magowie who died were stubborn. They went back again and again. Best to know when you cannot win."

Now, looking at Jenny, I took those keys from my pocket and dangled them in front of her. "The keys to the haunted attics," I told her. "So what do you think the first steps will be in dealing with the ghosts?"

"Entering the attics and seeing what they contain," she replied, her face lighting up with enthusiasm. "Seeing how big the problem is and what needs to be done."

"So what will our biggest difficulty be after we've assessed the situation?"

"Language," she replied thoughtfully. "You told me that you have to talk to a ghost and persuade it to go to the light. But Polyznian ghosts will talk Losta. They won't understand our language."

"So?" I demanded.

"We'll have to learn Losta!"

I nodded.

Jenny beamed at me. "I already know quite a few phrases that might be useful when dealing with a ghost. Grimalkin has been teaching me."

The prospect of visiting those haunted attics clearly appealed to her. If she could eventually send a soul to the light, she'd feel she was making real progress, which was important for her development and confidence. So despite my weariness, I had to make the effort.

"You can look after the keys," I told her. "There'll be no theory lesson tomorrow—you can have the afternoon off. Then soon after dark we'll investigate the first of the attics in order to get some idea of what we're dealing with."

The following evening I was sitting in my window seat again, staring down at the flickering campfires. A cold wind was blowing from the north. I could hear it whining past the tower. It wouldn't be long before the first fall of snow.

It was well after dark, and Jenny still hadn't arrived. I was beginning to worry. It wasn't like her to be late.

Then I heard rapid footsteps outside my room. The door opened, and Jenny burst in past the guard.

Something was badly wrong.

However, I nodded at the man to signal all was well, and he retreated, closing the door behind him. I turned to look at my apprentice. She was wearing my silver chain tied around her waist and carrying a rowan staff, but her eyes were wild and she was breathing hard.

"I'm sorry! I'm so sorry!" she cried, collapsing onto a seat.

"What have you done?" I asked, trying not to raise my voice.

She gabbled out her tale so quickly that I struggled to follow. She'd taken the keys and entered one of the haunted attics on her own. She'd expected to find ghosts but had stumbled across something far worse. There'd been what appeared to be a circular stone well. A glass had filled with blood and dropped down the shaft. Then the stones had begun to steam and some terrible entity had risen up out of the pit. The lights had gone out, and she'd been confronted by a monstrous being with six glowing eyes that reached toward her with its tentacles.

"I was terrified, but I reacted without thinking," Jenny said, hardly pausing for breath. "I dropped my staff, reached into my pockets, and grabbed a handful of salt and another of iron filings. Then I flung both straight at those frightening red eyes.

"I've never been so scared in my life. I knew that if it was some sort of ghost, it wouldn't work. If it was a demon or something else from the dark, it might not do much good either.

"The thing gave out a loud roar, and the whole chamber began to shake. The head dropped toward the pit, and the tentacles seemed suddenly shorter, shrunken. It wasn't destroyed, but the salt and iron gave me just enough time to escape. I snatched up my staff and ran for my life. I slammed the first door shut behind me. Once through the second door, I locked it—though I knew that this might not be enough to stop it. I feared that thing might get out into the castle and attack other people and I'd be responsible for their deaths. I'm sorry, Tom. I'm really sorry for being so stupid."

"Why? Why on earth did you do it?" I asked.

"I just wanted to prove to myself that I'm good enough to be a spook. I thought it would be easy. I've learned some useful phrases from Grimalkin. I know enough Losta to be able to say 'Think of a happy time in your life' and 'Go to the light.' I was hoping to come back and say that I'd done it, that I'd sent a soul to the light. But I didn't expect that . . . it wasn't a ghost. The prince told you that they were attics haunted by ghosts. I thought I might be able to do more to help you, take some of the burden off you when you're such a long way short of being fit."

My heart was thudding at the thought of the risk she'd taken. She could have been killed. And she was right—that entity might have been able to get out of the attic and into the castle. Many lives might have been lost as a result. Although Jenny had behaved irresponsibly, I tried to remain calm and I spoke slowly.

"We're in a foreign land now, not back in the County where we have generations of experience on how the dark manifests itself. Things are different here. We shouldn't take risks with the unknown. That was probably the most stupid thing you've done in your entire life!" I told her. "There are worse things than death. Some of the entities from the dark can do more than just put an end to your body. They can snuff out your soul—as if you'd never existed."

"I'll never be so stupid again. I've learned my lesson!" Jenny exclaimed. "It'll be good to leave the practice and get back to the theory!"

She was trying to put on a brave face, but she was still shaking with fear. I had to be cruel to be kind, to impress on her how serious her actions had been.

"It's not something to joke about, Jenny!" I snapped. "Yes, it was a lesson—one that I hope you'll never forget!

We have a duty to others. In some situations we might have to sacrifice our own lives. You stupidly put others at risk!"

"I'm sorry! I'm sorry!" she cried, tears streaming down her cheeks.

"But you're right about one thing. We do need to get back to the theory. That's exactly what we need to do," I told her firmly. "We need to find out a lot more about that attic before we go back there together."

"We're going back to face that?"

"Of course we are. I told you that being a spook was dangerous. And when we start a job, we finish it. You might have awakened something really dangerous— something that might be able to break out of that attic. We have to make it safe."

"How can we find out more about it?" Jenny asked, brushing away her tears.

"I'll talk to Prince Stanislaw tomorrow. I should have asked more questions when I spoke to him previously. That was no ghost . . . though the prince called it that. He speaks our language far better than I speak Losta, but—"

"That's not too difficult for him," Jenny interrupted sarcastically.

I stifled an angry response. One minute Jenny was in floods of tears, I reflected; the next, she was being cheeky again. *I would never have spoken to my master, John Gregory, in that manner,* I thought wryly. But Jenny had a natural impudence, and she'd just survived a very stressful situation. We both had.

"True," I told her, "but the prince's vocabulary is limited. I should have realized that we might not be talking about the same thing. At least that's something you can learn from my mistake. When dealing with something unknown, gather as many facts as possible before you get anywhere near it."

In my weakened condition, I hadn't been looking forward to going into the attics, but I'd still expected it to be a routine training exercise. Now I realized that even if Jenny and I had gone together, the encounter with the entity from the well would have been very dangerous. I'd been assuming we'd meet the ghost of some Polyznian nobleman or perhaps a guard—which would have given me some serious communication problems. I wasn't sure what the entity in the attic was, but it was clearly something extremely powerful.

"*Was* it some sort of demon?" Jenny asked.

I shrugged. "It certainly doesn't sound like anything I've come up against before. It might have been a demon or even something unknown, something that we County spooks have no record of."

I didn't divulge my true fears regarding what she'd encountered. Her account had shaken me to the core. I was far from home, and the threat was way outside my experience. I had enough problems without this. Jenny had probably awakened something that might threaten the whole castle and beyond.

It had to be dealt with.

The following morning, I checked the rooms below the turret and found no sign of any type of chimney leading down. The well that Jenny had described didn't pass through the kitchens or the throne room to reach the ground. She had called it a well, but I was certain it was really some sort of portal to the dark.

Prince Stanislaw was busy dealing with affairs of state, and it was late afternoon before he found time to receive me. As we walked along the battlements, our breath steaming in the cold air, I gave him an account of what Jenny had experienced.

"I expected to find the ghosts of people in those attics," I explained. "I think that what Jenny faced was some type of demon."

"Is demon not same as ghost? No?"

"Demons are far more powerful and dangerous."

The prince nodded thoughtfully. "Many years

ago—before my lifetime, before my father lifetime and his father—this castle was captured by Kobalos. Wicked enemy live here many years before driven back. Many years when they do as they wish. Their mages talk to dark ghosts in that attic. They whispered to dark things in dark pit that leads to hell. Some magowie who entered that room were never seen again. Others blasted by heat. Only bits of burn flesh remained."

I nodded. So we were dealing with dangerous Kobalos dark entities.

"Your apprentice chose most dangerous room to enter. Others not so bad. One has ghost of a Kobalos. We think he once mage but power now gone. He mutter to himself. Scare people but do no harm."

"Then I'll go and talk to his ghost next," I said. Maybe that ghost would know something about the entity that Jenny had encountered. Grimalkin had told me that most Kobalos mages spoke our language as well as Losta.

"Where is he to be found?" I asked. "In which attic?"

"The tallest tower in northeast. But rest tonight and save strength. We are almost ready to cross river and attack," the prince continued, gesturing down at the army below. "You speak to us tomorrow? Talk about plan?"

"Yes, I'll talk tomorrow," I told him. Grimalkin had finished helping me to rehearse my speech. She had already warned me about tomorrow. I was as ready as I would ever be.

"Just one thing," Stanislaw said. "Remember, we not tell them you just farmer boy. It is for the best. Keep to sorceress's plan, no? You agree? They follow better if it is so."

I smiled in agreement and then went off to tell Jenny that she wouldn't have to face the monstrous thing in the attic again until we'd talked to the ghost of a mage.

6
A Little Detour

I was nervous at the prospect of addressing the rulers of the principalities, even though I knew exactly what to say and how to behave.

When I arrived, they were already gathered around a large square wooden table in Prince Stanislaw's throne room. The mullioned window above showed scenes of forests, glades and lakes.

Grimalkin followed me in, carrying the map. Jenny was still posing as my personal servant, so her presence wasn't required. She'd been annoyed about that—her natural curiosity had made her eager to attend.

I looked around. Despite all my rehearsals, would I be able to carry it off? I wondered. Guards resplendent in ceremonial dress were stationed along the walls, each armed with a sharp spear and a stout club.

Despite the log fire burning in the grate behind the

throne, the long room was chilly. It would be a miserable place in winter. It had a high vaulted ceiling; torches flickering in brackets dispelled most of the gloom, but pools of darkness lingered in the far corners of that vast space. And far above us, in the attic, was the portal to the dark that Jenny had seen.

I looked up at the ceiling, remembering her account of the dark entity that had emerged from it, and shivered.

I was dressed in the garments that Grimalkin had brought with her from the County—garments that befitted my station as a prince. On each shoulder was embossed the red rose of the County; she had sewn them on herself. Those here to meet me were clad in their finery, and I had to look the part. As Prince Stanislaw had explained, it was in all our interests not to reveal that I was just a commoner.

Grimalkin, however, was in her usual garb, her skirt hitched up to aid movement. She wore the usual leather straps across her body, but the scabbards were empty of blades in deference to the occasion. Only the guards were armed.

So I didn't have the Starblade with me. The weapon had let me down when fighting the Shaiksa, but it had defended me against dark magic on other occasions.

There was no reason to expect a threat here, but I did feel naked without it.

Those gathered around the table smiled and nodded at us. They acted in a deferential manner, looking at me in awe. Grimalkin had prepared me for this, and I took it in my stride. I had risen from the dead—it was to be expected. A servant offered us glasses of wine the same shade of red as the County rose. Immediately it made me think of the glass that Jenny had seen filling with blood beside the portal, and I suppressed a shudder.

Grimalkin and I politely refused the offers. I simply walked over to the table and, after smoothing the map flat, pinned it into position.

Prince Stanislaw introduced each member of the company in turn, and I nodded politely, trying my best to remember the names, most of which were almost impossible to pronounce. But I had already learned that six principalities were represented. Prince Stanislaw's Polyznia was by far the largest; the next most significant was the mountainous Wayaland, closely followed by Shalotte, which was near the coast.

The easiest one to remember was Prince Kaylar of Wayaland, because in addition to his immense stature—he must have been at least seven feet tall—and broad, muscular body, he had a long black beard that almost reached his waist, ending in three plaits that curled upward, pointing at us like a trident.

This alliance of princes had provided an army that, according to the witch assassin, would total just over seven thousand fighting men. Four thousand would be mounted, and among the infantry there would be two thousand archers. We could also field three eighteen-pounder guns, each pulled by a team of mules. We had sappers, too—men who could dig tunnels and under-mine fortified walls.

In addition to the soldiers, two thousand ancillary staff would act in support. They included cooks, smiths, those responsible for stores, and a variety of servants to attend the royals. It was a lot of men to lead. And here was I, struggling to lead one apprentice!

Despite her earlier misgivings, Grimalkin was now pleased by what had been mobilized by the relatively small principalities. She believed that if the larger kingdoms to the south were to provide forces in the same proportion to their size, especially the Germanic ones, we would eventually have a real chance against the Kobalos.

We were a long way northeast of the County, which was separated from this battlefront by a huge continental land mass and the stormy northern sea. But if we didn't defeat it, in time the dark army that we faced would directly threaten the County.

I turned to face the princes and caught the eye of Prince Stanislaw, who gave me a faint smile and the lightest of nods. Then, trying to speak calmly and firmly, as the witch assassin had instructed, I told the first of my lies.

I pointed to the map, indicating Valkarky. "That is our objective. We should arrive in less than two weeks. It may take another week to successfully breach the walls of the city."

Grimalkin translated for the company, but I knew that Prince Stanislaw would already have understood the gist of what I had said.

"However," I continued, "first we shall make a little detour. After advancing steadily toward Valkarky for two days, we will then swing left and launch a surprise attack on this kulad!"

I pointed at it on the map and jabbed it forcefully with the point of my index finger. "It is called Kartuna, and the tower is of great strategic importance."

After Grimalkin had translated my words, I noticed that there were a few frowns. Prince Stanislaw raised his eyebrows, and Prince Kaylar of Wayaland spoke in a deep booming voice, tugging at his beard in some agitation.

"Prince Kaylar does not think that a wise move,"

Grimalkin translated. "He believes that by pausing to attack the tower, we will give our enemies time to gather their forces and meet us on the Plain of Erestaba. He says that we should sweep past such fortifications at speed, like a fist punching toward a jaw, and concentrate on our main objective."

I smiled and nodded at Prince Kaylar. "You are correct in pure military terms," I conceded, holding his gaze. "But Valkarky is guarded by much more than thick walls and steel weapons. The Kobalos have many mages who wield powerful magic—magic that may turn aside our cannon and strike such terror into our forces that even the bravest might flee. But this kulad here," I said, jabbing it again for emphasis, "is home to a mage who also uses it to store his magical power and artifacts. If we can seize this tower, Grimalkin, who is an expert on dark magic, can learn much that will aid us. She will discover a way to counter the occult forces that our enemies will deploy."

Prince Stanislaw nodded at my explanation, but the other princes had to wait for Grimalkin to translate.

While she did so, I met the eyes of each of them in turn, just as the witch assassin had coached me, finally returning to Prince Kaylar and giving him the longest stare. Then I told my second lie to the gathering. Lying made me feel a little uncomfortable, but it had to be done if Grimalkin's plan was to succeed.

"Once we have the knowledge that will protect us against their magic, we will head directly for Valkarky again. Within weeks it will be ours, and the Kobalos threat will be no more!"

After Grimalkin had translated these words, heads began to nod—even Prince Kaylar grudgingly conceded that this was the way to proceed.

Next, Grimalkin turned to face me and bowed.

"I would like to offer a little military advice, if I may."

"Yes, go ahead!" I commanded, as we'd rehearsed in the event of Grimalkin feeling the need to add anything to what I'd said.

She bowed toward me again and then addressed the princes directly. I wondered what she was telling them, but again they nodded and exchanged satisfied glances.

Ten minutes later we were back in my quarters.

"You did well," Grimalkin congratulated me. "You looked and behaved every inch a prince. If all goes well and our luck holds, we may return with valuable information and get most of those men back alive."

"What did you say to them at the end?" I asked.

"I told them that the Kobalos have two hearts. One lies in approximately the same position as a human one;

the other is smaller, but is close to the base of the throat. A Kobalos warrior may survive the piercing of his main heart, because the secondary one maintains the flow of blood to the brain. A wound that would certainly finish off a human might leave a dying Kobalos conscious and still dangerous. So I recommended that they inform their warriors that decapitation is the preferred method of despatching the enemy or, failing that, a double piercing of the chest. You remember that I advised you to kill the Shaiksa assassin in that way."

"How did you learn this? Browne never mentioned it, and it wasn't in your notes."

"My notes were a limited catalog of my experiments with Kobalos battle entities, not Kobalos anatomy. I have others that include my speculations on methods of countering their military might—you may read them if you are interested. Back in the County, I learned about the two hearts by dissecting the body of the haizda mage before I filled the grave with earth. I confirmed that finding by also dissecting the body of the Shaiksa assassin."

I nodded. Grimalkin was thorough and painstaking in her efforts to learn how we might defeat the Kobalos. Everything was woven tightly into the tapestry of her schemes . . . everything, including me. I felt trapped, bound within her plans, with no room for maneuvering.

7
The God Maker

THAT same night Jenny and I climbed the stone steps of the tallest northeastern turret, heading for the attic where the prince had said I would find the ghost of the Kobalos mage. I was wearing the Starblade at my hip and carrying a rowan staff, and my pockets contained salt and iron. Hopefully such precautions were unnecessary, but after Jenny's experience, I wasn't taking any chances.

I found the ascent hard work and felt dizzy and breathless before we reached the attic. I was a long way short of returning to full fitness. It was just a few days before we were due to cross the river and attack, and I really couldn't see how I'd be able to ride out at the head of an army. Sooner or later I would have to confront Grimalkin and make that clear.

The keys weren't marked, and I had to proceed by trial and error. I tried five of the large keys before the sixth finally opened the door. Jenny was carrying the lantern, and its light revealed a small anteroom with another door facing us. She had hardly spoken since we left my room. No doubt she was scared, which wasn't really surprising after her terrifying encounter with the thing from the portal.

"Is this anteroom similar to the one you passed through?" I asked.

"It's identical," Jenny said, shivering. "It even had a table and two chairs coated in a thick layer of dust, exactly like the ones here."

I could sense no warning chill telling me that something from the dark was close. Could Prince Stanislaw be wrong about this attic being haunted?

"Do you sense anything from the dark?" I asked. I wondered if my own gifts were working properly after the terrible experience that I'd been through.

She shook her head.

"Neither do I. Let's go into the inner room. We're in unknown territory here, so I won't have much chance to explain things. I'll need to concentrate, so the teaching must come second. Just listen carefully."

Jenny nodded, and I opened the second door into the inner chamber. This was very different from the room that Jenny had described. There was no water dripping from the ceiling, no stone well.

It was very dusty and cluttered with books: vast leather-bound tomes lay on the floor in precarious piles; the shelves were full to capacity but shrouded by thick curtains of spiders' webs. Long, low tables set against the far wall were bowed with the weight of enormous glass jars containing brown or green substances. It reminded me of the lair of the haizda mage back in Chipenden. No doubt Jenny would recognize these too, and they wouldn't help her get any calmer. She'd almost died at the hands of that mage.

Did those jars contain the seeds of monstrous creatures like the ones Grimalkin had grown near the lair of that mage? For a moment I wondered why the room hadn't been cleared. But it was obvious: Terrified by the hauntings, humans had obviously abandoned and then sealed them.

"Turn the lantern down low, Jenny," I said softly. "Some ghosts avoid light of any kind, and we don't want to deter this one."

She fiddled with the shutters and placed the lantern on the floor. Now it just cast a small circle of light onto the boards; the majority of the room was in darkness. It was now more likely that a ghost would materialize—though of course we were dealing with the unknown. If we did encounter a ghost, it would be the spirit of a Kobalos, and a mage to boot. Anything was possible.

Suddenly I felt an icy chill, that warning that something from the dark was drawing close. Slowly a faint column of light began to form in the right-hand corner of the chamber, close to a tall bookshelf. It flickered and shifted, taking on the shape of one of the Kobalos.

This creature was larger and broader than the haizda mage I'd fought back in Chipenden before our journey up here had ever begun. It wore heavy leather boots and a long gown not dissimilar to that of a spook—though the bare arms were covered in thick hair like the hide of an animal. The face had been shaved to dark stubble, and the big eyes were staring at me. If I was reading its expression correctly, it appeared curious rather than hostile, and showed a hint of sadness.

The shape flickered again. One moment it was gray and translucent and I could see the bookshelves behind it; the next, the crisp maroon material of its gown and its large brown eyes seemed solid and sharp, and it could have been a living, breathing mage that we confronted.

"What can you see, Jenny?" I asked.

"It's one of their mages. But I don't think he's hostile. There are waves of sadness coming from him."

Suddenly the ghost spoke in the guttural language of Losta. I couldn't understand a word and hoped that this mage had the same language skills as the haizda I'd fought back in the County.

"I'm going to ask him to speak in our language," I told Jenny. "If he does, I'll question him and maybe send the ghost to the light—if it's possible. So concentrate and listen carefully, but leave the questioning to me."

Jenny nodded, and I turned to the ghost.

"I don't speak your language. Can you speak mine?"

"You are brave to speak to me," the ghost replied in a deep, hollow voice. "All the other humans ran. Are you a mage?"

"My name is Thomas Ward and I'm a spook," I said. "My job is to deal with ghosts and similar entities."

"My name is Abuskai. I am a high mage."

"Do you realize that you're dead?" I asked.

That was the standard question a spook asked a ghost, the first step in preparing to send them to the light. But could a Kobalos mage be directed to the light? I wondered. Perhaps, like human malevolent witches and mages, he belonged to their equivalent of the dark. Or maybe there were domains completely unknown to us, where the dark of the Kobalos gather.

"Of course I do. I have been dead a long time," the ghost of the mage replied. "It wearies me to be trapped here. I seek release from my torment but cannot pass beyond this world."

"What holds you back?" I asked.

I was quite prepared to attempt to send this creature to the light by asking it to focus upon a happy memory from its life—the method that usually worked with the spirits of humans. But first I wanted to question Abuskai about the demonic entity in the well.

"There are magical barriers in place that prevent my escape. Alive or dead, I am no longer needed by those who now rule my people. I am discarded. What a fool I have been! I was the one who helped to bring about the change in the first place!"

"What change?" I asked quietly.

"The birth of our god, Talkus," the ghost replied. "I helped to bring it about. I created the foundation upon which he was constructed."

Talkus was the Kobalos god who had been born as the Fiend died. The horned Fiend, once the most powerful of the Old Gods, had been bad enough. He had been able to make himself far larger than a human and to halt time, making his victims powerless while he snatched their souls. He had been the source of power for many malevolent witches and other dark creatures and wished to dwell permanently on earth and bring to it a new age of darkness.

However, Talkus was far worse. While the Fiend demanded that humans submit to him, Talkus wished to destroy the human race—except for the females, who would be permanently enslaved to the Kobalos. Talkus had the shape of a skelt, a creature with many legs and a bone tube that it thrust into the flesh of humans to drain their blood. But perhaps the most terrifying thing of all was that, because Talkus was a new god, his powers were unknown. Talkus might be capable of anything, and we might have no defense against him.

Destroying Talkus could well be the key to defeating the Kobalos. I needed to find out how that could be done.

"What part did you play in his birth?" I asked.

"Through magic, through belief, I shaped him and gave him substance. A god is born when enough believe, when enough desire, when an architect shapes their thoughts. I was that architect."

I was stunned. It had named itself the architect. Was I facing the Kobalos who had planned and created this new darkness that we faced? If so, Abuskai was a god maker.

I realized that there was a potential for great danger here. Such a powerful mage, although a ghost, might be able to do us serious harm. We were dealing with the unknown. I would need to be careful not to anger it. I glanced sideways at Jenny. She seemed calm and was staring at the mage, who hadn't acknowledged her presence in any way. Perhaps it was because she was female. To a Kobalos she was a purra, no better than a slave and unworthy of engaging in conversation.

I hoped that was all and that Jenny was not in danger because she was female. For all I knew, perhaps the ghost found her presence offensive. I was glad I had warned her to leave the questioning to me. It might not tolerate any interruption from my apprentice.

"So what happened? How did you die? Why are you trapped here?" I asked.

"Kobalos mages constantly form and re-form their alliances. Within Valkarky, power shifts. Alliances conspired against me, seeking to subvert what I was shaping to their own ends. I was betrayed and murdered. Soon afterward, the king was also slain, and a triumvirate formed to rule in his place. They continued my work and brought the god Talkus into being, modifying my design and utilizing my magic for their own purposes. I have been cast aside without honor, slain and imprisoned here."

The triumvirate was the group of three powerful high mages who now ruled the Kobalos—I'd heard of them already. But Grimalkin had told me that it did not always contain the same three mages—she had slayed one of them on her visit to Valkarky, though it had not changed their policy of seeking to make war upon humans. No doubt it had only increased their enmity. But next time it might be different. Slay one, and the arrival of a replacement might well cause a new triumvirate to change its way of thinking. Could the war be halted by changing those who ruled the Kobalos? I wondered.

The ghost began to flicker and became insubstantial again, making me fear that it was about to depart. I needed to concentrate and keep the conversation going now, and speculate later.

Suddenly, despite my instruction, Jenny asked a question. "In one of the other attics in this castle, there is a dangerous demonic entity. What is it, and how can it be destroyed or driven away?"

The ghost gathered substance rapidly and looked solid enough to touch. Emotions flickered across its face: incredulity and anger. She really did need to listen to my instructions. I'd never have disobeyed my own master in that way. The ghost looked appalled at what she'd just said, and I grew afraid for her.

But the moment of danger passed. When the entity replied, it ignored Jenny and spoke directly to me. "Anyone who tries to destroy the thing your purra speaks of is a fool. It would seize and annihilate both his body and his soul. It is a being called the targon, which guards the gateways of fire that lead to the domain of Talkus."

"So the well in the room is a portal to your god?"

"Yes—one of the three doorways that I created!" The ghost's eyes gleamed with pride. "This is the room where I studied and planned. The portal chamber is where I crafted and created the future."

"Is there any danger that it could leave the attic and kill people outside?" I asked.

The ghost shook its head. "It is a guardian and cannot venture more than six feet beyond the gateway that it guards."

"What about the other attics in the south wing? What do they contain?" I asked.

"Echoes of what once existed, but nothing of importance. Maybe there are also human ghosts. Some of your people were questioned and sacrificed there."

All at once the ghost began to fade.

"Don't go!" I cried. "I want to ask you some more questions. And I'll try to help you escape from here. Just answer this, please—if the rulers of Valkarky changed, could the war end? Could Kobalos and humans ever live in peace?"

"It would depend upon those who ruled and upon the structure of that rule," the ghost of the mage said, becoming solid again, the hollow voice reverberating from the walls. "The last king of Valkarky was not as militant as the triumvirate. His father had fought wars against humans, and so had his father before him. But they were limited territorial disputes, whereas the triumvirate now seeks unlimited expansion and wishes to kill or enslave humans. There would always be border disputes and skirmishes, but with different rulers, Kobalos and humans could live in peace most of the time. Yes, that is possible."

I quickly asked another question. "You named yourself as the architect who conceived of and shaped the Kobalos god Talkus—and it is that god who now drives your people forward in this war. Is that what you wanted?"

The ghost flickered but answered my question.

"War was not the purpose for which I shaped Talkus," it replied. "Thousands of years ago, my people carried out a great crime, an act of insanity. We slayed all our females. I wished to rectify that act of madness."

I watched incredulity and horror flicker across Jenny's face. That was something she must have read about in Nicholas Browne's Kobalos glossary. However, hearing it from the ghost brought home the insane horror of that act. That defining moment had shaped the Kobalos society of today.

It was a terrible tale, and was hard to believe. The Kobalos women had been taken to a vast arena and slain, their throats cut, their blood drained. It took seven days to complete the terrible task. It was, as the ghost admitted, an act of madness. By that act, the Kobalos males had hoped to come to their full strength—they believed that the women made them weak, undermining the savagery that was the pure essence of a warrior.

Of course, they were then faced with the threat of extinction, but they had already planned a way to avoid that. Although humans and Kobalos are two distinct races, the Kobalos's use of magic made it possible for them to breed with human females—slaves that they call purrai. But only Kobalos males resulted from such unions.

"The god I began to shape would have helped us create our own females once more," the ghost continued. "Balance would have been restored and, in time, there would have been no need for us to use purrai. But the murder of the king and the coming to power of the triumvirate changed all that. They reshaped the new god for their own ends—that of war, and the acquisition of greater and greater power."

"Is it too late to change things again?" I asked, stunned by that revelation. The dead mage had actually been benign and had intended for good to result from his act of creation.

"There are those among my people who already strive for such change. I have talked to them. My spirit cannot leave this place, but they can and do project their minds to me. An alliance is already working to overthrow the triumvirate. It began with a small secret group called the Skapien, who are opposed to the slave trade. But recently there have been others in Valkarky who are more open and vocal in their opposition. Haizda mages are one of these dissenting groups, and as a result they have been outlawed by the triumvirate and are now being hunted down and exterminated."

"It would be better to change the rulers of Valkarky than have a war," I said to the ghost. "You say you have contacts with the Kobalos who oppose the triumvirate. Do you give them your support? Do you wish for the same thing?"

"I do," replied the mage.

"It would be useful for us to have contact with them too. Could you arrange that?"

I could see real possibilities here. There might be other ways than Grimalkin's to end this threat. Perhaps the Kobalos could be changed from within?

The ghost did not reply. It simply vanished.

I was disappointed, but it was a beginning. I would return here and talk to the dead mage again. I nodded at the lantern, and Jenny adjusted the shutters once more, filling that dusty room with brightness.

Then we left, locking both doors behind us.

"Could you have sent it to the light?" Jenny asked.

"I don't know," I admitted. "But I am prepared to try—eventually, that is. I think we can learn a lot of useful information from that ghost. We'll come back another night and try to speak to him again."

Jenny yawned.

"Are you tired?" I asked.

She nodded, stifling another yawn.

"Well, it'll be at least another hour before you get to bed," I told her. "We have something else to do before then. When you follow this trade, night work is something you have to get used to!"

Jenny Calder

8
The Dead Prisoners

My encounter with the demonic thing in the well had been terrifying. I was very nervous when Tom talked to the ghost of the Kobalos mage; I feared it might turn on us at any moment. Dead or not, it might still retain some magical power.

Tom had the Starblade, but I had no such protection. In any case, its magic had already let him down once. I was exhausted by both ordeals. The last thing I wanted was to face more ghosts. Surely they could have waited for another night?

However, I kept quiet—I didn't want Tom to think less of me. I played the dutiful apprentice and followed him up the steps toward another of the attics.

"You heard what the dead mage said about the other locked rooms?" Tom asked, stopping and turning to face me. He was breathing hard, wheezing terribly. I was worried that he might be overexerting himself.

I nodded. "Some are likely to contain the ghosts of humans."

"That's right. We won't be able to send them to the light because they'll almost certainly be from these northern lands and won't speak our language. We still need to see what needs to be done. Our job is to keep people safe from the dark, and that applies even when we're far from the County. That's our duty, so we're going to have to learn Losta—or at least enough of it to persuade a spirit toward the light."

He turned and began to climb the steps again.

"I know quite a few words already," I reminded him.

Tom nodded. "I see I have a bit of catching up to do," he replied with a wry smile.

At last he reached the attic and paused, struggling to get his breath back.

When we opened the door, we saw that there was no anteroom, just a large space that had clearly been used to torture prisoners. There was a brazier full of cold ashes, and on the wooden table lay a number of instruments: tongs, saws, hooks, blades, and long, thin needles—along with manacles to hold prisoners in position. I noticed dark stains where blood had soaked into the wood. There were also manacles set into the wall, with stains on the wooden floor beneath them.

My stomach heaved at the thought of what must have been done to those poor human prisoners. Up to ten of them could have been held here. Then I began to sense fragments of the horrific experiences the victims had gone through—flashes of contorted faces, sounds of moaning and screaming and a sudden overwhelming stench of blood.

I felt a sudden overpowering urge to get out of that room . . . but I took a deep breath and tried to steady myself.

"Cut the light to a minimum, Jenny," Tom commanded.

I placed the lantern on the floor at my feet and adjusted the shutters so that once again the room was in darkness but for the small circle of light on the boards that surrounded it.

I didn't like it in the gloom of that torture chamber. It was possible to imagine all sorts of things emerging from the darkest corners. But Tom knew what he was doing. Ghosts were less likely to appear when a room was well lit.

We remained near the door, still and silent. Suddenly I shivered and sensed a presence in the room. I could see nothing, but from the left-hand corner beneath the farthest of the wall manacles came a faint groaning.

Then, quite clearly, I heard the chains move against the stones—along with another sound like liquid running down the walls and dripping onto the floor. I could smell blood again.

There was a ghost present, the ghost of somebody in agony after being tortured. Instantly I knew a lot about the man. He'd been part of a small patrol testing the Kobalos lines. He was Polyznian, but he was not a subject of Stanislaw; his prince went by a different name. The ghost had been here many years, so maybe the ruler then had been Prince Stanislaw's father or even his grandfather? Most of the patrol had been slain, but the rest had been captured, questioned, and tortured.

I could sense the man's anguish; something that went far beyond physical pain. They had cut him with blades coated in a poison that caused extreme pain. But even worse was his realization that he would never get out of this place. His family lived far to the south, and he would never see them again. He had a small son and daughter and a child soon to be born. How would his wife, Karina, support their family without him?

I gave a sob and tears flowed down my cheeks, for the ghost didn't realize how long he'd been here. By now his wife would probably be dead and his children grown old.

Tom gave me a kind look and put a finger to his lips,

asking me to be quiet. I nodded and stifled another sob.

The next sound came from the table: a deep groan, and then a shriek of agony. Then I heard the noise of a saw cutting through something—but it wasn't wood.

The ghost was reliving the terrible moments of his torture and death. His captors were sawing through flesh and bone.

Unable to control myself any longer, I was sick on the floor at my feet. I didn't dare look at Tom. I could smell the stink of my own vomit, and I knew he could smell it too. I leaned back against the wall, shivering.

Tom pointed to the door. To my relief, I realized that we were leaving.

"I'm sorry," I said as Tom locked the outer door.

"You don't need to be sorry, Jenny," he replied, his voice kind. "It obviously affected you very badly. You must have experienced far more than I did. All I heard was the rattling of chains and a faint groan. Then I saw a few other vague luminous shapes. But I knew something really bad was happening on that table."

"They were sawing through his bones," I said, shaking with horror at the thought of it. "Why would they do that? What kind of a race are they?"

"Humans can be just as bad," Tom replied, leading the way down the stone steps. He sounded weary. He was still a long way from regaining his former strength. "They were probably trying to get information from him—troop strengths and movements—in order to save the lives of their own soldiers. I suppose that war brings out the worst in everyone. Our own civil war back in the County was terrible and tore families apart, brother against brother."

"But must the ghost endure his death over and over again?"

"Remember the dead soldiers I showed you on Hangman's Hill back in the County? This was also probably a ghast rather than a ghost, Jenny—the fragment of that poor soldier's soul left behind when it went to the light. But there must have been ghosts there, too. . . ."

"Yes. One of the manacled prisoners missed his family—he couldn't bear the thought of never seeing them again. He had two children and his wife was soon to give birth to a third. I think he'd been really happy at home. If we could get him to concentrate on that, it might be the way to send him to the light."

Tom nodded, but he seemed distracted, lost in thought.

"Are you all right?" I asked him.

He shook his head. "I'm far from right. And I think we'll have to wait until next year to sort out those ghosts."

I stared at him in astonishment.

"We're going home. In a few days, Grimalkin expects me to ride out to attack the kulad. It's madness. I've been thinking and worrying about it for days. The trouble I've had climbing these steps has convinced me. We'll travel back to the County before the snows trap us here. We'll go and tell Grimalkin now."

He'd given me no clue at all that that he'd been considering this option. When I'd asked to go home, he'd just brushed aside my pleas.

My heart soared with happiness. At last Tom had seen sense. I hated this cold, war-torn land and felt homesick for the meadows and green hills of the County.

At last we were going home!

9

An Anvil of Pain

TOM knocked politely, and then we entered the room I shared with Grimalkin.

She was sitting cross-legged on her bed and stared at us without blinking. The moment I saw her face, I could tell that she knew what Tom was going to say—whether she had scryed it or was simply reading the intent in his eyes, I don't know. Her gaze was anything but friendly. My powers didn't work with the witch assassin—she kept me out—but my instinct was that we might be in real danger from her if she was angry.

Tom stood facing her while I closed the door. I grew more and more anxious. I knew that Grimalkin wasn't going to like this. How would she react?

"I'm going back to the County tomorrow," Tom told her. "I'm not fit enough for what you propose. It'll take months for me to regain my strength, probably the whole of the winter, and I'm better off recuperating back home."

"You cannot leave now. It will disrupt my plans," Grimalkin spat. "Without you here, army morale will disintegrate at the first setback. The prince is expecting you to lead them."

I was furious when I heard her say "my plans." Why had Tom allowed himself to be caught up in her schemes in the first place? I wondered.

"Why does it have to be now?" Tom asked. "Wouldn't it be better to attack the kulad in the spring?"

Grimalkin shook her head. "The Kobalos will not wait for spring. They are a people of cold and ice. Winter is their time. Within months, their army will cross the river and overwhelm these small principalities. It is vital that we strike before that happens. What I can learn at the mage's kulad will not save these borderlands, but may well ensure the survival of the County. Our only chance is to act now."

I couldn't fault Grimalkin's reasoning; I expected Tom to yield to her will—I'd watched her controlling him ever since we left the County. Why should that change? She was very persuasive. But, to my surprise and delight, he resisted.

"I just can't do it. I'm weary . . . I'll be no good to you. You're better off without me."

"You must do it! You *will* do it!" Grimalkin growled, showing her pointy teeth.

"Don't threaten me!" Tom cried, an edge of anger coming into his voice. "We've been allies in the past and will be in the future, but I need to rest. You should listen to what *I* want for a change."

"How can you let down Prince Stanislaw and the warriors who believe in you? The odds are against them— many of them will die in the coming conflict. But they have seen you defeat the Shaiksa assassin and survive death itself. Only your presence will give them the confidence to cross that river. You cannot refuse."

"I *do* refuse! When I fall off my horse with exhaustion, it won't inspire anybody with confidence, will it?"

"You will do as I say!" cried Grimalkin, coming to her feet.

I couldn't stand this. It was plainly wrong, a spook taking orders from a witch!

"Do you think I can bear to see women enslaved and maltreated by the Kobalos?" Grimalkin shouted. She and Tom were standing face-to-face now, their noses just inches apart. "Do you expect me to stand by and see more slaves taken as city after city falls under the yoke of our enemies? No, it shall not be! I will destroy the Kobalos forces and pull down the walls of Valkarky until all is a frozen wasteland and not one of the creatures lives! And *you* will play the part that I have shaped for you!"

"No!" Tom snapped angrily, his own voice raised for the first time. "I have been shaped and controlled by you! You brought me here without explaining what would be involved. All along you planned to pit me against the Shaiksa assassin, but you didn't tell me until we reached the river. You never thought fit to warn me and let me make up my own mind about it. You led me into danger—into *death*—completely blind. I never asked to be a part of this. I need to be back in the County, fighting the dark in my own way. I've taken on an apprentice, and my duty is to train her properly. That's what I intend to do. I'll spend my winter doing exactly that."

Grimalkin let out a deep sigh and spoke again, her voice low. "For most of my life I have been motivated by vengeance," she explained. "I have only truly loved once. I have cared for others and been deeply hurt by their loss, but not totally devastated as I was when the Fiend slayed the child who was at the center of my life.

"I failed to protect that child, but with the help of others, particularly you," she went on, nodding at Tom, "I helped bring about the destruction of the Fiend. That was something that shaped me; that made me what I am. So I too have been forged into a weapon on an anvil of pain. Now I recognize that I was born for a specific purpose— to destroy the Kobalos. We will win in the end, I promise you that, whether you choose to help or not. But you have disappointed me. I expected more of you."

Tom sighed, his expression resigned. Now, once again, I feared that he would yield to her will. But then that determination I'd seen in the Tom of old came back.

"I'm sorry, but I can't help you this time. I'll travel back with Jenny tomorrow. If you still wish it, I'll return in the spring."

He turned to me. "I'll see you in the stables just before dawn. Don't be late."

Then he left, closing the door behind him, leaving me alone with Grimalkin. I looked at her fearfully, but she simply gave a sigh to match Tom's and then smiled at me.

"You look tired, child. Get yourself to bed. Things will seem better in the morning."

I was surprised by how pleasant Grimalkin was being. I would have expected her to be angry and snap at me.

I took her advice. No sooner had my head touched the pillow then I fell into a deep sleep.

Suddenly I was in the grip of what seemed like a terrible nightmare. The room was in total darkness, and someone was pinning me to the bed. I fought to get free, but it was useless. I was being held in an iron grip.

All at once I realized that it wasn't a nightmare after

all; it was really happening to me. I was on my back, and someone was stuffing something into my mouth—it felt like a ball of cloth. I began to cough and choke.

Then I felt two fingers being pushed up into my nostrils, and my head was filled with a stinging, burning sensation. I couldn't breathe, and I panicked, bucking and twisting, trying in vain to escape. But I couldn't get free—and then, suddenly, the fingers were removed.

I could breathe again, but I felt strange and light-headed, as if my soul was drifting away from my body into an ocean of darkness. It was as if I didn't care what happened to me. Nothing mattered anymore.

Then I was lifted up and slung over somebody's shoulder. I heard a door close somewhere behind me, then footsteps echoing along a passageway, but I could see nothing, and I suddenly realized that there was something wrong with my eyes. After a while the air grew colder and there was a breeze on my face and I knew that we were outside.

I could hear voices in the distance that grew louder as we approached—along with whinnies and snorts.

The person carrying me came to a halt and spoke. "Take good care of her. I'll see you in two days."

It was the voice of Grimalkin.

Thomas Ward

10
Beaten and Controlled

I was up well before dawn, and dressed quickly. I feared that the prince might try to prevent us from leaving if he spotted us. The main meal in the castle was a five-course supper with lots of ale, so few wanted breakfast. Down in the kitchens, the cooks and their assistants were still sleeping, so I helped myself to food and packed our saddle-bags with provisions. We'd have to buy more on the journey, but I had coin enough for that.

I waited for Jenny, but the sky was already beginning to lighten to the east and there was still no sign of her. I began to pace up and down impatiently. I didn't want to be spotted riding away. Finally I went up to her room. She'd been tired the previous night. Perhaps she'd over-slept. . . .

I rapped on the door impatiently and called her name, but it was the voice of Grimalkin that bade me enter. I opened the door and went in. I expected her to try to talk me out of leaving, but I was determined to stay firm.

Grimalkin was sitting cross-legged on her bed in exactly the same position as when I'd left the night before. There was no sign of Jenny.

"Where's Jenny?" I asked. "She's not at the stables."

"She's gone north, in the care of Prince Kaylar."

I stared blankly at Grimalkin, attempting to make some sense of what she'd just said. "Why would she do that?"

"I placed her in his care," the witch assassin told me. "He has ridden out toward the kulad with a small patrol to assess its defenses and monitor the movement of Kobalos forces in the region."

"She wouldn't have gone willingly!" I said angrily. "Why have you done this? What has she done to deserve being placed in danger like this?"

"You are right. She did not go willingly. I used a narcotic and a little magic, but nothing that will cause her permanent harm. I did it to force you into riding with us. I know that you will not go home and abandon your apprentice. We ride immediately. The best way for you to ensure her safety is to lead us as I planned. Is that not so?"

"Are there no lengths you won't go to?" I asked, angered

by Grimalkin's deceit. She must already have been planning this when she had spoken to me the night before.

She shrugged and gave a little smile. "I simply do what must be done. Within a week we will be back here. Then you may ride home with your apprentice."

I hoped that Jenny was all right. It was my duty to ride after her and ensure her safety as far as I could—after all, it was my fault for bringing her to this place—but I liked the girl and would have gone anyway.

I would ride out with the army. I had no choice now. But I was seething inside and worried about Jenny. Grimalkin could be ruthless, and she had displayed that quality now. Being taken toward the kulad would put Jenny in danger of death, and if the Kobalos caught her, she'd end up a slave, tortured every day to teach her obedience.

Grimalkin had beaten me, and now she controlled me once more. I wished I had never listened to her. I should have stayed in the County.

We left the castle and rode north. After two hours, we crossed the Shanna River, using the same ford where I'd fought the Shaiksa assassin, Kauspetnd. I remembered how I'd struck his head from his body; how it had rolled across the stones and into the shallow water, the blood swirling away with the current.

His saber had pierced my guts simultaneously, but I hadn't felt any pain. I recalled how I'd looked down at the hilt in astonishment, knowing that the blade had passed right through me. I'd watched my own blood trickling onto the stones. The pain came again—and with it the intense cold and fear of death.

I felt nauseous and swayed in the saddle, almost falling off into the water. I was weak for almost an hour afterward.

Our army marched in six columns; with the exception of Prince Kaylar, each prince rode at the head of his own cavalry, with his foot soldiers bringing up the rear. By far the largest was the central column commanded by Prince Stanislaw. I rode on his left, with Grimalkin on his right. In Prince Kaylar's place was his eldest son. He was only eighteen and not experienced in war, but Grimalkin told me he had trusted the warriors at his back and advisers at his shoulder.

He didn't belong here, and neither did I. I was only seventeen—barely old enough to function as a spook, never mind as the leader of this army. But I was doing my best, riding with my head held high, even though my breathing was labored and I ached in every joint.

It was vital that I make this pretense work. Otherwise,

we would not link up with Prince Kaylar's force and be able to save Jenny.

I was very anxious about her. Grimalkin had explained that Prince Kaylar's patrol was small, numbering no more than forty men. If the Kobalos spotted them, they'd soon be overwhelmed and either slain or taken prisoner. If Jenny survived such a battle, she'd end up as a slave in Valkarky. My anger at Grimalkin simmered away at that thought.

About an hour after midday, we reached the area known as the Fittzanda Fissure. I'd been expecting volcanoes, but there was only uneven, stony ground punctuated by crevices and ridges, with vents of scalding steam. The horses whinnied with fear, unwilling to cross them.

At times the ground shook, and deep rumbles could be heard beneath us, like the muttering of angry giants. The air was filled with dust and the stink of sulfur, and I was only too glad to leave the place behind and move onto the plain of Eresteba.

This was a flat, cold place with not a tree to be seen. The wind blew toward us from the north, making patterns in the long grass. I kept searching the horizon, hoping to spot our patrol, but also fearing to see a huge Kobalos army. I couldn't believe that they weren't already lying in wait for us. They must know that we'd crossed the river.

They must be busy setting a trap. Surely Grimalkin, who knew how dark magic could be used to scry the future, would see the danger? When I mentioned it to her, she just shrugged.

The sun began to set, and we continued until it grew dark. It was a cold night, but we couldn't build fires—they'd be visible for miles around on such a flat plain. The farther we got without being seen, the better; we certainly didn't want them to guess our true destination.

The Shaiksa had special powers: You couldn't kill one without other members of the brotherhood being summoned to avenge his death. The Shaiksa assassin I'd slayed at the river would have sent out his dying thoughts to his brother assassins.

So they might have already worked out that a human army would be coming across the river into Kobalos lands. I just hoped they didn't know that the kulad called Kartuna, rather than Valkarky, was our objective. I suddenly wondered if the Kobalos mages could scry like witches . . . perhaps they already knew of our intention?

I looked around the camp: Grimalkin and I were on the northern edge. No lights were showing, and apart from patrols and guards set to watch for danger, the men were asleep in their tents. Grimalkin and I, wrapped in blankets, sat outside the entrance to our own tent and talked about what lay ahead.

I was still angry with her, but I'd only put my grievances aside with great difficulty. I needed to work with her and ensure that our attack was a success if I wanted to save Jenny.

I looked up into the sky. The moon was covered with a cloud, and in the patches of clear sky I could see just the faintest visible sprinkling of stars. However, to the north the sky glowed and rippled with colored lights, and we could just make out one another's faces.

"Those strange lights in the sky—are they coming from Valkarky?" I asked Grimalkin.

"No. They come from farther north than Valkarky. As far as I know, they are a natural phenomenon," she replied. "The farther we travel, the more spectacular they will become."

I stared at them in wonder. It was good to know that they weren't products of dark magic.

"Is the kulad likely to be well guarded?" I asked.

"I don't expect to find more than fifty to a hundred warriors there," Grimalkin replied, her breath steaming in the cold air, "but it may not be easy to seize; our superior numbers will not help us. Most kulads are just simple towers with stone walls that can be breached by one of our three big guns. But mages also tend to fortify the land around their tower. Kartuna is encircled by a high stone wall. There could also be magical traps to slay or delay the unwary . . . or even creatures created by the mage to seek out warm human flesh and blood. And each hour of delay gives a larger Kobalos force time to intervene."

"What about the mage? How dangerous will he be?" I asked.

"Without doubt he poses the biggest threat," she answered. "When I was last in Valkarky, I managed to defeat and slay the third in rank of the ruling triumvirate. It was far from easy. The birth of Talkus will have increased the power of the mages. Lenklewth is the second most powerful high mage in the triumvirate—who knows what magic he now has at his disposal? Let us hope he is back in Valkarky rather than at home in his kulad!"

"If you succeed in getting what you need from the tower," I said, "the leaders of our army will be angry when I have to order a retreat to Polyznia."

Grimalkin shook her head. "But we won't tell them immediately. I need time to unlock the secrets of the kulad, and by then the first Kobalos forces will be approaching. Our only hope will be to retreat back across the river. The princes will be terrified when they see the huge numbers that face us. Even Prince Kaylar will not wish to linger then!"

"What then, after the retreat?" I asked. "Won't the Kobalos follow us to Polyznia?"

"I expect they will, and some of the cities will come under siege or be razed to the ground. But we will not stay. We need to rouse the larger kingdoms to the south. The Kobalos invasion will stir them into action. Do this with me, and you will get your wish—we will then journey back to the County and gather forces from our own land."

I was clearly included in Grimalkin's plans well into the future. I would go home with Jenny, but when my strength returned, I knew that I'd help her again: the Kobalos had to be stopped—if possible, before they reached the County. When that might happen was difficult to estimate, but it might take years. However, the threat was to the whole world of humans, and the sooner the Kobalos were vanquished, the better. I also felt indebted to Grimalkin. She'd helped me in the past, saving my life on more than one occasion. There was a strong bond between us despite our recent disagreements.

"But will they listen?" I asked. "Two years ago, even with the invading army drawing close, it was a long time before forces from the County entered the fray. We'd never convince our military to send troops to fight battles across the sea in the frozen north."

In that recent war, only when the County had been invaded had our soldiers been mobilized properly. Threats across the sea were never taken seriously until it was almost too late. I feared the same would happen regarding the Kobalos.

"Try to have a little more faith in me," Grimalkin said, glaring at me. "I do not speak of conventional forces. I will lead my sister witches back here. We will fight magic with magic."

"Then why didn't you bring them with us this time?" I asked. A raid using witches rather than ordinary soldiers might have been more effective. After all, the objective was to seize magical knowledge, and witches had expertise in dark magic. They would probably have been more than a match for Lenklewth.

"I tried to persuade them, but they wouldn't listen," Grimalkin told me. "In that respect, they are like the County troops—a threat in a far-distant land will not move them. But if I can seize some of the magical secrets in that kulad and demonstrate what we face, then they will change their minds."

I sat there in silence, mulling over what she had said.

All I could hear was the sighing of the wind and the breathing of the horses.

"I hope Jenny's safe," I muttered.

The witch assassin closed her eyes for a moment, took a deep breath, and held it, her brow furrowed in concentration. Suddenly she breathed out and opened her eyes. "Yes, she is alive and safe at the moment," she said.

"You've scryed that?" I asked.

Grimalkin shook her head. "It is a spell called sympathy," she replied. "It links the child and me, but it does not last long and is already beginning to fade. But in any case, we will join up with her and Prince Kaylar soon."

"It's getting colder," I remarked, starting to shiver.

"This is nothing compared to what we might eventually have to endure," Grimalkin said. "We face a dark army far greater than the Kobalos forces and larger than the terrible battle entities they have created. This army, led by their new god Talkus, includes other gods who support them—deities such as Golgoth, the Lord of Winter, who wishes to blast the green from the earth and create a road of ice along which their warriors may glide to victory. It may not be long before he moves against us." Her expression was grim, and I shivered again.

Soon after that, we retreated into the tent. I wrapped myself in my blanket and fell asleep within moments of closing my eyes. I awoke only once in the night—to the sound of Grimalkin gnashing her teeth and talking in a language I'd never heard before. But even that didn't keep me awake for long.

I soon found myself in a dream in which I was walking across the fells with my master, John Gregory. He was pointing out various places in the valley, telling me their names. I was happy and keen to learn—and it was with a deep sense of sadness, shock, and loss that I awoke to the realization that he was dead and I'd never see him again.

We continued across the Plain of Erestaba at a steady pace. The day was bright and clear, with a chill wind blowing from the north. We sent scouts ahead, but they saw no sign of the enemy or of the patrol led by Prince Kaylar. Grimalkin long-sniffed for future danger; she could detect nothing directly ahead, but she still seemed ill at ease.

The Pendle witches used spells of cloaking to hide both themselves and their possessions from others. The Kobalos mages could probably do the same, or use another form of defensive magic. Grimalkin feared that all might not be as safe as it seemed.

Midmorning on the second day, as planned, we turned westward and advanced quickly toward the kulad. I had expected to have encountered Prince Kaylar and his patrol by now, but there was no sign of them. I hoped Jenny was all right.

Early in the afternoon we halted for just half an hour to eat—though the army remained in formation, ready to proceed at a moment's notice.

I'd been briefed by Grimalkin for a short meeting with the princes. All I had to do was explain her plan as if it was my own. I was physically tired from the ride, but I was still mentally alert.

We formed a small circle, each prince attended by two or three servants. I began by greeting each prince in turn before issuing "my" orders. The more I did this, the easier it became to act as a leader. I was also becoming increasingly comfortable with the presence of Prince Stanislaw. He was very supportive and facilitated my dealings with the other princes.

"I intend to ride ahead and attempt to capture the kulad using a small force of about a hundred mounted men and a score of archers," I explained. I had to raise my voice because the cold wind kept whipping my words away. "Grimalkin will ride with me. We should reach Kartuna at dusk.

"The main body of our army should follow on behind," I continued. "Once there, you should encircle

the kulad and prepare our big guns—though they should
be deployed only if our first attack fails. We need to learn
what we can, so I want the tower and its contents to
remain intact."

Grimalkin translated my words into Losta. After
she'd spoken, Prince Stanislaw also said a few words, and
by then everyone was nodding as if they agreed with the
plan.

"Each of the other princes will supply the very best
of their men to accompany us," Grimalkin explained
for my benefit. "We will reach the kulad under cover of
darkness."

Soon we rode off. Anxious about his father, the son
of Prince Kaylar chose to accompany us. The others each
allocated us a group of their most trusted men.

As we headed toward the kulad, I wondered where
the patrol was. And what about Jenny? I was becoming
increasingly anxious about her.

Jenny Calder

11
Endless Nightmares

PRINCE Kaylar ordered that everyone should remain mounted. I could sense his anxiety: he kept fiddling with his beard, twisting each spike around his fingers in turn. It was about three hours after dark, and we were close to the trees that surrounded the kulad, which towered high above them. There were stars overhead, but the moon had yet to rise.

The prince had also ordered me to stay close by. I was now on horseback, but I had spent the first night of our journey unconscious, slung across his saddle. The following morning he had explained why I'd been drugged and taken away. He wasn't happy about it but had to obey the witch assassin and Prince Stanislaw. The plan was to force Tom to ride at the head of the army, and I knew it would work. He would not go back to the County and abandon me. Grimalkin had gotten her way again.

It was outrageous that I'd been treated in this way, and I

JOSEPH DELANEY

was determined to escape at the very first opportunity. But so far there had been no chance at all. I sensed that it was a point of honor with Prince Kaylar to keep me safe until he could return me to Tom's care. He was a man of high principles and was clearly ashamed of what he had done.

His son, a boy of eighteen, was with the main army, and was eager to fight and prove his bravery, but the prince feared that he might be injured or killed. He also had twin daughters of about my age and a wife he loved very much. He was here to fight and ensure their safety and the security of his principality, but he feared that he might die in battle and never see them again.

During our journey, we had seen no sign of Kobalos warriors. The vast plain had been empty. So we'd approached the kulad to test its defenses. Now that we were so close, I felt anxious. Were we just bait to draw our enemies forth and test their strength? That's what it seemed to me. I shivered with fear at the thought of being taken prisoner.

There would certainly be Kobalos warriors within that tower . . . but how many?

The prince had sent five men into the trees on foot. Three were to approach the tower; two were to wait among the trees, to look out for the enemy. Now we were awaiting their return.

116

Nothing happened for at least an hour. I could hear the wind sighing through the tall conifers, and once I thought I heard a distant scream. But when I tried to say a few hesitant words of Losta, the prince merely shrugged. Either he'd heard nothing, or it was something he'd expected and thought it of no account.

We continued to sit on our horses in silence. I watched the moon slowly rise above the trees, bathing us in its pale silvery light.

Suddenly the prince turned and held out a small dagger toward me, hilt first. "Understand?" he asked me in our language.

I accepted the blade, nodded, and tried to smile. I knew that it was not meant to fight off Kobalos attackers. Although he did not put his intention into words, using my gift of empathy I could sense it. If it became necessary, I should take my own life rather than fall into the hands of our enemies and become a slave.

I looked at it fearfully. I could never take my own life—it was wrong. I had accepted the dagger merely to please the prince. We must indeed be in great danger.

For a long time nothing happened. I sat on my horse, yawning, hoping that we could soon retreat to a safe distance and make camp.

✠

The attack took us completely by surprise.

Not one of the men who had entered the trees managed to call out a warning. They must have been ambushed.

Mounted Kobalos warriors surged out of the trees and were upon us, followed by others on foot. They advanced swiftly and silently, wielding sabers and battle-axes; even the hooves of their horses were muffled and faint.

But then I heard a terrifying noise. I had watched the archers of Polyznia practicing and remembered that deadly sound. It was the whistling of Kobalos arrows as they fell toward us, dark thin shadows against the moonlight. Now there were cries of pain from humans and whinnies of fear from the horses as the arrows found their targets, taking a deadly toll on our forces.

It was clear that we were greatly outnumbered, and I feared for my life. Some of our warriors held shields above their heads, but I had nothing to ward off the hail of arrows that fell all around me. It was pure chance whether I lived or died.

Prince Kaylar barked out orders to his men, and they quickly gathered themselves and stood firm, trading blow for blow. All I could do was strive to control my horse as it snorted and stamped beside him at the center of our warriors and the battle raged all around us. We were still some distance from the Kobalos blades and axes, but the volleys of arrows came again and again relentlessly. One would surely find its target soon.

Suddenly my horse screamed shrilly and bolted; however, it hadn't fled more than a few yards before its front legs buckled beneath it. I never glimpsed the arrow that brought it down, but I was thrown over its head and landed hard, the fall driving all the air from my lungs.

I lay there stunned, unable to draw breath. Hooves crashed down close to my head and, terrified of being trampled, I scrambled to my knees.

A horse thundered directly toward me, its hooves throwing up clods of mud. I crouched down, trying to protect my head, but at the very last moment it swerved aside. The rider reached down, a strong arm wrapped itself around my waist, and I was pulled up onto the horse behind him.

The man shouted something in Losta. I didn't understand his words, but I recognized that deep, booming voice. It was Prince Kaylar. He'd seen me fall and had ridden to my rescue. I wrapped my arms around his waist and pressed my head against his back, clinging on for dear life. Peering around, I saw that we were encircled by enemy riders; our own cavalry was nowhere to be seen.

The prince urged his horse into a gallop, straight toward them, desperately trying to break out. He wielded two huge swords, slashing right and left as we passed between the mounted Kobalos. I heard screams; saw one fall and another rock in the saddle. But then I realized that we were heading in the wrong direction—arrows were still whistling overhead.

The prince had taken the line of least resistance, but we were galloping toward the kulad, rather than away from it. I feared that other enemies might be waiting there. But having reached the shelter of the trees, the prince veered southward, his horse weaving between the tree trunks.

Before we could emerge from the trees, we encountered more of the enemy. The prince was brave and powerful, but he had no one to support him. We were alone, the odds were too great; he could not hope to win.

What happened next I will remember to my dying day. As we met the enemy, I felt the prince's body shudder and sway in the saddle. Then a warm liquid drenched my shoulders and back. The horse stumbled beneath us, and I looked up . . . and saw that the prince had no head. It had been struck from his body.

I screamed and fell off the horse, rolling into some scrub. It galloped onward, its headless rider swaying in the saddle. I lay there stunned. Waves of nausea rippled up from my stomach and I vomited onto the ground.

Finally I managed to control my stomach and peered out of the undergrowth.

I was surrounded by the Kobalos, and all I had was the small dagger that the prince had given me.

I had just one chance of surviving this: I had to use the gift that made me invisible.

Holding my breath, I began to focus, willing myself to blend into the background. I could hear Kobalos riders nearby. Had they seen me fall into the bushes? They would certainly have heard me scream. Would they search for me?

The answer to that question came almost immediately. The horsemen had ridden on, but a small patrol of enemy infantry was advancing toward me, prodding the ground with their spears. No doubt they had been set the task of finding me.

I hoped that if I kept perfectly still, the huge Kobalos warriors wouldn't see me. Of course, I couldn't be sure that my gift would be effective against them. They might sense me in other ways, using their sense of smell, for example. A random jab of a spear might pierce my body at any moment.

They were very close now. They thwacked the grass and twigs aside with their spears, then grunted, driving them deep into the ground. They were bigger than most men and clad in chain mail. Through the open visors of their helmets I could see thick, matted hair on their faces and eyes that glittered fiercely in the moonlight.

The right boot of the nearest Kobalos warrior passed within six inches of my head. The tip of his spear came very close to my left leg . . . but he strode on through the undergrowth and didn't see me. My gift had saved me—at least for a while.

I watched the line of soldiers recede into the distance, fearing that they might turn back and search the same area of ground again, but they continued through the wood.

After about five minutes, I climbed slowly to my feet. All was silent. The Kobalos were probably pursuing the small force that had been led by poor Prince Kaylar. I shuddered at the thought of what had been done to him, and my stomach twisted in revulsion. It was some time before I got it under control again.

Then I wept, thinking of the wife who'd lost her husband and the children without a father. As I reflected on what had happened, I shook with fear. If they caught me, I'd end up a slave. They would shape me into a purra— a female slave whose duty was to give blood freely, bear their children, and obey them in all things. Every day I would be cut with a blade to ensure my obedience.

I took long deep breaths to steady myself. I had to remember that I was a spook's apprentice. I needed to learn not to give in to my fears. I had to be brave.

What now? I wondered. Tom and Grimalkin must be leading the army toward the tower. The enemy had detected our approach . . . had it had been a trap all along? They might know that a larger human army was on its way.

I had to warn them—somehow I had to get through the enemy lines and out onto the plain. I was still terrified, but I couldn't just save my own skin and do nothing.

If I did manage to cross their lines, what direction should I take? I thought about it for a moment, then realized that I had to head roughly east. Tom had told me Grimalkin's plan. The army would have set off north toward Valkarky, and then turned west, heading for this kulad. I would be able to use the moon and stars to guide me. If they were in a narrow column, I still might miss them, but I had to try.

Suddenly I heard the sound of approaching boots. After a moment of panic I hid behind a tree, summoning my gift of invisibility once more and holding my breath. A Kobalos patrol was marching toward me in single file—a long column of armed warriors. Then I saw that two at the rear were in charge of four female prisoners.

The women were dressed in rags and chained together by their left ankles; I realized that they were purrai.

The patrol marched past, no more than thirty feet from where I was hiding. As the women followed, one stumbled and fell to her knees. One of the soldiers kicked her in the belly with his boot, and I heard the air whoosh out of her mouth. She groaned and collapsed forward onto her face.

The Kobalos warrior shouted something at her in Losta. He sounded angry—probably because he and his companion were being left behind with their prisoners. Then, suddenly, he drew his knife and slashed the woman's bare shoulder. She screamed and struggled to her feet, the blood running down her body to drip onto the grass. The soldier slapped her hard with the back of his hand, and her lip began to bleed. Tears were streaming down her face as they moved away.

They headed off toward the kulad, the woman's sobs gradually fading into the distance.

I began to breathe again, but I was shaking after witnessing the brutality of the Kobalos. How could the soldier cut a bound and defenseless woman like that?

This would be the fate of all human females if the Kobalos won the war.

I should have done something to help, I thought, even though

I knew I'd have had no chance against two armed warriors. I'd have ended up in chains too. But I would do anything to prevent myself from falling into that situation. If they attempted to chain me, I would fight to the very limits of my strength. It would be better to die in that way than to end up as a slave of the Kobalos.

Would Tom have intervened, had he been with me? I wondered. He still hadn't recovered from his ordeal, but I felt sure that he would have done something. The patrol had moved on, leaving just two warriors with the prisoners. Tom would have drawn the Starblade and attacked them. Now those four slaves would spend the remainder of their lives being mistreated. Their only hope was for humans to win the war.

I waited another ten minutes and then began to continue through the wood, moving away from the kulad. Glancing back, I could still see its threatening tower.

Emerging from the trees, I gazed out onto the plain. Scattered across the ground were the bodies of dead warriors and horses. I had come out a hundred yards from the place where the Kobalos had attacked. Nothing moved out there on the plain, but the enemy might be watching unseen from the trees. I had encountered the patrol of foot soldiers, but what about the mounted Kobalos warriors—where were they? No doubt they had pursued the remnants of Prince Kaylar's forces, but now they could be on their way back to the kulad.

It would be easy to spot me out here; even my gift of invisibility might not be enough. But I had to risk it. So after a moment or two studying the stars, I set off toward what I judged to be the eastern horizon.

Thomas Ward

12
Shape-Shifting

WE rode in darkness at barely a trot, for many of the horses carried two riders, a cavalryman and an archer. I was glad of the slow pace—I still had little strength or energy.

After several hours the moon rose, and in the far distance we saw the tower of Kartuna rising up above the pine trees like a dark, fat thumb.

Then we spotted something else: a lone figure walking directly toward us.

I can often recognize people by their walk, and I knew immediately who it was. "It's Jenny!" I told Grimalkin.

"Yes," she replied, "but I fear for the others."

I galloped forward to meet Jenny, leaping from my horse, and then she was sobbing in my arms.

"They're all dead. They're all dead but me!" she cried. "Poor Prince Kaylar—they . . ."

I patted her back and sought words of reassurance, but to my annoyance Grimalkin intervened. "Take your time, girl, and speak slowly." She seized Jenny's arm and drew her away from me. But Jenny pulled free and ran back.

Angrily Grimalkin tried to grab her again, but I stepped in front of Jenny.

"Leave her alone!" I snapped. "Don't you think she's suffered enough? *You* kidnapped her. She could have been killed!"

Grimalkin hissed with fury but took a step backward. "We need to know precisely what happened," she said.

I turned back to face Jenny. "Do you feel well enough to talk?" I asked.

She nodded and began her story. Most of our force dismounted and gathered around. Every so often Grimalkin halted Jenny's account so that she could translate it into Losta for the others.

Long before she had finished, Prince Kaylar's son was on his knees, tearing his hair and weeping at the news of his father's death. It was a terrible tale. It seemed likely that Jenny was the only survivor of the patrol.

I assumed that Grimalkin would call off the attack on the kulad—or at least wait for the rest of our army to arrive. Instead she spoke quietly to me, proposing an immediate advance with only a dozen soldiers.

"It seems very risky!" I told her. "We need some way to call for help if we get out of our depth. We could use a triple whistle to summon the others."

Grimalkin agreed, but I was still unhappy with her proposal and told her bluntly of my fears.

"What if they know we're here?" I said. "They might have known of Prince Kaylar's approach in advance. How can we hope to do better with so few? There must be hundreds of warriors in the kulad."

The witch assassin stared at me, clearly angered by my challenge. "It is a risk we must take!" she spat. "Time is against us—a large Kobalos army even now is riding toward us. I *must* have the knowledge that lies in that tower. That is what matters. Tell them now!" she said, gesturing toward the gathering. "Tell them what must be done!"

Filled with misgivings, I obeyed, and the witch assassin then translated my orders.

So it was that Grimalkin and I led a force of just a dozen men toward the kulad.

Jenny was left behind. She didn't object. She'd been scared badly by her encounter with the Kobalos.

Grimalkin strode beside me, outlining her plan. The

tower was surrounded by a high wall and a moat that could be crossed by a drawbridge. It was the only way in. While she approached the wall, we were to stay among the trees and keep perfectly still. Once she had gained access, we were all to follow, at her signal.

Most of the Kobalos would be quartered below ground. The only way we could win was by attacking swiftly. We had to reach the very top of the kulad, where the Kobalos high mages routinely had their quarters. Once there we could defend that position while Grimalkin learned what she could.

We halted just short of the first trees and turned to face Grimalkin. She spoke to the warriors in Losta, repeating what she had already told me. Then she closed her eyes and began to mutter. She was casting a cloaking spell to hide our approach.

As her muttering rose into a light musical chant, I glanced at the men who were coming with us. Six of them had long bows; these were very accurate at a distance, but were also deadly at short range—they could pierce the toughest armor. I knew all this because Grimalkin had spent hours taking me through the capabilities of our forces. The other six were swordsmen, the cream of our army. One was a champion and had been due to face the Shaiksa after me.

A cinder path led into the wood. I noticed that it was steaming, creating a mist that reached up into the branches of nearby trees. Why should that be? Why should the ground be hot beneath it?

I'd no time to consider this further because Grimalkin had completed her spell and was ready to advance. We entered the trees to the left of the path. I took the lead, Grimalkin at my heels, with our small band following in single file. We moved cautiously, making as little noise as possible. There was no wind and it was very gloomy, with clouds now obscuring the moon.

I sensed the dark mass of the tower ahead, then heard the snort of a horse. The sound came from somewhere to the left of the tower, and it was followed by a whinny. I signaled that we should halt, my heart lurching with anxiety. Were there Kobalos warriors ahead, waiting to attack us?

"It's just the stables!" Grimalkin hissed into my ear. "They're inside the wall. Keep going toward the kulad!"

I felt angry with myself. I was too jumpy—I still hadn't gotten over the trauma of my death. It had sapped my confidence and set my nerves on edge.

Finally we came to the edge of the trees and saw the tower directly ahead. It was constructed from huge blocks of dark purple stone that dripped with water. Keeping within the trees, I led us to the right, toward the cinder path.

Grimalkin put her hand on my shoulder and whispered once more into my ear. "I'll try to gain entry to the kulad now. Keep the men back until I signal that it's safe to follow."

I turned to the warriors and gestured that we should crouch low. Then I pointed first to Grimalkin and next to the kulad as if ordering her forward.

She stepped boldly onto the path and approached the high wall; it didn't drip like the tower, but glistened as if covered in beads of sweat. I saw that the drawbridge was up and wondered how she planned to cross the moat.

In seconds the answer became clear, and I heard the warriors around me gasp in astonishment. It was no longer Grimalkin who stood there with her back to us, facing the drawbridge. It was a huge Kobalos warrior dressed in full armor. And when she called out, it was not in her own voice, but in a harsh, deep guttural tone of command.

From conversations with the witch assassin back in the County, I knew that this was not true shape-shifting, but a spell of illusion—though it was totally convincing. She *was*, to all intents and purposes, a Kobalos warrior.

No reply came from the tower, but she got the answer

that we all wanted. With a clank of chains, a rasp of metal, and a creak of wood, the drawbridge began to descend. Once it was in position, Grimalkin stepped closer to the moat and waited. With shrieks of tortured metal, the portcullis began to rise. When it was fully up, she crossed the drawbridge, passed through the gate, and disappeared from view.

We waited for several minutes, and I started to become anxious again. Had she been discovered? Had something happened to her? The Kobalos mages had powerful magic. Would Lenklewth, the second most powerful mage in the triumvirate, somehow know of her deception?

I needn't have worried. Grimalkin reappeared under the portcullis. She had reverted to her own shape once more, and beckoned us forward. We ran across the drawbridge and gathered inside the wall. There were several Kobalos bodies on the ground, and they had died violent deaths at her hands.

I noted the looks of astonishment on the faces of our men. They were clearly impressed by what she'd achieved.

I'd hardly had time to take that in when Grimalkin pointed to the open door of the tower. At a word from her, three of our archers took up their positions, guarding the door and protecting our rear. The others followed us quickly into the tower.

A staircase led upward in a widdershins spiral, but the ceiling continued uninterrupted above our heads, so we couldn't see how far up it went or whether our enemies were waiting to ambush us. There were no landings, just openings that gave access to each floor. I could smell new wood; the floors appeared to be of fairly recent construction.

Grimalkin pointed upward, and I took the lead racing up the steps, the Starblade gripped in my left hand. We climbed very swiftly, our boots thundering on the wood. At the first floor, Grimalkin put a hand on my shoulder to pull me to a halt, and I heard her sniff three times. She was long-sniffing for danger, trying to detect Kobalos who might be concealed above—though I felt no chill running up and down my spine, no sense that the dark was nearby. Hopefully, that meant that Lenklewth was not in his kulad.

Apparently satisfied that all was well, the witch assassin released my shoulder, and I led the way to the next floor. As I passed the opening, I glanced into a large room. It was empty, and the polished wooden floor looked new. I wondered why it wasn't furnished.

The next floor was the same, and the one after that. But then there was a disturbing noise from behind us . . . the shriek of metal, the clank of chains. The portcullis was being lowered.

The three archers had been instructed to guard the gate. The noise could mean only one thing: they were already dead or out of action. Our enemies were behind us.

Grimalkin signaled that we should halt and listen. Suddenly we heard boots pounding up the wooden stairs toward us.

She turned quickly and snapped out an order in Losta. I knew that there wasn't time for her to translate for my benefit, but the men froze for a moment and looked doubtful. They were wondering why *she* was giving the orders, so I nodded in agreement, and the soldiers obeyed.

At our rear, two of our three remaining archers turned to face the approaching Kobalos and knelt, nocking their arrows and pulling their bows taut. Behind them, three of our swordsmen crouched down, weapons at the ready.

"Let me take the lead," Grimalkin said. "There may be magical traps ahead. I will trigger them, but if I'm immobilized, be ready with the Starblade."

I pointed upward as if giving her the order to take the lead.

Grimalkin ran up the steps, and I followed with the remaining soldiers. Now Grimalkin and I had only one archer and three swordsmen to help us penetrate the lair of the mage.

The next floor was empty, and the next. There were other doors in each room, but Grimalkin didn't bother to check these. Whatever lay behind them, she had no doubt established that they presented no danger.

I began to wonder if there was anybody at all in the upper floors. It now seemed likely that our attack had been foreseen. The Kobalos might have abandoned the top rooms of the tower, trapping us and sending warriors up the spiral staircase after us . . . more warriors than we could ever hope to defeat.

I was at Grimalkin's shoulder when we reached the top floor—the place where she thought Lenklewth stored his magical artifacts.

We emerged into a small tiled antechamber that led to an open door.

When we peered through, the large room beyond it seemed to be filled with mist. The witch assassin entered slowly, and I followed, gripping the Starblade. Half the room was occupied by a huge sunken bath filled with what appeared to be very hot water. Clouds of steam rose from it, so dense that Kobalos could have been lurking unseen in the corners of the room. Then I saw that a small bridge crossed the bath and led to another door.

Grimalkin stepped forward and sniffed loudly three times. She took a second slow step. I could tell from her cautious approach that she was still wary.

The thought came to me that something might be hiding beneath the surface of the water. It looked extremely hot, but that meant nothing. A Kobalos high mage, or one of his creatures, might be unaffected by scalding water.

Grimalkin stepped onto the bridge and took a couple of paces forward. I followed, looking down nervously at the steaming water. She signaled to the four warriors behind us to remain where they were.

We crossed the bridge and went through the door into a spacious room with a flagged floor. At its center stood a large oak desk, the edges inlaid with strips of silver. Weapons were displayed on all four dark-paneled walls: axes, sabers, and spears—along with weapons I had never seen before, some a bit like County scythes, but curved into spirals.

The room was empty. Thankfully, the mage was not at home. We looked about us, examining our surroundings. Some of the carved wall panels depicted warriors and battle scenes. The image on one was duplicated in the single large painting that hung on the wall— a huge Kobalos warrior on horseback. It was extremely lifelike and seemed to demand our attention. We both stepped forward to examine it more closely.

The warrior's left eye was transfixed by a long spear that was protruding from the back of his head; he was falling off his horse.

"That is the last king of Valkarky," said a deep voice from behind us. "He was killed by that lance, which they called the Kangadon, meaning the lance that cannot be broken. It was afterward that the triumvirate of high mages began their rule!"

It could have been the Kobalos high mage who had first made himself invisible before distracting us by using further magic to make us focus upon the painting.

But I knew that voice. . . .

We both turned to confront the speaker.

I stared at him in astonishment and then anger. It was the dark mage Lukrasta.

13
Blood and Spittle

"WHERE is the Kobalos high mage?" Grimalkin demanded, glaring angrily at Lukrasta.

"He is very close," he replied, a touch of mockery in his voice. "Would you like to speak to him?"

I stared at my enemy, the one who had taken Alice away from me. A long mustache hung down over his lips, which were very pink, as if suffused with blood. They were parted in a smile, revealing sharp white teeth.

He was on our side—an ally in the fight against the Kobalos—but I still considered him my personal enemy and struggled to keep my feelings in check. I met his arrogant eyes, and anger flared through me.

The last time we'd met, we had fought with swords. I'd won, and he had been at my mercy, but Alice had begged for his life. I'd listened to her, though this was not the only thing that had influenced my decision to spare him. Part of me—the part that came through my lamia blood—had wanted to kill him. However, from my father I'd inherited a sense of right and wrong. The mage had been at my mercy, but I was unable to slay him in cold blood.

Now I gripped the Starblade tightly, knowing that it would protect me against his magic. As I did so, I wondered where Alice was. When I'd fought the Shaiksa assassin, she and Lukrasta had combined their magic to control me. They might do it again.

"Yes, if he is your prisoner, I *do* wish to speak to him!" Grimalkin declared angrily. "There is much to be learned. But why are *you* here?"

Lukrasta smiled and seemed about to reply, but then, from the antechamber, we heard a sudden scream and the sound of arrows being loosed. Grimalkin and I ran to the doorway, but the steam from the bath was now so dense that we could only see vague shapes that seemed to be struggling to stay upright. There were curses, a groan of pain, another scream, and then silence.

I thought Grimalkin would leap forward to join the fray—but to my surprise, she took two rapid steps backward and moved into a defensive crouch, long blades at the ready. She almost collided with me, and I had to step aside hastily.

Then I saw what had caused her to retreat. A huge insectlike creature with a long snout was crawling toward us, its thin multijointed legs stepping delicately across the bridge. It was a skelt.

These deadly creatures had long, sharp bone tubes that they used to pierce their prey and suck their blood. Standing upright, they were taller than a human.

The skelt was quickly followed by two more, which scuttled toward us. I realized that they must have been concealed in the scalding water.

Skelts had once been rare, but I had seen hundreds of these creatures in one of the domains of the dark. They had cut the body of the Fiend into pieces and carried them to a lake of boiling water, where they had disappeared.

I suddenly remembered that the powerful new Kobalos god Talkus was supposed to take the form of a skelt. For one terrible moment, I feared that he might be here.

However, I had no time to reflect upon this. We quickly backed away into the mage's room, and the skelts pursued us, water dripping from their bodies, tendrils of steam twisting up toward the ceiling. Why didn't Grimalkin attack? I wondered. Were there too many? Did she fear the presence of Talkus too?

Then I heard a deep voice behind us. It wasn't

Lukrasta's. It had a harsh, guttural quality . . . it wasn't human.

"Witch, you are not the only one able to shape-shift!"

I looked over my shoulder and saw, in the place of Lukrasta, a Kobalos warrior who must have been all of seven feet tall. He was clad in full armor, though his head was bare. The sight of his shaved face sent a tremor of fear through my body, for this was the mark of a mage.

My heart sank into my boots. It had to be Lenklewth, the powerful mage Grimalkin had hoped to avoid.

"In me you have met your match!" he hissed at the witch assassin.

She stepped toward him, blades at the ready, eyes glittering with fury.

He gestured with his left hand, and to my shock and dismay, Grimalkin fell to her knees, her blades slipping out of her grasp to fall upon the flags. Her face was twisted in agony, and suddenly blood spurted from her nose and began to drip down her chin. Then red rivulets trickled from each ear.

I watched in horror. The mage had tricked us, drawing us up into his tower, and now he had brought Grimalkin to her knees with a mere gesture. She had seriously underestimated his capabilities. I had never seen her vanquished like this, reduced to such pitiful weakness. It was terrifying to witness such a thing.

Now he turned toward me and made a similar gesture. I felt nothing, and I saw him frown. I realized that the Starblade was protecting me from his magic.

Grimalkin seemed to be struggling for breath, but then I saw that she was desperately trying to say something. At last she forced out the words with a spray of blood. "Kill him now!" she gasped. "But you *must* keep hold of the sword!"

I raised the Starblade and stepped toward Lenklewth. My sword had not enabled me to see through his shapeshifting illusion, but it would protect me against a direct attack by dark magic.

However, I was still not strong, and I had not practiced with the sword since I'd returned from death. I would no longer possess the skill and strength that had let me defeat the Shaiksa assassin at the river ford. My arms trembled.

"You have more resistance than the human witch," the mage rasped.

As a seventh son of a seventh son, I had some immunity against dark magic, but I knew that it was mostly the blade that was deflecting it. I had to hold on to it at all costs.

I heard a scratch-scratching on the flags behind me.

Out of the corner of my eye I saw that two of the skelts were behind me. The desk was between us, but more skelts were now scuttling across the bridge and entering the room.

The danger was increasing by the moment, so, wasting no time, I swung my blade toward Lenklewth's head. The Starblade felt heavy and unwieldy, and I knew my blow would fail. Despite his size, he stepped back nimbly and avoided it with ease, then spun away and seized a huge double-bladed battle-ax off the wall. He crouched down, gripping it with both hands, waiting for me to attack.

As I advanced toward him, he straightened to his full height, raising the ax high above his head. Then he swung it down at me in an arc. Had the blow landed, it would have cleaved me in two. I barely managed to step aside before it clanged against the flags.

I darted in before the mage could raise the ax again and aimed the Starblade at a point high on his shoulder, where neck and shoulder armor joined. The blow rang against the metal but failed to find the vulnerable point. Again we circled each other. Already, after just one attack, I was breathing hard and my legs felt weak.

Grimalkin was on her hands and knees, head down. A small, viscous puddle of blood and spittle was forming on the flags underneath her open mouth. She'd been rendered helpless by the mage's powerful magic.

I knew I had to finish this quickly, because I had little stamina. I was concentrating on my opponent, calculating my next move, when suddenly I felt a sharp stabbing pain in the back of my calf. I looked down and saw that a skelt had pierced me with its bone tube. At that moment of distraction, the mage struck. He swung his ax at me horizontally, and I barely managed to block the powerful blow.

The Starblade went spinning out of my hand and clattered to the floor.

I quickly stooped to retrieve it, but I was too late; I was already beyond its protection.

The mage smiled, and suddenly I couldn't breathe. Bile rose up in my throat. I was choking, drowning.

Within seconds I knew no more as Lenklewth's magic cast me down into darkness.

14
Prisoner of the Kobalos

I awoke with a blinding headache; when I sat up, the world spun about me. I felt sick and struggled not to vomit.

After a few moments, the worst of the nausea had left me, and I looked around the small room in which I'd been imprisoned. There was no window, but a rusty spike on the wall to my left impaled a candle; the flickering flame showed me the dismal interior of my cell. The floor was flagged and the stone walls were splattered with blood. Many were old, dark stains, but some looked new. People had died and been tortured here.

In the corner lay a heap of dirty straw—my bed—and there was a hole in the floor. I got to my feet and walked across to examine it. Immediately I recoiled; it stank of urine and excrement. I knew what it was for—and knew also that before long I would be forced to use it.

Next I noticed a jug by the door. It contained water. My mouth was dry, but could I trust it? Could it be poisoned?

Why bother, I asked myself, when they could just use a blade to finish me off any time they wished?

I groaned when I remembered how quickly I'd been defeated. How easily the mage had disarmed me! I felt ashamed. I should have kept hold of the sword. Grimalkin's gift of the blade had been our one chance, and I had let her down. All that training had been for nothing.

But then my thoughts took me in another direction, and I grew angry. Weak as I was, I should not have been put in that position in the first place. I'd warned Grimalkin, but she'd ignored it and kidnapped Jenny in order to make me bend to her wishes.

I walked over to inspect the wooden door. It was stoutly made, the lower half clad with steel. There were no bars—no way to see out of the cell, not even a keyhole. Back in the castle was the special key made by Andrew, the brother of my dead master, John Gregory. Andrew was a master locksmith, and that key had allowed me to escape from other dungeons and places of confinement. But it wouldn't have helped me here. No doubt the door was securely bolted on the other side.

I sniffed the water before taking a sip. It was warm but tasted fine. Everything in this tower was warm. There must be some source of heat underground. Maybe there was a hot spring? I thought. Then I remembered the Fittzanda Fissure, where the ground shook and jets of steam spurted up from the ground. The tower could be built upon a similar area of volcanic instability.

Driven by thirst, I began to gulp down the water. After a few seconds, I was almost sick and had to stop. So I put down the jug and began to pace backward and forward, trying to think.

We'd been defeated so easily. The Kobalos mage had set his trap, and we had rushed into it like lambs to the slaughter. He had assumed the likeness of Lukrasta, and I'd been totally fooled. My usual sense that something from the dark was near had failed me. Kobalos high mages were exceptionally strong in their use of dark magic. What was even more worrying was the way that he had also duped Grimalkin and quickly overcome her with his magic.

In her desperation to learn the secrets of Kobalos magic, she'd been reckless. Jenny's account had told us that the kulad contained a large force of enemy warriors, yet we had attacked it with just twelve men. And we hadn't known for sure that the mage would be away in Valkarky.

I suddenly realized that in order to take on his likeness, Lenklewth must have known about Lukrasta. He must have met him—perhaps he had already destroyed him. I had no love for Lukrasta, but if he had been defeated already, it did not bode well for our chances of survival.

In the distance I heard a scream. It sounded female. Perhaps it was one of the human slaves the Kobalos called *purrai*? I knew that they treated them with great cruelty. Or had the scream been wrenched from Grimalkin's throat? I wondered.

Only once had I heard her cry out in pain—when I had helped her mend her broken leg. To regain her former mobility, she had used magic and a silver pin to hold the broken bones together. When I had tapped the silver pin home, she had screamed in agony. Silver causes great pain to a witch—but Grimalkin would have to live with it for the rest of her life; this was the price she had to pay if she wanted to continue as a witch assassin.

However, I would not have expected her to cry out under torture. What terrible thing was being done to her in order to draw that scream from her lips?

No! No! I told myself. *That cannot be. That cry cannot be from Grimalkin!*

Agitated, I continued to pace to and fro, pausing just

once to take another sip of water from the jug.

I've always been good at judging the passage of time; if I wake up in the middle of the night, I can usually estimate what time it is. But now it seemed as if my normal senses and abilities were blunted.

Nor could I tell how much time had elapsed between the moment when I was plunged into unconsciousness by the mage and the moment when I had awakened in this cell.

I wondered if there was any chance of being rescued. The few warriors we had led into the tower would all be dead now, slain on the stairs by the Kobalos. Yes, it had been a well-executed trap.

But what of the hundred or so we'd left beyond the trees? My heart sank when I realized that we'd get no help from them. Surely Kobalos warriors would have already driven them off or killed them.

Jenny had been with them. She might already be dead.

Poor Jenny! She would never get her wish to become a spook. I had brought her here to her death, or perhaps to something worse—enslavement by the Kobalos.

My heart plummeted even further when I thought of the danger to our army of seven thousand. The mage, Lenklewth, had known we were planning an attack and would have made provision for them as well. No doubt a

Kobalos army was now approaching from the north; soon they'd be surrounded.

I continued to pace up and down.

Time dragged on. Eventually, exhausted, I sat down with my back to the wall, facing the door. I fell asleep, to be awakened by the sound of the bolt being drawn. The door was eased open, and a woman stared into the cell.

I couldn't see her face: there were others standing beside her holding lanterns, and she was in silhouette. Quickly she ducked into the cell, set something down on the floor, and retreated. The door clanged shut again, and the bolt was drawn across again.

I had noticed at least three other women, dressed in tattered clothing and armed with clubs. The one who had entered my cell had bare arms that were covered in scars. So they were purrai; the wounds were inflicted by the Kobalos as part of their training, or perhaps as a punishment. These purrai were sometimes snatched from their homes by the Kobalos, but most were born in captivity.

I got to my feet and walked over to the door. On the floor was a small bowl containing something that looked like lumpy gray porridge. I tasted a bit and confirmed it. It was a little too salty for my liking, but I ate it all. I needed to keep up my strength for whatever lay ahead.

I slept again—for how long I do not know—and was awakened once more by the rattle of the bolt. This time the door was flung violently back so that it bounced from the wall.

Instead of the women, three fierce Kobalos warriors were standing in the doorway, staring into the room. Unlike the mage I'd faced earlier, their faces were unshaven, and their eyes glared at me with such anger and hostility that I thought for a moment that they intended to slay me on the spot. Had the mage ordered my execution? I wondered.

One was armed with a huge double-bladed ax, and he faced me, legs apart, weapon at the ready, while the other two entered the cell and dragged me outside. They forced my arms behind me and pushed me down a flight of steps; I nearly fell headlong down them.

Were they taking me to be executed? The thought made me tremble with fear. At first I'd had no memories of what had happened to me after death, but recently images of horror and pain had come back. They'd seemed like nightmare visions, but I now feared that they were dim recollections of what I'd experienced; I'd felt a terrible pain in my shoulder. Someone had been screaming—the noise had set my teeth on edge. Then I realized that the person screaming was me.

I didn't want to go through that again.

Somehow I managed to stay on my feet. Down and down we went, passing the floors I remembered from our ascent. We went past the door through which we'd first entered, and I knew that we must now be heading deep underground.

15
The Shameful Death

FINALLY we came to a large door, and the Kobalos warrior rapped on it three times with the hilt of his saber. It opened wide, and I was thrust inside.

Two things surprised me: the vast size of the cellar, and the large number of Kobalos who occupied it. They were dressed in full armor but for their heads. Some of the body armor was splattered with blood, as if they had recently been fighting.

The noise was deafening. The Kobalos communicated by shouting at the tops of their voices, spitting into one another's faces and spraying food from their mouths in an effort to be heard.

More than a hundred of the soldiers sat at long tables, chomping and chewing at their food. Before them were set huge plates of meat, some of it charred and blackened, some almost raw; blood matted the hair around their mouths and dripped from their chins. Seeing me, they let out great bestial roars and beat rhythmically upon the table tops with their huge, hairy fists.

I was pushed along between them until I reached the head table, which was raised on a dais. Beside it, in the huge open fireplace, yellow flames flickered up into the dark mouth of a chimney.

Its two occupants looked down upon the other tables. One was the high mage, Lenklewth, who was warming his hands at the fire. The other was a warrior whose hair was braided into three long black pigtails, marking him out as a Shaiksa assassin; he was likely to be as dangerous and skilled in combat as the one I'd fought. Neither one wore armor. Instead they were dressed in leather jerkins decorated with strange whorls and loops of gold thread.

Then I looked up and saw two wide marble shelves on the wall directly above the fireplace. I realized that they were altars. On the top one was a statue of a skelt, its thin, multijointed legs, body, and long, sharp bone tube crafted out of what appeared to be volcanic rock. It was shiny and black but for its eyes, which were ruby red. Without doubt this was a likeness of Talkus, the newly born god worshipped by the Kobalos.

But impressive and astonishing as that was, on the lower shelf was something that defied belief. It was clearly a depiction of Golgoth, the Lord of Winter, who had allied himself with the Kobalos and their new deity. This statue wasn't carved from black rock, but from white ice. The circular mass of ice was topped by an oval head with two black eyes. A multitude of clawed limbs and tentacles protruded from it, some hanging down below the shelf, close to the flames in the fireplace. By all the laws of nature they should have been melting, but the heat of the fire had no effect on them.

I was thrust forward and pushed down onto my knees. One of the soldiers grasped my hair from behind and forced my head forward into a bow, banging it against the flags. Three times he did this, as if determined to dash out my brains. For a moment I saw stars while my stomach lurched and I almost lost consciousness. I kept perfectly still, fearing more violence. I could feel the blood trickling down my forehead.

My head was jerked up again so that I was looking at the high table. Lenklewth was talking to the Shaiksa assassin in Losta, gabbling rapidly. By now I understood a few words of the language, but only when it was spoken slowly and clearly. The warriors at the other tables were silent, listening to what was being said.

Suddenly the mage changed languages and addressed me directly.

"What was it like to be dead?" he demanded. "What did you see?"

In response to his question, something flashed into my mind—a fragment from my experience after death. Something sharp and white was cutting into my shoulder, and I felt hot breath on my face and heard shrill screams, like the noise made by a pig when its throat is slit. In a second it was gone, and I was left gasping, my heart in my mouth. I tried to reply but my voice came out as a croak and I started coughing. At the second attempt, I managed to force out my lie.

"I remember nothing from the moment I collapsed in the water to when I was awakened."

"Do you think you were really dead?" Lenklewth asked. "Or was it just trickery from the human mage?"

I had often asked myself this question. Had my death been faked in some way? Had Lukrasta used his dark magic to create some sort of illusion?

"I don't know, but others tell me that beyond question I was truly dead," I replied.

"I do not believe that Lukrasta had the power to bring someone back from the dead," the mage growled. "It was simply a clever trick that fooled most humans and achieved what he intended. The story of your resurrection is still spreading. Cities far to the south are responding and would have rallied to your flag. Unfortunately for them, you are now in my hands and as good as dead. There might have been sufficient opposition to give us pause, but now it will quickly be snuffed out. Lukrasta's plan has already failed."

My master, John Gregory, had taught me to engage any captor in conversation; one could gain valuable information that might be used at a later time. I decided to do just that. I would flatter this mage.

"So you knew all about Lukrasta in advance? Your magic must be very powerful to foretell the actions of such a formidable human mage."

Lenklewth stared at me for a few moments before replying. I was suddenly worried. What if he could read my thoughts?

He spoke in Losta again, addressing the gathering. When he had finished, a great roar went up, and they began to beat the tables with their fists again. This went on for at least five minutes, until Lenklewth raised his hand and they fell silent.

I hadn't understood a word of what he had said, but it had certainly pleased his warriors. It seemed to me that he had accepted my flattery at face value and communicated my words to his followers.

Once more he spoke to me, a triumphant smile on his face.

"I believe that your human witches use mirrors to see into the future—a method they call scrying. Your mage, Lukrasta, used a different process to achieve the same end. But there is a third way. I am a high mage of the Kobalos, and I use something that we call tantalingi. It is far superior to any human technique. I set a trap for Lukrasta.

"First I sent a Shaiksa assassin to offer combat on the banks of the Shanna River. How easily you humans took the bait! Tantalingi showed me that it would attract the attention of the human witch called Grimalkin. I foresaw that she would bring you to fight the Shaiksa.

"I saw beyond her too; I glimpsed the mage Lukrasta, but it was a while before I understood what part he would play, because the future changes with each new decision. Lukrasta decided that you and the witch would become his tools. You defeated the Shaiksa, but he engineered your seeming death and rebirth. The prophecy of you as a leader was powerful, but Lukrasta took it even further. Your resurrection was to be a clarion call to gather a powerful human army who would follow you to war.

"But none of you, not even Lukrasta, saw the trap that I had prepared! Foolishly believing that she could seize Kobalos mage magic, Grimalkin was drawn to this kulad like a moth to a flame. Now I have you both in my power!"

This revelation hit me like a hammer blow between the eyes. Grimalkin had used me, but these creatures had used me, Grimalkin, and Lukrasta, in that order. The levels of scheming were like the layers of an onion, and I was right at its center, the puppet of them all. Anger blazed within me, and it was only by a huge exertion of will that I stopped myself from launching an attack upon the Kobalos mage.

Lenklewth reached down and lifted something into view, placing it on the table in front of him. It was my Starblade.

"This is a most impressive magical artifact. It's hard to believe that it was created by a mere human. The witch Grimalkin is very talented. I was going to have her executed, but now I think it would be better to enslave her. A year or two in the skleech pens with the other purrai will teach her humility. We can use her skills to serve our people. And as for the sword, it is of use only to you, so I will melt it down and forge a new weapon from it. The metal is precious and rightfully belongs to us anyway. The witch assassin entered our territory and stole it. And then, soon, we will deal with you."

He looked at the Shaiksa assassin, nodded, then

turned back to me. "Remain here while we pray and then feast. Do not attempt to move. Even one flicker of an eyelid will bring an instant reprisal. Later I will give you to the Shaiksa, who will have the satisfaction of avenging his brother assassin. This death will be no simulacrum; it will be offered as a sacrifice to our gods. You will not survive the assassin's blades. He will cut you many times and kill you slowly. It will be the shameful death—the once we call slandata and reserve for rebellious purrai. Only when you cry and beg for death, as they do, will he deliver the killing blow and release you from your torment."

The experience of death was still sharp in my memory and I had an extreme fear of it. But it seemed to me that I could not avoid the fate the mage had planned for me. All I could do now was, perhaps, choose the manner and moment of my end. If I launched a sudden attack on the mage, he would have to defend himself. Perhaps that would gain me a quicker and less painful death. I would wait for my chance.

The mage and the Shaiksa assassin then knelt on the floor, facing the two statues of their gods. I heard movement behind me: the whole gathering was kneeling now. Hands were no longer gripping me, but I knew that at least two Kobalos warriors were standing just behind me.

The mage began to speak in Losta, but the tone and cadence were different from normal speech. Every so often he paused, and the voices of those behind me answered in deep rumbling voices like a chorus. They were praying to their gods.

It seemed to me that the statue of Talkus moved slightly; its sticklike limbs twitched, while the bone tube went up and down. However, I put that down to my imagination—not to mention the discomfort and stress I suffered.

But something was certainly happening to the representation of Golgoth, and a sudden chill ran down my spine. Something from the dark was approaching. The mage could have accounted for this, but there were other indications to support my reaction. The fire suddenly died in the grate, and I could feel cold radiating from the ice statue.

Was Golgoth merging with the statue? Would he be present in the room as witness to my sacrificial death?

The mage and the Shaiksa assassin cried out and held out their hands toward it, then bowed so that their foreheads were touching the floor. After a few moments, they got to their feet and stared toward the ice statue in silence.

At last the worship ended and everyone returned to their seats.

Lenklewth ignored me and began to talk to the Shaiksa. All around me I heard sounds of feasting, punctuated by roars and the beating of fists on wood. It went on for a long time. I forced myself to remain calm, trying not to think about what lay ahead.

Then, very suddenly, the high mage came to his feet, and there was absolute silence. He gestured, and I heard the assembled warriors rise as one. I inclined my head a little so that I could see what was going on. They were abandoning the feast, leaving food uneaten on the tables. What was happening?

That was the last thought I had for some time: the response to my slight movement was violent and immediate. Once more my hair was seized from behind, and a huge fist struck my left temple. There was an explosion of light and I lost consciousness.

The next thing I remember, I was being dragged to my feet and pushed backward. I staggered, lost my balance and crashed down onto the floor once more. I looked about me and saw that, but for the mage and the assassin, the room was empty. The Kobalos warriors had been dismissed, but I wondered what errand they had been sent on.

Lenklewth was still sitting at his table. It was the Shaiksa who had dragged me to my feet; he was holding a wide-bladed dagger.

The fire was now just embers in the grate, and the air felt cold. The mage and assassin were now both wearing body armor, but I was naked to the waist, my upper garments stripped off me. Moments later I realized why.

Before I could react, the assassin stepped forward and, with the tip of the dagger, cut me across the chest from left to right.

The pain was sharp and burned like fire. I gasped in agony. Then I glanced down at the wound and saw that it was very shallow; only a faint line of small, bright red beads of blood showed where it was.

Before I could retreat, the Shaiksa cut me again, this time from right to left, making a diagonal cross. The pain I felt seemed out of all proportion to the wound, and I staggered backward. However, I was determined not to show the agony I felt. I would not weep—though I couldn't help letting out a groan, and my eyes filled with tears.

The Shaiksa looked at me in satisfaction, readying the knife to cut me again. "The blade is specially treated with a poison that causes extreme agony. Already the tears are falling from your eyes. Soon you will scream and beg!"

I tried to summon one of the gifts that I had inherited from Mam. I would attempt to slow down time and halt it. If I could achieve this, then I could seize the Starblade.

Nothing happened. The pain was so intense that I could no longer concentrate. Any thought became impossible.

Looking along the cellar, I saw that the door in the far wall was slightly open. Could I reach it and escape? The Shaiksa was blocking my path, and I would never get past him.

It was then that my instincts took over. I realized that I had but one chance here. So when he attacked again, I leaped up and ran.

I ran toward the Starblade. It was still on the table in front of Lenklewth. The high mage saw me coming, but he didn't move. For a moment I thought I'd taken him by surprise, and hope soared within me. The blade was almost in my grasp when a blow sent me backward onto the flags. I rolled over and over, away from the table.

Lenklewth hadn't touched me; he had simply blasted me with mage magic. I came up onto my knees, but before I could rise, the Shaiksa assassin cut me on my back. This time, despite all my efforts, I let out a scream of agony.

I heard Lenklewth roar with laughter. He began to

beat his fists on the table, just like his soldiers had done earlier. Trying to ignore the waves of pain, I staggered to my feet. The assassin came in fast, but I sidestepped. He missed and overbalanced, presenting me with an opportunity. I punched him hard on the left temple.

It had little effect. He shook his head like a dog after a swim, then straightened up. His cruel eyes watched me, a predator tormenting its prey.

"So far my cuts have been light," he said softly, "but now they will be more damaging. I will start to slice away your flesh."

I backed away, fear rising in my throat. He was an assassin, trained to kill, while I was unarmed and half naked, my flesh vulnerable to his blade. I looked around, wondering if there was a weapon in the room other than the Starblade. There were weapons on the wall, but they were behind the mage.

There was nothing; not even a sliver of hope.

The room seemed to be growing ever colder. Was Golgoth exerting his power to acknowledge the sacrifice of my life?

Then, all at once, I heard a strange sound: the clatter of a blade. I glanced back in astonishment.

The Shaiksa had dropped his dagger onto the flags and was staring at me, an expression of bemusement on his face. A rivulet of red blood was running down the front of his armor, and I saw that a small dagger was buried up to the hilt in his throat. That hilt was a vivid green; it glittered like the dew upon dawn grass. As I stared openmouthed, the rivulet became a river, splattering down onto the flags, and the assassin collapsed onto his knees and began to choke.

Out of the corner of my eye I glimpsed a movement. It was less than a shadow; nothing more than a subtle change in the light. But the next moment someone was standing by the table, obscuring my view of Lenklewth.

As I gazed at the apparition, it turned swiftly and purposefully.

I saw that it was a girl. Her hair was gathered up on top of her head, which accentuated her high cheekbones; her dress, which came down almost to her ankles, was the dark green of December holly.

She was holding the Starblade.

It was Alice.

16
Pause for Thought

"ALICE!" I called out in astonishment.

She made no reply but threw the Starblade toward me, and I caught it by the hilt. The moment I did so, she vanished.

I didn't stop to wonder how she'd suddenly appeared from nowhere. All that mattered was that I had the sword in my hand, so Lenklewth's dark magic could no longer hurt me. I had to concentrate on what needed to be done.

Wasting no time, I advanced toward the mage. As I did so, the fire flared up in the grate, the flames licking the tentacles of the statue of Golgoth.

The mage lurched to his feet, overturning his chair, and started to make complex passes in the air above his head while muttering a spell. His eyes showed what could have been desperation, though it was more likely to be anger at his inability to destroy me with his magic.

I ran at him, aware that I needed to finish this quickly, while I still had the strength to fight.

The mage darted toward the far wall. This time he seized a huge sword in both hands and stepped forward to meet my attack. He brought it across horizontally, just as he had with the ax when he had dashed the sword from my grasp.

Now I brought the Starblade up to block that scything stroke, and there was the clash of blade against blade. This time my grip was firm, which boosted my confidence.

Then, as Lenklewth raised his weapon again, I gave two quick lunges in succession: one aimed at the throat, the second high on his left arm.

Both were blocked by his armor, but the force of the blows sent him staggering backward. For a moment my weariness had been shed and I went after him, whirling and spinning as Grimalkin had taught me, coming in under his guard.

Again my sword was deflected by his armor, but I pressed him harder. However, now my breath was coming fast, and my limbs seemed to be growing heavier.

Suddenly I heard a sizzling and saw that, behind the mage, the limbs of the statue were melting and dripping into the fire.

I realized that I needed to find a gap in Lenklewth's armor or aim for his head. I had to do it quickly, before I became too weak to fight.

As I prepared to strike, I heard heavy boots running down the steps toward the cellar. My heart sank—I assumed that Kobalos warriors were coming to help the mage, but then I saw an expression of dismay on his face. These were human warriors wearing the blue tunics of Polyznia under their metal breastplates, half a dozen of them, splattered with blood from their battle.

I experienced a moment of triumph—and then the mage vanished.

At first, because these men only spoke Losta, I didn't know what the situation outside was. For all I knew, our enemies could be on their way. So we had to be quick—find Grimalkin, then get out of the tower.

So I simply pointed upward, calling out, *"Poska!"* That meant "Follow!"—one of the few Losta words I knew. I ran up the steps, checking each cell in turn, the men following at my heels. I pointed to the first empty one and said, "Grimalkin?" I hoped that they would understand.

The next five were also empty; then, through a grille, I saw a body on the floor, illuminated by a wall candle. It looked like the witch assassin.

The door was barred and locked. I drew back the bar,

then gestured impatiently, pointing at the lock. Two of the warriors hurried off immediately, but it was at least ten minutes before a key was found.

Grimalkin was tightly bound with twine, and a gag had been stuffed into her mouth, kept in place by strips of cloth. Her bare arms were badly cut, but she was conscious and her eyes glared angrily.

In moments we had her free. Once the gag was removed, she coughed for a few moments before climbing to her feet and questioning the warriors in Losta.

Then she turned to me. "Prince Stanislaw is here with our full contingent," she told me. "He surrounded the kulad before advancing into the trees. The Kobalos warriors fought to the death; no prisoners were taken. But now we have little time before the rest of our enemies arrive in force."

"Ask them if Alice is safe!" I demanded.

Grimalkin did so and then nodded. "The girl is safe. The advance party took no part in the victory here of the larger army."

We hurried out of the tower. The cellar steps were slippery with the blood of dead Kobalos. Outside there were more bodies, slain by Prince Stanislaw's infantry.

It was a relief to be out in the cool night air. At one time I hadn't expected to leave the kulad alive.

"I would be dead now but for Alice," I told Grimalkin. "She saved me."

"Alice was here?" she asked, a shocked expression on her face.

"Yes—she appeared out of nowhere, threw the sword to me, then vanished again."

"You can tell me the full story later. First we need to speak to the prince."

After she had spoken to Prince Stanislaw, we walked through the trees together, out of earshot. I told her exactly what had happened. Soon we reached the cinder path, still steaming with the heat from the geyser deep underground, and crossed over. We entered the trees again, and I saw that, despite the cold here, there was no frost on the grass.

Finally I told the witch assassin what the Kobalos mage had said. "Lenklewth claimed he was able to see far into the future using a Kobalos method that was superior to scrying. He saw our plan; he also glimpsed the machinations of Lukrasta. He set a trap and lured us into it—but I want to know why he didn't see how badly it would end for him, how he would be defeated, his men slain. . . ."

"Even the best of those who peer into the future

cannot foretell everything—especially their own deaths," answered Grimalkin, her breath steaming in the cold air. "It is a blind spot that affects all seers, creating a fog around contingent events. He knew that our army would soon reach the kulad, but no doubt he thought he could defend it until the larger Kobalos forces arrived."

"Yes, I think he sensed an imminent attack," I added, remembering how the mage had suddenly come to his feet and the room had fallen silent. "He sent his warriors out to defend the tower."

"He was not far out with his timings, either," said Grimalkin. "Our enemies will be here before noon tomorrow, an army many times larger than our own."

"Alice must have been using magic to watch us," I mused. "Otherwise, how did she know when to intervene at the very moment I faced death?"

"No doubt that is so," said Grimalkin. "Her control of dark magic grows ever stronger. But I wonder why she felt it necessary to leave so suddenly? I would like to speak to her. . . ." She sighed and then turned to me. "Come. Let us go and talk to the prince again. We need to prepare for the coming battle, but this time leave the talking to me."

"What about Jenny?" I asked. "I need to talk to her."

"First the prince, then Jenny," Grimalkin insisted.

We entered Prince Stanislaw's tent; it was lit by thick wax candles in tall wooden holders. Wooden plinths bore carved stone heads of humans—probably previous rulers and heroes of Polyznia.

None of the other princes were present—only Majcher, Stanislaw's high steward, a big man with a proud bearing who scowled at us. He never looked happy. I wondered if he was grieving for the death of comrades, or maybe Prince Kaylar.

Prince Stanislaw addressed us in our own language. "Welcome," he said. "My scouts tell me enemy army approaches. It outnumbers us many times. It is shaped like crescent. Right horn lies between us and river. We cannot win, yet it is too late to retreat."

I nodded. "Yes, we have no choice but to fight," I said. Then I gestured toward Grimalkin, who also spoke to him in our language.

"We can save most of the cavalry and perhaps three quarters of the infantry," she declared. "But you must do *exactly* as I say. The enemy will soon encircle us. We need to break through and escape back across the river."

The prince frowned. For a moment I thought he was about to object. Why should he follow her advice after such a disastrous attack upon the kulad? It had cost him many lives, not least that of Prince Kaylar.

But then his expression softened. The prince already knew the truth about me, and he was shrewd. In spite of her recent failure, he recognized Grimalkin's martial abilities.

"If we break out and cross river, what we do then?" he demanded.

"There are two possibilities," she told him. "One is that they will follow us across the river and lay siege to your cities. But I think the second is more likely. The failure of Lenklewth's plan will have given them pause. I believe that the Kobalos will now wish to assemble an overwhelming force before making that crossing. Then they will advance until their conquest is complete."

"You seem certain," the prince said, meeting her eye.

"I am very certain. I am a witch and have scryed it. That is their plan at the moment. It may change. If it does, I will inform you."

He nodded. "What wish you to be done?"

"The three eighteen-pounders must be brought close together, facing south. Then I need a body of cavalry who are prepared to fight a rear-guard action so that most of our infantry can escape. Unfortunately, it will cost some of them their lives."

"There will be many volunteers," the prince assured her. "My men are brave. I will choose the best."

This was what Grimalkin had always intended: to break through the enemy forces and escape back across the river.

But she had failed in her plan to gain knowledge of mage magic. She would return empty-handed. There had been many deaths; more would follow. And it had all been for nothing.

The pain of the Shaiksa's blades still hurt, but it was not as severe as the anguish in my heart. My glimpse of Alice had brought back all my confused feelings about her—the love and closeness of our friendship, tainted by her betrayal of me.

17
The Earth Witch

It was less than an hour before dawn, and the sky to the east was growing lighter. I was restless.

After Grimalkin had attended to my wounds, I'd spoken to Jenny. She was starting to calm down after her ordeal. I intended to talk to her again later, but for now I urgently needed time by myself to think things through and try to resolve my confusion about Alice.

I had not come through my most recent ordeal well. I was more afraid of death than ever before. The experience of the pain of death had taken away some of my courage.

I walked through the trees, circling the kulad, wondering if any of us would survive the coming battle.

It was then that I heard a faint sound: music drifting on the breeze, reaching my ears from a distance. At first I thought it was a human voice. I came to a halt and listened more carefully. The leaves overhead rustled in the wind, and for a moment the sound was gone. Just when I started to think I'd imagined it, the song came back louder than ever. No, it was not singing. It was some sort of instrument.

It seemed familiar. Who could be playing?

Then I finally remembered: It was the pipes of Pan, the Old God of nature and life itself.

Two years earlier, I'd encountered him in Ireland. Once you had heard that enthralling music, you could never forget it. Why was he here? I wondered.

I tried to locate its source, and suddenly realized that it was coming from the kulad. I began to walk directly toward it, slowly at first, as if in a dream; then I felt an urge to run. I was being summoned by magic. The Starblade at my side was failing to defend me against that spell of compulsion.

There could be two reasons for that. Either there was no intention to harm me, or the spell was too strong even for the sword. Back in Ireland, Alice had been snatched away into the dark, but Pan had returned her. He had helped us once. If it was Pan, I felt sure that the Old God meant me no harm.

As I ran, I looked up at the tower looming above me. It was in darkness but for a light flickering in the topmost window, from Lenklewth's chamber.

I crossed the drawbridge, passed under the portcullis, and walked toward the tower. There were two guards on the door. I wondered if they were aware of the music . . . perhaps only I could hear it? I nodded to them and entered the tower. As I climbed the stairs, I noticed that the bodies of the slain had been removed for burial, but there were still bloodstains on the walls and floor of each room. The music was growing ever louder and more compelling, drawing me upward.

I began to run up the steps until I reached the outer door of the mage's chamber. The huge bath still steamed, and I looked at it warily. The skelts had vanished with the mage, but what if they'd returned and were lurking there?

I went on through the white mist and crossed the bridge to the inner door, then stepped inside, expecting to find Pan.

Pan wasn't there, but Alice was.

The first time I'd met Alice, she had been wearing a tattered black dress tied at the waist with a piece of string. More recently, when she'd left me and gone off with Lukrasta, she'd worn a dress of dark silk and a fine black coat trimmed with fur. Now she was wearing what I'd glimpsed when she'd saved me—a long green dress. Alice had painted her fingernails green, too, and wore a short fur-trimmed jacket the color of bark. There were two small daggers at her belt; each had a green hilt, identical to that of the dagger buried in the throat of the Shaiksa assassin.

Just one thing hadn't changed since our first meeting on the path that ran up the hill from Chipenden to the Spook's house: Alice was still wearing her pointy shoes.

I remembered the warning issued by my master, John Gregory, at the beginning of my apprenticeship: "Watch out for the village girls. Especially any who wear pointy shoes."

It had been good advice, but I'd ignored it and gotten involved with Alice. A part of me wished I'd never met her.

"It's good to see you, Tom," she said, a faint smile on her lips.

I wanted to say something cutting and sarcastic, but I bit my tongue and attempted to restrain my anger. However, my feelings were too strong, and rather than thanking Alice for saving my life, I had spoken the bitter words before I could help it.

"Where's your friend Lukrasta?" I demanded.

The smile left Alice's face, and a look of anger flickered across it. Then it faded to sadness.

"Lukrasta is dead. He was killed by the Kobalos. It's all gone badly wrong. We tried to penetrate their city and learn the secrets of their magic, but we made the same mistake as Grimalkin. We underestimated them. They were lying in wait. I barely escaped with my own life."

For a moment I wondered whether Alice was telling the truth, but it was just a momentary doubt. The expression on her face drove it away.

It was a shock to learn that Lukrasta was dead. Thoughts and feelings began to swirl around in my head. First I felt a glimmer of hope—if he was dead, then perhaps Alice and I could be together again. But I was immediately overcome by fresh anger as I realized that she was only here because Lukrasta was dead!

"So now you've lost him, you've come back to me. . . ."

Alice shook her head slowly. "I've come back to *help* you. I saved your life, didn't I? I'm here to try and save you all, Tom. Without my help, many of you are going to die. It ain't possible for you all to escape. Grimalkin's got great self-belief—she can't imagine failing—but not even she can achieve that."

There was silence as I mulled over what she had said, and suddenly I heard the music again. It seemed to be all around me, filling the room.

"That music—is that Pan?" I asked.

Alice nodded. "Yes, Pan's close by. He'll add his strength to mine to make up for the loss of Lukrasta."

"Do you mean Pan's on our side?"

"He's on the side of life, Tom; on the side of everything

that's green, on the side of everything that springs from the earth. The Old Gods are taking sides. Soon Talkus, the Kobalos god, will control most of 'em. The first that bowed to him was Golgoth, the Lord of Winter. He's a lot to gain from the expansion of Valkarky and the ice spreading southward, bringing blizzards and perpetual winter. But Pan will never give in."

"Grimalkin said that Talkus and Golgoth were part of the dark army that seeks to destroy us. So is Pan really part of our army? Does he really support humans?"

"Pan wants a green world teeming with life, so he'll fight with us—he'll help to hold the ice back. That's how it started, Tom. That's how I ended up with Lukrasta."

"What do you mean, Alice? What did that have to do with Pan?"

"When I went into the dark to get the Dolorous Blade, Pan was angry at my presumption at entering his domain without permission. So I had to pay a price, or he wouldn't let me leave. He made me promise that I would help him if he asked. Didn't have any choice, did I? Otherwise I'd have been trapped in the dark forever. So I agreed.

"Wasn't long before he told me what I had to do—link my powers with those of Lukrasta. I had to leave you and fight the Kobalos with the mage. You can't break your word to one of the Old Gods. It was useless to resist. Then, when I tried the Doomdryte ritual, Lukrasta arrived, and that was the beginning of our alliance."

The Doomdryte ritual was a reading from the book of that name. If you made one mistake, mispronounced a word or hesitated, you could be destroyed. Alice had risked that to gain power to fight the Fiend. But it was Lukrasta's book. It was believed that it had been dictated to him, word by word, by the Fiend. So as soon as Alice began the ritual, Lukrasta had appeared before her.

"You make it sound like you had no choice, Alice. Are you sure you aren't just twisting the truth? Grimalkin was there. She said that as soon as you saw the mage, you changed and wanted to be with him."

Grimalkin's cool assessment of what had taken place between Alice and Lukrasta had hurt me more than I could bear.

"I just accepted the inevitable, Tom. Belonging to him enabled me to get close to him. It gave me a chance to help you. It gave me a chance to save you."

I remembered seeing Alice on the balcony of Lukrasta's tower in Cymru. The image of them kissing came into my mind so clearly and strongly that for a moment I was back there in the past. Anger and jealousy surged through me. I took a deep breath, trying to stifle those emotions.

"But did you have to kiss him, Alice? Couldn't you just have worked with him? Did you have to sleep in his bed?"

"It was the only way. He expected it. He's used to people doing his will," Alice continued. "I was able to save your life more than once, Tom. Lukrasta wanted to restore the Fiend to power in order to oppose the Kobalos. He'd have done anything, he would, to achieve that. He would have squashed you like an ant. But you listen to someone who kisses you and holds you close, Tom. You listen to someone who sleeps in your bed. Don't you see that? That's why I did it.

"He wanted to come with me to the Spook's garden to steal the Fiend's head. Nobody there would have survived that, not you, not John Gregory—not even Grimalkin. But because I was close to him, I was able to change his mind, Tom. I persuaded him to let me go alone. That way nobody got hurt too much . . . apart from the boggart. It fought so hard, I was forced to hurt it more than I wanted."

"That note you left me in the tower—you said that you never wanted to see me again. You said that you'd gone to the dark. Was that true as well?" I said bitterly.

"The mark on my thigh is now a full dark moon. Ain't no going back from that, is there? Like I said, now I belong to the dark."

When Alice was much younger, the mark had appeared as a crescent. She had fought against going to the dark, but from time to time she'd been forced to use dark magic to save both of us. And each time she'd done it, the crescent had grown. The full moon marked her new status. She did indeed belong to the dark.

"But it could be a lot worse," Alice said.

I laughed out loud—it sounded ugly and forced. "What on earth could be worse than being a malevolent witch?" I demanded.

"I belong to the best bit of the dark. I belong to Pan. I never wanted to be a bone witch or a blood witch, or a witch that has a creepy familiar like a toad or a spider, so it's worked out fine. I've ended up being something different, something that no Pendle witch has ever been. I'm an earth witch who serves Pan. My magic comes from the ground. It comes from the elements. It comes from the earth itself. The truth is, that's what I was always meant to be."

I stared at her in silence. My heart felt as cold as stone, but part of me was fascinated by what she'd just said. As far as I knew, we spooks knew nothing of earth witches. My master had never mentioned them, and there had been no reference to them in his library. It was a completely new category of witch.

Anger flared within me again and drove away my curiosity. I asked her a question: "If Lukrasta were still alive, would you be with him now?"

"Open your ears, Tom! If you'd listened to what I said, you'd know the answer to that. Of course I'd still be with him—I'd be doing the will of Pan. But now that he's dead, the bond between me and Lukrasta is over, ain't it?"

"Do you miss him, Alice?"

She stared at me for a long time before replying. "You can't be close to someone and not miss 'em when they're gone. He was kind to me. He wasn't all bad. None of us are. If I didn't miss him, I wouldn't be human, would I? I feel sorry for him, I do. They did terrible things to him before they killed him, Tom. They stitched his lips together so that he couldn't chant spells. They chopped off his hands so that he couldn't make magical signs. He was in agony. But I couldn't help him."

"You did terrible things to me too, Alice. You joined your power with Lukrasta's to overcome the Starblade, didn't you? You forced me into a mistake that caused my death. That's true, isn't it?"

Alice hung her head, unable to meet my eyes. "It's true," she said softly. "I was shocked when Lukrasta told me what we had to do. I argued that we needed to find another way. But there wasn't one. So even though I hated hurting you, I had to go along with it. But we did it for a purpose: so that you could come back from the dead and give these people hope, so that we all might have a chance of survival. Despite the pain you suffered, it was worth it. Ain't nothing different from what your own mam would have done! Think about it, Tom. She would have sacrificed me to destroy the Fiend. She would have done it for the higher good. Ain't that true?"

Then it was my turn to bow my head.

Yes, it was true. Mam had created a magical ritual to destroy the Fiend; my part in it was to slay Alice with my own hands. But this didn't make me feel any better.

"What was the winged creature that appeared to the magowie?" I asked. "The one that seemed to bring me back to life. They called it an angelus. Was it some sort of angel?"

"No, Tom, it was a tulpa. It's the name for a magical thought form. You create such a creature using your imagination. At first it just lives inside your head, but in time you can project it outside yourself so it has substance in the real world. Lukrasta taught me how to do it. Look, Tom, we can talk this through later, when this is all over. Now I need to find Grimalkin and help her salvage what we can of this army."

As we left the kulad together, I saw the guards' eyes widen in astonishment at the sight of Alice. We walked in silence toward the encampment beyond the trees until we reached the tent I'd shared with Grimalkin and Jenny.

Alice's words were spinning inside my head. She'd given me an explanation for her behavior, but it didn't make me feel any better.

On the horizon, the clouds were pink with the approach of dawn, but the ground was still in shadow. A lantern flickered inside the tent. I opened the flap and stepped inside; Alice followed.

Jenny was sitting cross-legged on her blanket, making entries in her notebook. She looked up, and her eyes widened at the sight of Alice.

"Jenny, this is Alice," I said, nodding toward her.

Alice smiled, but Jenny just stared.

Grimalkin was on her knees, sharpening one of her short-bladed throwing knives on a whetstone. When she lifted her eyes, she smiled warmly at Alice, showing no surprise at all.

"I hoped you would come and join your strength with ours," she told Alice, rising to her feet and sheathing the blade. "This changes everything."

Jenny Calder

18
Grimalkin's Plans

I'M sick to death of this bleak northern country. How I hate the endless tall conifer trees and long for the sight of a sycamore or an oak. The cold has gotten into my bones, and I never feel warm. I'm terrified, too: A huge army stands between us and the river. How can we possibly hope to fight our way through them? I fear that I may never see the County again.

As far as I can tell, Tom hasn't reprimanded Grimalkin for abducting me. He's just accepted it. We've only spoken briefly when he asked how I was feeling, and I haven't had a chance to speak to him alone yet, but I hope he hasn't changed his mind about going back to the County . . . if we survive tomorrow.

Grimalkin doesn't talk about her long-term plans, but she is always optimistic. Even now she's been busy working out how to defeat the Kobalos. Last night she left her notebook open and I had a look—I couldn't help myself.

She intends to teach the infantry new maneuvers, tactics she has learned on her travels through foreign lands. Their marching pace will increase; when attacked, they will quickly assume defensive positions—sometimes in a square formation, sometimes in triangles or star shapes. Sometimes a thousand men will form five squares and, using shield walls, long spears, and bows, stand firm, driving off enemy cavalry; then they will advance rapidly, only to form a triangle when attacked again.

It sounds very complicated, but the witch assassin clearly believes that it is something that can be accomplished.

She also plans to employ scores of blacksmiths, using molds set in sand pits to craft huge armaments. At first I thought she was just intending to forge more of the large eighteen-pounder guns, but her sketches tell a very strange story. The long barrels of the weapons she has designed are twisted, and rather than cannonballs or round shot, their projectiles consist of pieces of metal connected by chains. Some of these are round like small cannonballs, but others are helical, triangular, or thin hollow cylinders.

She's also sketched small carriages that she calls chariots. Some have long, sharp blades attached to the rims, which spin with the wheels. Others have runners for ice and snow. From these, huge blades curve upward like wings. They are the wings of the angel of death; anyone or anything that the chariots pass is cut into pieces.

The further I read, the more fantastical Grimalkin's ideas became. She intends to manufacture musical wind instruments that she calls joshuas. They are very long; each needs to be supported by a dozen men. I don't know how such music might motivate an army. Far better are the drums and bugles used by the County. *The mind of a witch is mysterious indeed,* I thought. *Who could possibly fathom it?*

But Grimalkin's notes have convinced me of one thing: She herself has no intention of returning to the County. She will stay here and fight right through the winter. I only hope that she doesn't change Tom's mind and persuade him to stay as well.

Moments ago, something else happened that made me feel very uneasy. Tom came into the tent with the witch girl, Alice. How she got here I don't know, but I wish she'd stayed away. She gave me a quick glance that was far from friendly, and then the two of them began a long conversation with Grimalkin. I pretended to be reading through my notebook, but I was paying close attention to all that passed between them.

Alice told Grimalkin that the human mage called Lukrasta was dead. I wonder what that will mean for the future . . . will Tom now become close to Alice again? If so, things don't look good for me. She doesn't like me one bit—she'll want Tom all to herself. There'll be no place for me at Chipenden. I'm sure she'll persuade him to end my apprenticeship and send me away.

I wish I could get inside her head and assess her true feelings, but she is a powerful witch, like Grimalkin, and I can't.

It is strange that a spook should be in alliance with two witches. Surely it goes against everything a spook stands for.

But what does it matter? Few, if any of us, will survive what the dawn brings.

Thomas Ward

19
The Final Winter

I<small>F</small> the coming of Alice, with her powerful magic, brought me new hope, the dawn light brought renewed fear.

For the first time, in the far distance, I could see the vast Kobalos army that faced us. The flags of each of the principalities fluttered at the head of our small force, but the Kobalos army boasted flags and banners almost beyond counting. The predominant reds and blacks stood out against the white frosted plain and gray snow-laden sky.

They were here to slay us all. Lenklewth had escaped, and they would all now know what had been done to the Kobalos from the kulad. They'd want revenge.

It was not just the size of the army that daunted us. Towering above the cavalry and infantry were creatures with many legs that resembled gigantic millipedes. They blew jets of hot breath from the vents on their shoulders, and above their heads, clouds of dark steam pulsed in the freshening wind like low clouds threatening a storm.

Grimalkin stared at the enemy lines for a long time. Then she turned back to face me, her expression grim. "See those enormous creatures in the distance? They are the varteki, grown to their full size."

"Ain't no doubt about it," Alice confirmed, "and the varteki are deadly in battle. Lukrasta thought that, next to their gods, they were the greatest threat posed by the Kobalos."

"We have our cannon," I said, gesturing toward the three huge weapons. They were arranged in a line pointing south; already the gunners were making them ready to fire. "If those men have the same skill and ability as County gunners, they could do a lot of damage!"

"Even the varteki will be vulnerable to eighteen-pounders!" Grimalkin agreed.

"But you can't kill 'em all," Alice pointed out. "Some will survive, and they'll cause havoc. They'll burrow through the earth and attack from beneath, won't they?"

"Some will. We must kill as many as we can, and then move quickly. We must fight our way clear and save as much of this army as we can."

Grimalkin and Alice exchanged glances. Then, without another word, they headed off together, deep in conversation, for almost an hour. I didn't like being excluded. When we'd fought the dark in the past, our discussions had been open. There'd been none of this skulking around out of earshot. There was obviously something they didn't wish me to hear. What secrets had they shared?

The presence of Alice unsettled me. I was grateful that she'd saved my life, but still jealous of the time she'd spent with Lukrasta. Physically I felt much stronger, but my mind was in turmoil. I saw again that I had lost a lot of my courage.

I looked across at Jenny. She was standing by her horse, patting its neck. She looked pale and scared, so I went across to reassure her.

"Don't worry, Jenny," I told her. "Another hour, and we'll be safely through the enemy lines and heading toward the river and safety. The prince selected that horse for you. It's good, reliable, and won't be panicked. All you have to do is stay in the saddle. It'll be fine, I promise you."

Jenny nodded and forced a smile onto her face. "I wish I was as brave and confident as Alice. She's not one bit afraid of Grimalkin. I can see why she was once your closest friend. Have you become friends again now?"

"Not really," I replied, "but it's a good thing that Alice

has joined us. She could make a difference."

"Using her magic, you mean?"

"Yes. The Kobalos have powerful mages; Alice will help to counter their power."

Jenny didn't reply.

The enemy had been advancing steadily for almost an hour, but now they had come to a halt and waited less than a mile away. Some were on horseback, but the majority were on foot, dwarfed by the monstrous creatures that served them. As the varteki exhaled, their hot breath continued to form clouds in the cold air above them.

A silence had fallen, broken only by the occasional whinny of a horse or a soldier clearing his throat. Our army was ready, the blue uniforms of the Polyznians forming the vanguard.

Were our enemies preparing to advance? I wondered. After consulting with the prince, Grimalkin had already decided to take the initiative. She had explained her plan of attack at length; it would begin with the firing of our cannon.

From a distance we watched the gunners go about their business. They had the calm, methodical efficiency of the County gunners. It seemed so long ago that I'd watched them attempting to breach the walls of Malkin Tower.

I'd been told that our guns were eighteen-pounders, the same as those used back home. But although the bore was the same, the barrels were much longer and, rather than being smooth, were embossed with grimacing faces and skulls. The barrels were now being elevated by means of levers and ratchets. The gun carriages had already been positioned so that the weapons were pointing toward the largest group of varteki.

Despite the cold, the gunners were working in their shirtsleeves. I'd noticed that County gunners did the same. Probably it was to avoid their jackets getting soiled. The military was very strict on the requirements for a smart appearance for soldiers of all ranks. Only the sergeant still wore the dark blue jacket of the Polyznia military as he supervised the aiming of the guns, without getting his hands dirty. Despite the fact that the enemy might charge toward us at any second, the gunners appeared to be in no rush. They were calm and methodical. The important thing was to get it right.

The cannonballs had been arranged into long rows between the guns. I remembered that County gunners usually stacked theirs in neat pyramids. But I acknowledged that everything seemed well organized here. I could not fault it. I noted the large tubs of water to cool the barrels; they were prone to overheating and then exploding, which could send shrapnel in every direction. The canvas bags of gunpowder were kept well away from the water.

The central gun would be fired first. Gunpowder had already been tipped into the mouth of the cannon before being rammed home with a long rod. Now one of the gunners lifted a heavy cannonball, inspected it, and then, with a nod of approval toward his sergeant, hefted it upward and rolled it smoothly into the long barrel.

Finally the sergeant barked a command in his best parade-ground voice. He was speaking Losta, but I assumed that the order was "Fire!"

There was a reed fuse sticking out of the top of the gun and another soldier lit it, then stood well clear. All the gunners had their hands over their ears. We were standing about a hundred yards away, but I did the same—I'd experienced the deafening thunder of an eighteen-pounder before.

The gun carriage jerked back a few paces, and the cannonball hurtled through the air toward the monstrous varteki, to the rear of the front line. Even with my hands over my ears, I could still hear the shriek of its passage through the air.

It struck the ground about thirty yards short of the enemy, sending up a cloud of dust, then bounced twice and flew into the line of waiting Kobalos. Distant screams and groans from the fallen Kobalos filled the air. But the line quickly closed to fill the gap.

A cloud of smoke hung over the central gun, but the trajectory of all three barrels was adjusted: there was the clicking, metallic sound of ratchets.

Less than a minute later, the three cannon discharged with a simultaneous clap of thunder, followed by the banshee wail of the projectiles falling toward our enemies. This time they struck their intended target.

I knew immediately that we had caused serious damage to the enemy. The screams and bellows didn't sound human. Horrible shrieks rent the air and unsettled our horses even more than the noise of the cannon.

Within a minute, a second volley had struck the same area, and after a third fusillade, the guns were repositioned, each now seeking out the remaining varteki. They were now firing at will, but the targets were found again and again, and I noticed a smile spread across the sergeant's face in recognition of a job well done.

This was the first stage of a battle in which our smaller army would try to break through the lines of a force that greatly outnumbered us. So far, so good. It had begun well.

As for my own part in this, little was required of me other than to survive and reach safety. When the time came, I was to ride close to Grimalkin, Prince Stanislaw, Alice, and Jenny, surrounded and protected by the prince's personal guard.

I couldn't understand why the Kobalos didn't attack now. It seemed crazy to stay in the same position and take such punishment, especially when their army was so much larger than ours. I *could* understand that the rank and file might be required to stand firm under withering fire, to show discipline or bravery. But the varteki were being targeted; our gunners were rapidly depleting their most powerful weapon. Did the Kobalos also have weapons that could kill over a distance, or would they use some sort of dark magic against us?

I wondered what part Alice intended to play in this battle. On first seeing her, Grimalkin had exclaimed, "This changes everything!" So would Alice use her powerful magic to help our cause? At the moment, she was just standing beside Grimalkin, staring at the Kobalos lines.

I patted Jenny on the shoulder, then walked across to stand beside Alice. "Are you going to use your magic against the Kobalos?" I asked her. "We're going to need it."

Alice nodded. "Not yet, but the moment will come when I can make a difference. I'll use it then, Tom, and not before. I only have so much strength, and I want to make it count."

Suddenly a dark orb fell through the air toward the gunners and splattered wetly over the central cannon—a yellow brown goo with streaks of white, like excrement dropped by some gigantic bird. I looked up just in time to see the next one coming, traveling in a high arc from the Kobalos lines. This landed on the cannon on the left. Their targeting was extremely accurate, I realized.

"They are probably using big catapults," Grimalkin explained calmly. "They are every bit as accurate as our cannons. Soon we will see how effective their missiles are."

I watched as the barrel of the central cannon began to steam, and I heard a hissing sound; the surface of the metal was bubbling and spitting. Seeing the threat, two of the gunners staggered toward it with one of the smaller tubs of water. They intended to try and wash away the noxious substance, but they were too late.

Suddenly the whole barrel began to twist and distort. The men backed away as it began to send out globules of molten metal.

The third projectile missed its target by a few feet,

landing on the ground near the sergeant and two of the gunners and splattering them with yellow-brown droplets. They reacted immediately, running around in circles and beating at their faces and heads; they were screaming in agony.

I shuddered in horror as the sergeant's blue jacket steamed and blackened as if consumed by invisible flames. The skin on his face and hands began to bubble and fall off in long strips.

The second gun was already beginning to suffer the fate of the first: The barrel was distorted and would clearly no longer be of use. Seconds later, the third gun was also silenced.

Whatever means they had used to launch those deadly orbs, the accuracy of their targeting had proved to be at least the equal of ours. I looked up fearfully, but could see nothing. They had simply ended the threat from our guns.

Everything fell silent. For a moment I thought the Kobalos might be using dark magic against us. The silence grew and intensified, and then a cold wind suddenly sprang up, blowing toward us from the massed ranks of our enemies. Snowflakes began to whirl down out of the ominous gray sky.

And a dark thought winged its way into my mind.

We might well be dead soon, slain in the first big battle between humans and Kobalos. Valkarky would expand, bringing ice and snow to cover forever what had once been green.

Was it a coincidence that the snow was falling just as the battle started? Was Golgoth already starting to blast us with cold?

Could this be the first snow of the final winter, one that would never end?

20
The Space Between Worlds

Distracted by the snow, I had failed to notice something else . . . when I next glanced across, the enemy line had changed. The central section seemed to be bulging outward. Then I heard the distant thunder of hooves, and my heart lurched. The Kobalos cavalry was charging toward us.

In response, there was a single bugle call from somewhere close to Prince Stanislaw, and our archers began to sprint forward into the space between the ruined guns and the advancing enemy.

This was part of the plan that Grimalkin had put forward. The original intention had been to send the archers forward earlier, to protect the guns and prevent them from being overrun in the event of such an attack as this. Now that the guns had been destroyed, the archers would still attempt to halt the enemy cavalry.

The two thousand archers got into position rapidly, forming two lines facing the enemy cavalry. Within seconds, they had each nocked an arrow from the quivers on their backs, aimed their longbows, and at a shouted command, fired.

The arrows fell in a long downward curve, swooping like a flock of predatory birds, sharp beaks seeking out the flesh of the enemy. The trajectory seemed perfect, and I tried to estimate the result.

The snow was thickening and it was hard to see now, but the enemy seemed unaffected. Back in the kulad I had noted the armor worn by Lenklewth; his warriors had been no less well protected. Their armor had overlapping plates with few chinks to allow an arrow to penetrate. The helmets covered the head; only the narrow visor and the join at the neck were vulnerable. Our arrows were unlikely to cause harm.

This first fusillade had been a way to release tension, exercise muscles, and engage the skills of our archers before they got down to the real business. Grimalkin had been quite clear on what would happen next: They would not use the same tactic again.

Now they simply waited, allowing the enemy cavalry to get closer. The two lines of bowmen were offset;

the ones on the back line were positioned so that they could fire between the two men in front of them. They drew back their bows as one, no longer aiming high but straight ahead.

The foremost of the Kobalos cavalry were less than a hundred yards away now, and still our archers did not fire. I could hear the thunder of the hooves; see the fierce eyes of the enemy glaring through the narrow slits in their helmets. My hand gripped the hilt of the Starblade where it still rested in its scabbard. If the archers failed to halt them, the Kobalos would be among us in seconds.

When the enemy riders were less than fifty yards away, the archers finally fired.

Polyznia had excellent blacksmiths, able to forge first-rate weapons. At close range, their steel-tipped arrows could penetrate metal, flesh, and bone. Horses screamed and fell. Kobalos warriors pitched forward, many dead before they hit the ground. Those that followed couldn't halt in time and went into their fallen comrades, crashing down in a tangle of limbs, the living intertwined with the dead.

Enemy riders were now circling to the rear, trying to find a way through the piles of bodies to reach us. The archers fired again, and more Kobalos were flung from their saddles to join those already on the ground.

Again and again flights of those deadly arrows struck

home, until there were none left to attack. Not one Kobalos warrior had retreated; they were prepared to fight to the death, with no concern for their own survival. That made them a truly formidable race.

In the distance, the enemy lines looked unchanged. Although they had lost perhaps a brigade of cavalry, they no doubt had many others in reserve.

However, rather than waiting for the next attack, the archers retreated, summoned by a bugle call. As they rejoined our ranks, another thin, high note cut through the cold air. In response, the largest detachment of our cavalry began to move forward in two long columns, which would join together beyond the fallen Kobalos.

These were the blue-jacketed elite, the Polyznian lancers, all polished leather and shining buckles. They did not wear helmets, and each fair-haired rider carried a long lance across his right shoulder. Their mounts were immaculately turned out, as if for the parade grounds rather than a battlefield, but the men exuded confidence and determination.

When they reached their positions, I heard another bugle call—the order to charge.

With a thunder of hooves, they galloped into the swirling snowflakes, heading directly toward the Kobalos lines.

It was exhilarating to watch that charge. It filled me with hope, but that was tempered by nerves and fear. This was the moment of truth, because their advance was also our own signal to move.

It was intended that the lancers would cut a swathe through the ranks of the enemy, clearing the way; we would follow as best we could. The plan was that each of the remaining cavalrymen would allow an infantry soldier to share his horse. Those foot soldiers left behind would have to run and fight as best they could, although some of our lancers had volunteered to offer protection during the retreat.

Swords already drawn, the prince's guard fell into position around us. Grimalkin had already leaped onto her horse. I clambered up onto my mount and gave Jenny an encouraging smile as she did the same. I noticed that Alice was still on foot; she was staring intently at the distant lancers, who were closing with the enemy.

Her face was very serious, and she was frowning slightly. Alice still had the appearance of a pretty young girl, but I could see something else. I could see the mature woman that she would one day become. I could see her determination. Radiating from her was the power of a will that would tolerate no opposition to her intentions.

I had assumed that Alice would share Grimalkin's

horse. To my surprise, she came over and pulled herself up into the saddle behind me, wrapping her arms tightly around my waist. I looked over my shoulder in surprise, but the guards were already moving forward and I had no chance to speak.

We advanced, our trot soon becoming a canter. We were heading straight toward the enemy lines, following the path of the lancers. I sensed a horse and rider go down somewhere on my left. Whether they'd been hit or the horse had stumbled, I didn't know—the result would be the same, the rider trampled and left for dead. It was vital to stay in the saddle and keep moving with the rest.

The snow was falling thickly now; although I could hear a few faint screams and shouts, everything seemed slightly muffled and distant. Our route was clear, but there was fighting somewhere far to our right; there was a clashing of swords as humans battled Kobalos. Prince Stanislaw was ahead of us, and we were still protected by his guard. I looked around for Jenny but couldn't pick her out; as long as she didn't fall off her horse, I reflected, she would be fine.

In the distance, far to my left, I glimpsed one of the terrible varteki. It towered above the battlefield, three huge tentacles writhing like the branches of an enormous tree in a gale. But then the snow closed in, and it was lost to my view.

It was a blizzard now—I could hardly see the horse in front of me. We seemed to be floating rather than galloping. The snow was no longer driving straight into my face. It was parting like a curtain before it touched my skin, and I couldn't hear anything at all except my own breathing.

All at once I began to feel strange and dizzy, and I feared I was about to fall off my horse. Alice tightened her grip upon my waist. I felt nausea in my belly . . . and then everything changed.

There was suddenly no snow, no battle; nobody but Alice and me staring out over a vast, featureless plain of gray sand. My horse had come to a halt, and I could feel it trembling beneath me. Above us the sky was the same color as the sand. There were no clouds, no sun, no stars—just the same quality of light that might be expected back in the County at dusk. In every direction, the horizon was obscured by a distant white mist.

I realized that Alice had used her magic to bring us to this strange place. But I needed to be back in the battle. I wanted to be sure that Jenny was safe and that everybody got back across the river.

"Where are we, Alice?" I demanded angrily. "Is this the dark?"

"No, Tom, this is the space between worlds," she replied. "From here we could be back in Chipenden in an instant or, with great difficulty and danger, find our way into the heart of Valkarky. But the Kobalos mages can use it too."

"I didn't want to come here, Alice—my place is with the others!"

"That's *why* we've come here. More use to the others here than back in that battle, we are. This is *exactly* where we need to be. I'm going to do my best to save those soldier boys. Lenklewth will no doubt try to stop me. He's very strong, that Kobalos mage—he could make it difficult. So we've got to sort him out first. The Kobalos high mages are aware the instant anyone enters this place. That's why they were ready for us when we used it to get into Valkarky. Our presence here will alert him. Lenklewth will come after us. . . . Then you can kill him."

"You make it sound easy, Alice."

"You've got the Starblade, Tom. His magic can't hurt you. Just make sure you don't drop it this time."

That jibe made me angry. Alice must have heard from Grimalkin how I was beaten by Lenklewth. Or, more likely, she'd been using her magic to watch what happened.

"Not only is he a powerful mage—he's been practicing combat skills all his life! He's a warrior mage!" I snapped. "He knocked the sword out of my hand with a blow from an ax. I did my best."

"Of course you did, but now you've got to do better. A lot of men are going to die if you fail here. You have no choice. You *have* to succeed!"

"What about your magic, Alice? Can't you use it to defeat him?"

"If things go badly, I'll do my best—but even if I win, it will drain most of my power. It'll take a while after that before I'm strong again and that'd be too late to save those soldier boys. That's why you have to kill him."

I fell silent.

It was then that the ground began to tremble. I looked down and saw the gray sand shaking, forming constantly shifting patterns. Then, directly ahead, something suddenly thrust its way up through the sand like a sapling, thick as a human arm. I remembered the last time I'd seen such a scary thing. It had been at the center of the village green in Topley, back in the County. I realized that it was a vartek burrowing up to the surface!

My horse was terrified and reared up so sharply that we were both thrown off. I landed heavily, but the sand cushioned my fall. I came up onto my knees to see it galloping away into the distance.

Two more writhing tentacles followed it. Each had a sharp, hard bone tip like a blade.

Then the monstrous head of the creature erupted from the sand.

Lenklewth had sent a vartek to kill us.

21
A Globule of Acid

I was wrong in one respect: It was indeed one of the fearsome vartek, but Lenklewth had not *sent* it. He'd arrived *with* it. He was sitting behind its huge head, on a brown leather saddle strapped about its neck. He wore a long coat of chain mail and a helmet, though I could see his eyes and forehead through the open visor.

As I staggered to my feet, the vartek pulled itself up onto the surface, its belly almost touching the sand. The many thin insectlike legs had a green sheen, but its upper body was covered in black, shiny scales.

It opened its elongated jaws wide, and its foul breath washed over me. The acidic stench made my eyes sting, and I started to cough and choke. The creature's bulging eyes regarded me carefully, and I looked at its fearsome teeth in dismay. They moved around in its mouth, constantly changing angle.

I stood my ground, but I knew that at any moment the creature might spit a globule of acid at me. The varteki I'd fought previously had not had a rider. Was this one subject to the mage's will? Would it only spit at his command? Could I provoke the mage into fighting me in single combat?

Out of the corner of my eye, I saw that Alice had gotten to her feet and was walking toward me.

I drew the Starblade and held it aloft, looking up to meet Lenklewth's eyes. "Get down and fight!" I challenged him.

He gave the same booming, manic laugh I'd heard in the cellar when he'd beaten on the table with his fists. The vartek straightened its legs, rising up before us, and opened its jaws even wider.

Something hit my shoulder, and I fell sprawling onto my side, somehow managing to keep hold of the Starblade. As I struggled angrily to my feet, I saw that it was Alice who had pushed me.

But then I looked at the place where I'd been standing. The gray sand was bubbling and steaming under a globule of acid: the monster had spat it out so fast that I hadn't seen it coming.

Once more Alice had saved my life. Now I had to do my bit. It was up to me to finish this mage off quickly and allow her to use her magic to help our army.

The vartek widened its jaws again, but this time Alice raised her hands high above her head. In response, the sand rose up in front of her, blossoming into a great gray cloud. Then she clapped her hands, and the vortex of dust whirled toward the vartek.

The creature screamed as the grit flew into its eyes; it jerked backward and twisted away from us. Lenklewth rocked sideways in his saddle and was almost unseated. Then Alice grabbed me by the arm and dragged me directly toward the vartek. For a moment I thought she was crazy, but she'd been more quick-witted than I.

We ran straight under its body; for the moment this was the safest place to be. The creature couldn't spit at us if we were beneath it—though I saw that there were other dangers. I looked at the stick-thin legs. They were covered in fine hairs, and at the tip of each was a slimy green bead of moisture.

"Keep away from its legs!" I shouted. "They're sticky with poison!"

We kept moving beneath the monster as it scuttled along, staying clear of each long row of legs. But then I realized that the vartek's body was sinking down. I reached across and pulled Alice onto her knees in order to protect her.

Lenklewth was clearly controlling the vartek; now he was trying to use its tremendous weight to crush us. As its bulk dropped toward us, I gripped the Starblade with both hands and stabbed upward, gripping it tightly. I remembered what we'd learned in our last encounter with one of these battle entities. The upper surface of the creature was covered with hard scales, but the underbelly was soft and vulnerable. My sword slid into its belly, up to the hilt.

The vartek let out an unearthly wail and jerked upward on its trembling legs, its whole body quivering. The sword was almost dragged out of my hands. As the blade came free of its belly, black blood gushed downward onto the sand, splattering over my breeches.

"The neck!" Alice shouted, pointing.

She was right. That would be the vartek's most vulnerable point—the arteries in the neck would carry blood to its brain. And this was where Lenklewth was seated.

As I got to my feet and ran forward, I saw the three broad brown leather straps holding the mage's saddle in place. I stretched up onto my toes and whirled my sword overhead in an arc, cutting through them, hoping that Lenklewth might be sent tumbling off.

The straps parted. The tip of the Starblade had also cut into the vartek's flesh, and I stabbed upward into the neck again and again. The vartek's screams became frantic, its whole body convulsing.

"Tom!" Alice cried out.

Her warning came just in time. One of the long thin tentacles came snaking toward me through the creature's legs. The sharp bone at its tip suddenly swung up toward my neck. I lunged forward, and the Starblade cut right through it. The stump sprayed black blood as it withdrew between the many legs.

I started to renew my attack on the vartek's neck, but it had straightened its legs again and was out of reach of my sword. It was still bleeding, but a creature that size must hold a lot of blood. I wondered how long it would take before its strength failed. And what was Lenklewth doing now? I couldn't see whether he was still seated on the vartek. Even though I'd cut through the brown leather straps, the saddle hadn't been dislodged.

All at once another tentacle snaked toward me, uncoiling like a whip. I barely had time to bring up my sword, but I managed to deflect it. I was forced to parry for a second time, until finally I was able to sever that one too.

It was then that Alice used her magic again. With the forefinger of her left hand, she pointed upward at the vartek's throat. It was as if a long, thin, invisible blade had extended into the flesh of the vartek. As she moved her hand, a gash in the creature's neck began to widen. The rivulet of blood became a steady stream, and then a torrent that gushed out with each slow pump of the beast's heart.

She turned and headed back to the creature's underbelly, where I'd made the other cut, and repeated the action. Now the vartek was hemorrhaging from two places. Black viscous blood was pouring onto the ground beneath it.

Distracted by this, I failed to see the third tentacle uncoiling beneath its body. But this time I wasn't the target . . . it snaked toward Alice.

Before I could call out a warning, she spotted it and stepped aside. The sharp bone tip passed within an inch of her eyes. But at that moment the creature scuttled sideways, and before Alice could move away, one of its legs brushed against her arm.

She cried out and flinched, looking down in dismay; her arm was smeared with green poison. She gave a groan of pain and bit her lip. I saw that the skin was already starting to blister.

22
Poison

I pushed my sword back into its scabbard and, without thinking, scooped up a handful of the gray dust. Then I gripped her hand, extended her arm, and let the sand fall onto the blistering flesh.

I hoped that it would soak up some of the slimy green poison. She was shaking, her eyes wide with pain and fear. I carefully blew off the dust and looked at the damage. Some grains remained stuck to her arm, which was caked with blood, so I carefully wiped it clean with my cloak.

Now I could see the swollen dark blue veins beneath the greenish skin. I wondered how much poison had gotten into her system.

I saw that Alice's eyes were rolling up into her head, and the fingers of her right hand were scrabbling toward the pocket at the hip of her long green dress. Knowing that this was where she kept her herbs, I reached across to retrieve the pouch—but before I could do so, the beast above us started to collapse.

I sensed its bulk descending ever closer, and, gripping Alice's hand tightly, I pulled her along toward its head. The vartek's lower body was already in spasm, each thump reverberating through the ground. The only way out, avoiding its poisonous legs, was by the head.

But I thought we would never reach safety in time. Alice was whimpering with pain as I dragged her forward. We could have died there, crushed beneath the gargantuan vartek. For one terrible moment I thought we had no hope of escape.

However, in the vartek's death throes, the right row of legs collapsed, and the creature twisted onto its side so that the left legs were raised up in the air. I quickly changed direction and passed beneath them, pulling Alice to safety with just moments to spare; almost immediately it twisted back onto its belly, raising a great cloud of gray dust.

Supporting Alice with one hand, I retrieved the pouch from the pocket of her dress and held it out to her. She fumbled awkwardly with it, so I undid the drawstring, opened the neck, and pulled out an assortment of herbs and leaves. I held them out in the palm of my hand—I had no idea which one might help her.

Alice hesitated; then, with a shaking hand, she selected a small piece of leaf. It was pale green with yellow spots and lighter white areas that looked like mold. She put the leaf in her mouth, pushing it under her tongue.

"Is there anything else here that can help?" I asked.

I glanced back at the dying vartek. I could hear the cracking of bones and gurgle of liquids. The muscles, now relaxing in death, could no longer bear the creature's weight. Its internal organs were being crushed as the vast body settled down on the sand, the legs still twitching.

But where was Lenklewth? I wondered. The saddle was empty.

I turned back to Alice; she hadn't replied, so I repeated my question.

She shook her head, so I shoved everything back into the pouch and handed it over. No sooner had she pushed it back into her pocket than her legs buckled beneath her. I only just managed to catch her before she hit the ground.

Alice was unconscious, breathing heavily. I carefully stretched her out on her side so that she wouldn't swallow her tongue. I saw that she was really struggling for breath now. I was desperate with worry, but there was nothing more that I could do. How virulent was the poison? I wondered if she could use her magic to fight its effects? Maybe she was too weak now? Maybe she was dying?

A lump came into my throat. We'd been apart for so long, and I'd missed her. How cruel it would be if I were to lose her again now!

I sensed a movement behind me and turned to see Lenklewth. At last my enemy had showed himself. He was standing beside the vartek's huge head.

The mage wore a coat of mail that flared out over his hips, almost brushing the sand. It extended up to encase his neck, but his head was bare.

Why? I wondered. Why would he face me bareheaded when he had been wearing a metal helmet? Had it been dislodged when the vartek collapsed? That combination of body armor and helmet would have made him almost invulnerable.

Then I knew. He had removed it deliberately. Lenklewth *wanted* me to go for his head. He would be prepared for it. Beneath my cloak, I was just wearing my lambskin jacket. I was totally exposed to his blades.

Then the mage spoke to me. "Nothing survives that poison," he gloated. "The little human witch is dying. In moments you will join her!"

His words were designed to prod me into some reckless move. No doubt he assumed that his ruse had succeeded, because I ran at him fast, the Starblade already in my hand. He drew his two sabers from their scabbards, and with a confident smile readied himself to meet my attack.

I stopped short of him, just out of reach of his blades. Then I spun like Grimalkin; I spun as she had once taught me; I whirled the dance of death—first to the right with the clock, then widdershins.

I felt strong and fast, back to my former self. But how long would that last?

As I reversed direction, I brought my sword across in a horizontal arc—not aiming for his head, as he expected. With all my force, gripping the hilt with both hands, I struck his shoulder.

Grimalkin had told me something of the power of the Starblade. The mage would be wasting his time using magic against me; it would nullify his most powerful spells. And although rusty in appearance, it kept its edge, never needed sharpening, and could not break.

Now I learned something else: It could pierce the strongest armor.

Lenklewth's armor was first rate, but the Starblade sliced through it like butter, deep into the flesh of his shoulder. He cried out in pain and dropped one of the sabers. He brought his remaining weapon up in time to block my next blow, but the third got through his defenses, slicing another piece of armor away from his chest.

The blade felt light and responsive—a far different weapon than the first time we'd fought.

I was forcing him back toward the dying vartek. My fifth blow tore another piece from his side. Now blood was oozing from his cuts, forming red rivulets that streamed down the long coat of chain mail to splatter onto the sand.

I knew I had to finish him before my strength failed. Alice might yet recover. She still might be able to use her magic to help our retreating army. But first I had to kill this mage. Only when he was out of the way would Alice be able to act without hindrance.

I was still whirling and spinning, driving Lenklewth backward, when the huge vartek stirred behind him. It opened its jaws wide, as if to spit poison again; instead, a great sigh erupted from its throat. I could see its eyes twitching behind the pink lids covered with brown wart-like protuberances. No doubt these offered some protection when the vartek burrowed into the earth. The creature suddenly opened its left eye and raised its head. I think Lenklewth sensed the danger, because he glanced back over his shoulder, presenting me with the opportunity to slice away more of his mail.

My blow never reached its target. The vartek lunged forward and seized him in its long jaws, gripping his upper torso. I heard Lenklewth's bones crack. He opened his mouth to scream, but then the vartek tossed him into the air, caught him, and swallowed him whole. In a second he was gone.

I stepped backward in alarm, but the huge creature closed its eyes again and gave another great sigh, its acidic breath washing over me. It settled down and continued the slow process of dying.

I stared at it for a few moments, my whole body shaking. Then I took a deep breath, sheathed my sword, and walked back to where Alice lay.

She was still breathing deeply. I wondered if she was dying, sinking ever deeper into a coma from which she would never awaken. I sat down and watched her while a number of emotions churned within me.

Despite all she had done, despite my feelings of bitterness, I still loved Alice. Tears came into my eyes as I looked at her. I realized that I still felt jealous; her explanation of how Pan had demanded that she form an alliance with Lukrasta had not convinced me.

Then I remembered why Alice had brought us to this space between worlds. It had been to lure Lenklewth here so that I could kill him, thus freeing her to save our army. By now, our cavalry might have escaped over the river, but the infantry would be easy prey for the Kobalos horsemen and varteki.

Finally my thoughts turned to my own predicament. Without Alice, there was no way I could escape this place.

After a while I sat cross-legged on the sand beside Alice. The vartek was totally silent now. The only sound I could hear was Alice's slow, steady breathing. She was no longer struggling for air. That was something.

There was nothing I could do. So much had happened in a short space of time. I felt exhausted. Part of me wanted to give up, to close my eyes and never open them again.

All I could do was sit there, close to despair.

23
The Earth Screamed

SUDDENLY Alice opened her eyes very wide and began to choke. Full of concern, I reached toward her, but she got to her knees and vomited a thin green liquid into the sand.

I knelt beside her and put my arm round her shoulders in reassurance. At last the spasm passed and she stared at me, breathing heavily, her arms crossed over her stomach. Her brow was pale and slick with sweat.

"That hurt," she said at last. "Twisted my insides something rotten, it did. But I'm rid of it now."

"Are you going to be all right?" I asked.

Alice nodded. "I just need a few minutes to get my breath. I used my magic to draw the poison out of my blood and into my stomach while I kept the leaf under my tongue. It's a special leaf, an emetic that makes you vomit. I swallowed it to make myself sick. I'm a bit shaky, but it'll pass. I need some rest, but I've got something to do first. You dealt with Lenklewth?"

I nodded. "The vartek finished him off. Now they're both dead."

"Dangerous creatures, varteki. The Kobalos use torture to train them. Got its revenge, it did. It serves Lenklewth right!" Alice exclaimed.

I helped Alice to her feet and she took a couple of shaky steps forward, as if checking that her legs were strong enough to bear her weight. "First we need to get your horse back," she said, giving a thin, high whistle. She had to whistle twice more before the horse came into view, trotting toward us.

"More magic?" I asked with a smile.

Alice nodded. "It only took the tiniest bit—but now I've got to do something much bigger. I hope I've got the strength for it. . . . We ride that way," she said, pointing off into the distance.

We rode for almost an hour, Alice once more seated behind me. All I could see was gray, featureless sand, a vast plain of it. I began to grow anxious. Alice had brought us here very quickly; why was it taking her so long to get us back to our world? Had she drained her magic? Was she no longer strong enough to do it?

Eventually it began to snow. Within minutes, the

snowflakes were whirling down in a fury. Then I had a brief feeling of nausea and heard the sound from the horse's hooves change. The soft sand had given way to rock and loose stones. It had no covering of snow. Steam was rising from the ground, and I could smell sulfur.

Alice had succeeded. We were crossing the Fittzanda Fissure, that unstable area that marked the old boundary between the Kobalos and human lands. Moments later, the ground began to shake—nothing more than a few trembles, but it was a warning of danger; the earth's crust was very thin here, and not far beneath was molten rock.

Soon we began to pass bodies, some already coated with snow. Many wore the blue uniform of Polyznia. Some were covered in blood, clearly dead from their wounds; others bore no mark to show what had killed them. They could have died of exposure and exhaustion.

A terrible thought entered my mind. What if Jenny had fallen off her horse? What if she was lying out here somewhere, dead or wounded?

In some places, dead horses and riders lay together. The lancers had paid a heavy price for their action. But I counted at least as many Kobalos corpses, along with their long-haired horses. It was clear that an advance party of the enemy had clashed with our infantry and cavalry.

The snow was lighter now, little more than sleet, and the visibility was improving. Ahead I could now see the uniforms of our infantry, among them the blue of Polyznia, the red of Wayaland, and the green and gray of Shalotte—hundreds of them, retreating in the same direction as us. They were no longer in orderly ranks; just a mass of men desperate to reach the river before the enemy caught them.

I looked back over my shoulder and saw the main Kobalos army in fast pursuit. Grimalkin's tactic had been to delay them with a series of cavalry charges. But that would also have cost lives and couldn't continue for long. The last of our lancers would now have crossed the river, leaving the poor stragglers to their fate.

Ahead of the advancing Kobalos, I could see a number of monstrous varteki, tentacles raised. We were almost at the southern edge of the fissure now. The stones were giving way to soft snow; the earth no longer trembled. We rode on for another five minutes before I heard Alice whisper into my ear.

"This is the place, Tom. This is where I have to do it. Leave me here and ride ahead."

"I won't leave you, Alice. I'll stay here until it's over."

Without protest, she slid down from the horse. She made as if to walk away, but the moment I was on the ground, she turned back to face me.

"I might not survive this, Tom, so there's something I need to say to you." She took a step toward me. She came really close and then wrapped her arms around me and held me tight against her. Then she kissed me.

It couldn't have lasted more than a couple of seconds, but her warm lips seemed to melt into mine; it seemed like an eternity of bliss. Then she stepped away and stared right into my eyes.

"I'll tell you something now that I want you to remember. This is the truth. From the moment I first saw you, I knew we were meant to be together. I loved you when we both lived with Old Gregory in Chipenden. I loved you when I was with Lukrasta. And I love you now. Either believe me or call me a liar—that's up to you. But it's the truth."

My eyes filled with tears and I opened my mouth, not knowing what to say. But it was too late in any case. She was already walking toward the enemy. Then she came to a halt.

Alice hadn't told me what she intended to do. That wasn't necessary. It was clear enough.

She'd said that she was an earth witch. Now she was going to use the earth itself against our enemies.

She raised her arms high above her head, her fingers

splayed wide. For a moment everything was silent. Then, very faintly, somewhere in the distance, I heard the music of Pan, the thin, reedy sound of his magical pipes.

When Alice called out, her voice was high-pitched and strident. At first I thought she was screaming, but there was something elemental about it, like wind keening over rocks or the shriek of a storm.

Then there came an answer. The earth screamed—a thin, piercing sound, higher but in harmony with Alice's cry. It was a sound that could make ears and noses bleed and burst blood vessels in eyes. I covered my ears, but my horse reared up in terror, forcing me to hang on to the reins to stop it from bolting.

Now, between Alice and the Kobalos army, the earth growled and hissed in anger, venting gouts of steam from where it had been imprisoned beneath the rock. Suddenly there was an eruption of fire, fierce flickering orange tongues of it, as rocks and earth were hurled skyward in explosion after explosion. Beneath me, some distance from the fissure, the earth shook and roared out in fury.

Suddenly I remembered one thing Alice had said to me, and I gasped in horror: she'd said, "I might not survive this."

We'd only just been reunited. Terrified of losing her, I dragged my horse forward until we were level with her.

What I saw was appalling and heart-wrenching.

Blood was streaming from her nose and eyes; it was running in thin rivulets down her face and dripping onto her pointy shoes. Her face was twisted in torment, her mouth wide open in what looked like a scream. If she was indeed screaming, it was impossible to hear because of the tumultuous eruptions all around us.

I could do nothing to help. All I could do was hope that it ended soon.

The eruptions lasted no more than a minute or so. Afterward, it was hard to estimate how many of the Kobalos and their creatures had died in that inferno. When it began, they had not advanced far into that area of devastation. The vast bulk of their army was untouched. But it had halted their pursuit of our infantry.

Alice had saved the lives of many of our soldiers. They would be able to escape the Kobalos and cross the river.

Now she lowered her arms, turned, and staggered toward me. I just managed to reach her before she fell. Her breathing was rapid, and she looked utterly weary. I wiped the blood off her face with the sleeve of my gown.

Grimalkin had once told me that it was possible for a witch to expend so much of her energy that she died. I feared for Alice, but with a trembling hand she pointed to the horse, and I helped her into the saddle before clambering up in front of her. She wrapped her arms around my waist and buried her face against my shoulder.

I wondered if she had the strength to hold on, so I rode on at a slow trot.

As I crossed the river ford, I saw that Grimalkin was waiting on the far bank. Most of the army was retreating south toward Prince Stanislaw's castle, but she had waited for us and had already erected our tent.

I could see no sign of Jenny, and my heart sank into my boots. I feared the worst and hardly dared to ask Grimalkin about her.

"What about Jenny? Is she all right?"

She nodded. "Yes. She has gone back to the castle with the others. She wanted to wait here, but I forbade it."

I quickly told her what had happened, and she eased Alice down from the saddle and carried her inside.

"Are we safe here?" I asked as Grimalkin stretched her out carefully on a blanket.

"We are safe for now. After all that has happened, the Kobalos will not cross until they have built up an overwhelming force, and that will take some time," she said. "I prefer to work on Alice here."

I watched anxiously as the witch assassin ministered

to Alice, muttering spells into her left ear and using ointments and herbs—the latter taken from Alice's own pouch. I waited anxiously, but Alice was unconscious.

"She will not die, but her chances of a full recovery are in the balance," Grimalkin explained once her work was done. "A witch can draw upon too much of her magic, using her last reserves, until the very essence of her being is drawn forth too. And to some extent, that is what Alice has done. She was already hurt by the poison from the vartek."

So we kept vigil beside Alice, awaiting the outcome of Grimalkin's efforts to save her. She woke briefly the following day and looked up at me. We stared at each other for a long time without speaking, but she kept squeezing my left hand.

"I thought I was going to lose you again," I said softly.

Alice smiled. "Thanks for waiting for me, Tom. Thanks for staying beside me. The pain was terrible, but you gave me strength just by being there. I told you to go because I didn't want you in danger. But the biggest part of me wanted you to stay. Had I died there, the last thing I'd have seen would've been you. That gave me comfort."

"I couldn't have left you, Alice. I won't ever leave you again."

"There'll be no need, Tom. There may be good reasons

for us to be separated physically, but in our hearts we'll be together always now, whatever happens. I can promise you that. Ain't ever going to go off and leave you again."

Later, Alice was able to eat a little soup, and by the third day she was feeling much better, though she was still too weak to stand and slept most of the time.

From time to time I thought of Jenny alone back at the castle and wished that Grimalkin had not sent her there. But I could do nothing about it

The snow had stopped for now, and the wind had veered to the south. Soon it became warmer, and the snow and ice began to melt. It was almost as if Golgoth had retreated after what Alice had done.

At last a Kobalos patrol came to the riverbank and stared at us but did not cross. They made camp, and soon their fires had covered the river with a brown haze.

We had achieved next to nothing. Grimalkin had failed to steal Kobalos magic, and our warriors had died for nothing. Yet, but for Alice, it could have been a lot worse.

Wrapped in our blankets, Grimalkin and I sat in the opening of the tent, gazing back across the river toward them. I could hear the distant screeching of varteki and the cries of other things that were not human.

"Do you think they'll wait until spring to begin their offensive?" I asked. That was what most armies did.

Grimalkin shook her head. "They are creature of the winter cold," she said. "Snow and ice will not hinder them. As I said, it is a question of numbers. When enough Kobalos and their battle entities are in position, they will attack. We must prepare to defend ourselves."

"Could we repel such a superior force?" I asked.

"We can hinder them and slow their progress. As we fall back deeper into the territory of the southern nations, their soldiers will come to our aid. They will have no choice, because the Kobalos will be on their soil."

"The Starblade protected me against the magic of Lenklewth," I told her, explaining how I had fought and defeated him. "But it did more than that. You told me it couldn't break and that it would always be sharp. Well, it certainly didn't break. It actually seemed sharper than ever. It sliced right through the mage's armor."

Grimalkin smiled. "That is good to hear. The armor of a Kobalos high mage has no equal. I think the Starblade is growing in strength. That is another of the features I built into it. The blade will absorb from you what you are and what you are becoming. If you are weak and full of doubt, the power of the sword will diminish. You have certainly been weak and lacking in confidence since your return from death, but you are putting that behind you. You believed that you could defeat the mage, and it drew upon that self-belief and became a more formidable weapon."

"You almost make it sound as if the sword is alive!" I said with a grin.

Grimalkin's expression remained serious. "The longer you wear and use the Starblade, the closer it will be to you. It will draw upon your essence and personality. In time it will become an extension of your own self."

I thought about that for a bit. When I'd fought the mage the first time, the blade had seemed heavy and unwieldy. I'd put that down to my own weakness. But when I'd fought the final battle against him, the Starblade had been light and responsive.

Suddenly my thoughts turned to the future. "I still intend to return to the County," I told the witch assassin.

"If that is your choice, you are free to do so, but I would rather you stayed."

"I need to go. Back in the County, I'll regain my strength, and I'll be able to train my apprentice properly. What about the prince? Won't he try to keep me here as a figurehead for his army?"

"I will tell him that you have urgent business back in the County, but that you will return in the spring."

"I will. I'll keep my word. I'll travel back here in the spring."

"That will be too late," said Grimalkin. "By then these kingdoms will have been overrun. The battle will be far to the south. But the lie will suffice to keep him happy for now."

The following morning, Alice was fit to ride, so we traveled to the castle of Prince Stanislaw. The mild weather was holding; it was still possible to travel back to the County. So I decided that a couple of days' rest would do no harm.

I wanted to be sure that Alice was fully restored to health before we left.

24
White String

I was walking up the path that led back to the Spook's house, carrying the sack of provisions I'd bought in the village. It was growing dark, and I was late. My master wouldn't be best pleased.

Then I noticed a movement under the trees to my left and saw a girl coming slowly toward the path. She made no sound as she approached. She could almost have been floating. I came to a halt and looked at her. She was very pretty, with high cheekbones, long black hair, and large brown eyes. She came right up to me.

"Don't you know me, Tom? Don't you remember who I am?"

I felt sure I'd seen her somewhere before, but my head was befuddled and I couldn't bring her name to my lips.

I noticed that her shoes were very pointy. My master had once told me something about such shoes—some kind of warning—but I couldn't remember what it was. The girl's black dress was tied at the waist with white string.

She saw me staring at her waist and smiled, then untied the string and held it out to me.

"What's this for?" I asked in puzzlement. "What do you want me to do with it . . . ?"

Then I woke up and stared at the ceiling for a long time. I remembered the retreat from the Kobalos and how Alice had kissed me. She'd said that she loved me. Had she really meant it? Or was it simply that she thought she was going to die and wanted to say a proper good-bye? But later she'd said our hearts would always be together, even if we were separated by distance.

Was it really possible that we could be together? Could we eventually live together at Chipenden? I hardly dared to hope.

"If we don't leave soon, we'll be trapped here for the winter," Jenny complained with a frown, gazing out of the turret window at the ground far below.

The army camp was now a sea of mud, but a cold wind was blowing from the north again, and on the horizon the sun was sinking into clouds that threatened snow. I was beginning to see the cold as an enemy. I wondered if the advancing cold really was being directed by Golgoth. That was what Grimalkin believed.

Jenny voiced her worries about being trapped at least three times a day. I tried not to let it irritate me. After all, I was a spook, and she was my apprentice. It was my duty to be patient. And I couldn't really blame her. We were both wrapped in sheepskin jackets despite the fire in the grate. The castle was chilly and full of drafts.

We'd stayed here almost a week, twice as long as I'd originally intended. But Alice had now made a full recovery, and I could set off for home with a less troubled mind.

We certainly couldn't delay any longer. There was a double threat: a full-scale Kobalos attack and the snow. Either one might trap us here.

"Cheer up!" I told Jenny. "Try smiling at the world. It might just smile back!"

She did her best, but her smile was forced.

"Look, we'll set off for home tomorrow before noon. How does that sound?"

"You really mean it?" she asked, her eyes brightening with hope.

"Yes. We need to get away before the serious snow arrives."

Just then the door opened, and I saw a pair of pointy

shoes stepping into the room. Instantly the smile fled from Jenny's face, for it was Alice.

I glanced from Jenny to Alice and back again. My apprentice was a pretty girl, without a doubt. She had a warm, bright smile, and her mousy hair seemed to change with the light, glinting red in the sun.

Her eyes were her best feature: the left one was blue, the right one brown. Sometimes they twinkled with merriment and mischief; occasionally they seemed sad and soulful; and very rarely—I'd glimpsed it just once or twice—her gaze became very old and knowing, as if something wise and infinitely compassionate gazed out in pity on a world that fell far short of what it had hoped for.

But pretty as Jenny was, Alice made her look very ordinary. Alice was just seventeen, and with her high cheekbones, vivacious eyes, and shining black hair, she had become a spectacularly beautiful girl. Although she had gone to the dark and was now a witch, she did not have the shifty eyes or slyness of her mother, Bony Lizzie. Alice held her head high and looked everyone straight in the eye.

But Jenny and Alice had something in common. They didn't like each other. So I had to find some way to make them become friends, or at least learn to tolerate each other.

"There's snow on the way, Tom," Alice told me, completely ignoring Jenny. "This time there won't be a thaw until the spring. We need to set off home tomorrow, or we'll be stuck here."

"I'd already decided to leave tomorrow," I replied. Then I realized what she'd said. "You said *we*. You're coming with us?" My heart leaped with excitement. I'd expected to say good-bye to Alice and not see her again for many long months.

"Yes. Somebody has to make sure you get home safely!" she said with a wicked smile.

I glanced at Jenny. She looked far from happy. No doubt she'd expected to be traveling alone with me. The last thing she wanted was Alice's company.

"Doesn't Grimalkin need you here?" I asked. "The Kobalos army could cross the river and attack at any time."

"She wants to get me away safely. Then I can use my magic when it might tip the balance of some big future battle. That ain't going to happen until next year. Maybe it'll be far to the south, when the larger kingdoms there have mobilized their troops; maybe it'll be back in the County. Grimalkin believes that the coming battle here will be a rout and just hopes to form an organized retreat."

Alice turned toward Jenny and gave her a smile. There was no real warmth in it. "Why don't you get yourself off to bed, Jenny?" she suggested. "You'll need to be fresh for the journey."

Jenny stared at her but made no move to leave.

This time Alice spoke without smiling. "Look, I need to speak to Tom alone."

Jenny came to her feet, picked up her notebook, and went out without another word, not looking at either of us. She didn't exactly slam the door, but it closed with a bit more force than was necessary.

"Try to be a bit kinder to her, Alice," I said. "She's a long way from home and just wants to get back. She wanted to be a spook's apprentice, not end up in the middle of a war in a cold northerly land. She almost died out there; she was sitting on the same horse as Prince Kaylar when he was slain."

I remembered the horror in her eyes when she'd told her story. The Kobalos had struck the prince's head from his shoulders and she'd been drenched in his blood.

"I'll try, Tom, but she only seems to think about herself. She irritates me. I think it was a mistake to take her on as your apprentice."

"She's brave, Alice, and she's gone through a lot recently. I took her on, and what's done is done. I can't go back on that. She's my responsibility now. I hope to train her and make a spook out of her."

Alice smiled. "Then I'll try to make allowances for her. . . ." She sighed and turned to the window. "Let's sit down over there, Tom. I want to watch the sun set. I like to see the stars, and the glow of the campfires."

"You never seemed to get that much pleasure from it before—"

"Before I became an earth witch, you mean?" Alice interrupted.

I nodded.

"I've always liked sunsets and dawns, ain't no doubt about that, but now the feeling is even stronger. I feel closer to the earth. I love its rhythms—light giving way to dark, and small changes in the weather. The earth seems alive to me. Maybe it is."

"Don't you know?"

"There's lots that I don't know, Tom. Some of my knowing is just instinct, but there are gaps."

"Are there other earth witches?"

"In the future there might be more. Pan tells me that I'm the first. But no more questions for now, Tom, please. I just want to sit and watch. Do you mind?"

"No, Alice, I don't mind. If it makes you happy . . . that's all that counts."

She sat on the window seat next to me, and then reached across and held my hand.

For a moment we sat in silence. She gave my hand a squeeze. "Do you remember how we held hands that night on the way to Staumin?"

I smiled again. "I dreamed about it the other night. In fact, I keep having dreams about you!"

"Are they nice dreams?"

I nodded and squeezed her hand back.

The moment I did that, Alice came to her feet.

My heart sank. I thought I'd offended her in some way and she was about to leave, but instead she sat on my knee and put her arms around my neck. Then she kissed me very slowly . . . it went on for a long time.

Jenny Calder

25
Wolf Meat

I'D expected the journey home to be hard, and from the beginning I was proved right. We left the castle a couple of hours after dawn, much earlier than Tom had planned, because heavy snow was already drifting in from the north.

Tom and Alice rode ahead side by side while I brought up the rear. I'd noticed a change in Tom's behavior since Alice had arrived. He smiled a lot more. It was clear that her presence made him happy. He certainly seemed to prefer her company to mine.

I still wanted to become a spook, but I wondered if I'd be better off being trained by somebody else. The trouble was, it would be difficult to find someone suitable. I disliked Judd, who worked the area north of Caster, and I knew he was against training a girl. And as for the other spook I'd met—the one called Johnson—we'd disliked each other at first sight. He hated witches and was obsessed with hunting them down. I suspected that he probably disliked most women.

We were traveling south, so at least the snow wasn't gusting into our faces. But it was very cold, and even with my hood up, my ears were slowly freezing.

I had been glad to get away, but now I began to wonder if we had left it too late. Once we left the forest, the landscape was flat, bleak, and featureless. Already a film of snow covered the ground, obscuring the road. The sky was a dark gray and full of snow. Soon it would form drifts, and I feared that the route would become impassable.

Somehow we stayed on the road—no doubt helped by the witch's dark skills. But the daylight hours were short, and soon we were forced to make camp. The snow had eased, and after Alice made and lit a fire, using one of the small bundles of wood we'd brought with us, we had a hot herbal drink and small pieces of cold venison, which were chewy but tasty.

The three of us shared the tent, and although I remembered the witch assassin's growls, mutters, and teeth grinding, I wished Grimalkin was with us rather than Alice. Here there were other, more disturbing, noises. Alice laid her blanket down very close to Tom's, and I could hear them whispering to each other in the dark. Once Alice gave a low giggle, which surprised me; she usually scowled more than she laughed. At one point I thought I heard them kissing, and I was forced to cover my ears with my hands. It took me a long time to get to sleep.

The following morning, the snow was coming down much harder and we set off without breakfast. I began to wonder how much farther south we'd have to travel to get clear of it. Tom had said it might be something to do with the Old God, Golgoth, the Lord of Winter. He might be driving the snow and cold south to aid a Kobalos attack. In that case we might never be clear of it. But before noon, it had eased to a light sleet, and we stopped and rested for an hour.

This time we had soup, made by Alice, to go with the strips of cold venison. It was spicy and delicious, and so hot that I could barely sip it. It warmed me up, and I was in a better mood as we moved on.

But my good spirits didn't last long. In the morning we had ridden in silence, but now Tom and Alice began to chat. She became very animated and kept laughing at everything he said. I suppose I was just jealous. Nobody was talking to me, and they seemed to be enjoying themselves.

I began to drop back. I didn't want to hear what they were saying. At one point, Tom turned around and shouted to me to keep up. I kicked my horse on, but after five minutes I began to fall behind again. After all, despite the sleet, they were still clearly in view.

I suppose I must have been daydreaming, because suddenly I looked up and could see no sign of them. For a moment I panicked. I urged my horse forward, but they were nowhere to be seen. At last, to my relief, I saw them waiting for me ahead. Tom looked angry.

"You have to keep up, Jenny!" he snapped as I approached. "You could easily get lost in these conditions. It might get worse at any time."

"I'm sorry," I muttered, trying to avoid Alice's gaze. She looked far from happy with me.

We rode on. I kept up, but soon they began to talk and laugh again. They were totally absorbed in each other, and by small increments I began to drop back a little.

What happened next took me completely by surprise. I heard a rushing noise to my left, and I was suddenly hit by a wind so strong that it almost knocked me out of my saddle. With it came the snow. Within seconds, what had been sleet was transformed into a blizzard of thick, whirling snowflakes. I could no longer see Tom and Alice ahead, so I urged my horse forward to catch up, expecting them to wait for me.

But somehow I must have wandered off the road. I could see no sign of them, and I began to panic. I tried shouting, but the wind snatched my voice away.

Within minutes I realized that I was truly lost. I tried to keep calm, although my heart was thudding in my chest. They would find me, I told myself. Alice would use her magic. It would be easy for her.

Then I began to wonder whether she really would. She didn't like me and probably wanted me out of the way. She wouldn't want an apprentice hanging around once we got back to Chipenden. I thought she might pretend to Tom that she was searching while making no effort at all.

I kept calling out, but there was no response. There seemed no sign of the blizzard easing. I was getting colder and colder, and the light was going. Was it getting dark already?

Then I started to imagine things. I thought I heard a rider coming up behind me, but when I turned round, I could see nothing. I was really cold and drowsy. I could hardly keep my eyes open.

Back in Chipenden I'd felt a bond slowly growing between me and Tom, and I'd enjoyed being trained by him. But things had changed for the worse once we'd journeyed here. Recently I'd been feeling increasingly alone. But I'd never felt so bad as I did now. I was lost and isolated. And I was scared.

Things were already really bad, but then they got worse: my horse stumbled into a snowdrift, and I was sent flying over its head.

I landed in the soft, deep snow unhurt; not even winded. I just lay there, too weary to climb to my feet. It was so nice to simply lie back. I didn't even feel cold anymore. Something inside my head was telling me to get up, but I didn't have the energy. It was much easier to stay where I was, so I drifted off to sleep.

I realize now that falling asleep was the worst thing I could have done. The cold was drawing the heat and life out of my body and making me sleepy. I could so easily never have woken up. I could have died there.

But I *did* wake up. Suddenly I was sitting up, leaning against a mound of snow. In front of me was a fire, and I was bathed in its bright, flickering warmth. There was a pot bubbling over it, and a delicious smell of stew. I could hear horses breathing and snorting nearby.

I assumed that Tom and Alice had found me; I felt guilty for thinking badly of the witch. Then I noticed something beyond the fire. It was awhile before I realized what it was: a wolf's head sitting in a pool of blood that was soaking into the snow and ice. Strips of raw red meat lay beside it.

Then someone crouched down, put a hand on the back of my head to steady it, and brought a cup to my lips. A voice said, "Drink, and you'll feel better."

It wasn't Tom's voice. It had an odd rasping quality. I looked up, cried out in fear, and tried to crawl away—for it was one of the Kobalos.

The creature was dressed in a long black overcoat, a saber at its hip. His face was bestial, but shaved in a way I'd seen once before. I realized it was a haizda mage.

Back in the County, I had once been captured by one of these mages. It had hung me by my feet from a ceiling and drained my blood very slowly. I'd felt the life draining from me, and I'd been close to death when Tom had rescued me. The experience still came back to me in my nightmares. It was hard to tell the difference between that haizda mage and this beast bending over me now.

"I mean you no harm," the creature said. "Look. I will leave the cup here. You need not be afraid."

He placed the cup on the ground, then retreated to the far side of the fire and sat down cross-legged, facing me.

I didn't move, but I soon realized that the mage could catch me any time he wanted. Keeping my distance would make no difference. So I crawled forward, picked up the cup, and began to sip.

I stared at the mage across the flames. Although his hands were covered in dark fur, his face, with its elongated jaw and sharp teeth, was wolflike. His eyes glared at me with a mixture of amusement and arrogance.

I glanced again at his sharp saber, which was stained with dried blood. Had the beast used that to kill the wolf? The terrible memory of what had happened to Prince Kaylar suddenly flashed into my mind. Again I felt the warm blood flowing over me and saw the stump of his neck as I clung to his torso. I shuddered at the thought that the creature might use his saber to cut off my head.

"I think I have good cause to fear you," I said, my voice trembling. "I don't want to end up as one of your slaves. I fell into the hands of one of your kind, and he drained my blood until I was near death."

"In truth, I *would* like to drink a little of your blood, child—I can smell its exquisite odor. But I am a haizda mage, and despite the temptation, I am capable of disciplining myself. As for slaves, I have had a few, the minimum needed to comply with our laws. But I wish for no more slaves. The law will change, and I will help to bring it about. I repeat . . . there is no need to be afraid," the creature rasped. "I only wish to speak to your master, the spook called Ward. That is all. I have something to tell him that will be to his advantage. I have been following you for some time. I know that you are his apprentice. What is *your* name?"

"Jenny," I replied, taking another sip from the cup.

"My name is Slither," he told me. "Well, little Jenny, are you hungry? There is meat simmering in the pot. It is juicy and tender."

The name Slither seemed familiar to me. Where had I heard it before?

"Is it wolf meat?" I asked, staring at the head.

"Yes, a tender, delicious female. There is nothing wrong with eating wolf. They eat humans and Kobalos if they get the chance. Sometimes we are meat for the wolf. Now it is our turn. Why don't you try some?"

He approached the bubbling pot and began to spoon stew into a bowl. Then he came round the fire and set it down on the snow-covered ground. Once he'd returned to his previous position, I came forward, picked up the bowl, and tasted the stew. Wolf meat is delicious.

I began to spoon it into my mouth but paused nervously as Slither came to his feet—though he simply walked across to the wolf's head, picked up one of the raw strips of meat, and began to gnaw at it. More beast than human, he clearly liked his meat red and raw. But while he was eating, he was occupied, so I carried on eating too.

As I watched him, I remembered that Grimalkin had mentioned the name Slither. She had once encountered a haizda mage by that name. He had been her ally. Could this be the same one?

Once my belly was full, the warmth of the fire began to make me feel drowsy. I fought to keep my eyes open. I didn't like the idea of being asleep and vulnerable in the presence of the haizda mage. I kept nodding off and jerking awake, but before long I drifted to sleep.

The next thing I remember, I was standing up. Someone was breathing gently into my face. The breath was warm and spicy and pleasant, and my knees suddenly became very weak. I would have fallen, but an arm went around my waist, supporting me.

I struggled to open my eyes, but my lashes seemed to be stuck together. When at last I pried them apart, I realized to my horror that I was staring up into the eyes of the mage.

"There will be no pain," he rasped. "I will just sip a little of your blood, and then you may sleep. And you will remember nothing of this in the morning. Then I will reunite you with your companions."

I felt weak and helpless, unable to resist. He gently tilted my head back, and I saw his teeth bearing down on my throat. It was then that I remembered something that Tom had once told me about haizda mages.

They took only a little blood and let their victims live. A haizda mage was a farmer; the humans who lived close by were his cattle, and he took care of them. They were a valuable resource—he wanted to take blood from them again in the future. But sometimes a haizda mage's desperate need for blood overcame his restraint.

Sometimes he drained the victim until the heart faltered and stopped. Remembering that, I was suddenly terribly afraid.

26
Not Safe Anywhere

ALL at once I was sent flying backward. It wasn't so much a physical contact as a displacement of the air, a powerful gust of wind. Now there was someone standing between me and the mage.

"Keep your filthy hands off her!" It was an angry female voice.

I knew who that voice belonged to. It was Alice.

She struck out at the mage with her left hand, her nails raking down his cheek. He staggered away with a gasp, blood trickling from the five deep scratches. Alice came over and put her arm around my shoulder protectively.

"Take a deep breath, Jenny. This ain't nothing to worry about. Stand behind me if he attacks," she said softly into my left ear.

And then, out of the darkness, Tom came striding toward the mage, the Starblade ready in his right hand.

"Kill him, Tom!" Alice commanded.

Suddenly I realized that the mage hadn't drawn his saber. Did that mean he didn't want to fight? That he wasn't our enemy? And he'd said he had something important to tell Tom. . . .

"No!" I cried. "He said he has something to tell you—something to your advantage. His name is Slither! He's the one Grimalkin told us about!"

Tom came to a halt and lowered his blade slightly. "You were an ally of Grimalkin," he said, taking another step toward the mage. "That would make you our ally. If so, why did you attempt to take Jenny's blood?"

"It is in my nature to do so," Slither rasped. "I only wanted to sip a little. She would not have been harmed. I intended to return her safely to you. But for me she would be dead now. I found her unconscious in the snow."

"That's true enough," I said. "I fell off my horse and didn't have the energy to rise. I fell asleep there."

"Let's talk to him," Alice said. "Let's find out what he has to say."

We sat on opposite sides of the campfire, with me between Tom and Alice.

"You are welcome to eat from the pot," Slither said. "It is good meat, freshly killed and cooked."

"It's wolf meat," I said. "It's tasty, but I felt really sleepy again after eating it. Maybe he put something in it."

"You slept because you were weary, little Jenny. The meat is good. Eat or do not eat, it is up to you," Slither replied.

I noticed that the scratches on his face had dried to five thin crusts of blood. I wondered if Kobalos mages healed more easily than humans.

Tom stared at him across the flames before speaking. "Why are you here? What do you want to tell me?" he asked.

"You talked to Abuskai, the dead mage trapped in the tower. He told you there were groups among our people who are opposed to the present regime. Is that not so? The Skapien are a secret group of Kobalos within Valkarky who are opposed to the slave trade in purra. They are growing in number. My haizda magic allows me to talk to the dead mage and then liaise with such groups. You asked if he could contact those opposed to the triumvirate, did you not?"

Tom nodded.

Slither licked his lips with his long tongue. "I am that contact. As they wish to kill all haizda mages, the triumvirate is now my enemy. That makes us allies," he said, nodding toward each of us in turn. He was panting like a dog, though in truth he looked more like a wolf. When his gaze turned upon me, I flinched.

"Lenklewth is dead. Will that make any difference?" Tom asked. "Will the triumvirate change when he's replaced? Abuskai didn't think it would."

"I agree with the dead mage, little human," Slither replied. "Each of its members is selected from the hierarchical pool of high mages; most dream the same dreams of conquest and expansion. Abuskai is the only one I know who thinks differently. I have been communicating with him for some time. As I said, he is the link between me and other dissident groups."

"Would you fight against your own people?" Tom asked.

"I have already done so. Among those I have slain are Shaiksa assassins. They never forget. Even now they hunt me down. You too are marked for death because of the Shaiksa you killed. Grimalkin is also their target. They seek to kill the little witch too," he said, pointing at Alice. "But we haizdas do not behave in the same way. We put such things behind us. I know you killed one of our order back in your homeland, but I do not seek vengeance for that. What is done is done."

Tom shrugged. "He was about to kill Jenny and would

have killed me. I did what was necessary."

"You were in your rights to slay him. You acted within our laws." The mage stared at Tom, his eyes flickering with intelligence. "But he had no right to slay purrai so wantonly. He had killed three before you encountered him. A good haizda mage husbands his human herd carefully; if any die, it is usually by accident. The one you slayed was young; he was only in the third year of his novitiate, and may be excused."

"Then why did he come to the County alone, with his training incomplete?" Alice asked, speaking for the first time.

"He was escaping from our homeland," Slither answered. "We haizdas are being hunted down and exterminated by the agents of the triumvirate. They do not like our independence. We operate far from Valkarky, and they cannot control us. What they cannot control, they wish to kill."

"You said you'd something to tell Tom," Alice said. "You're our contact and ally, but there's something else, ain't there?"

Slither licked his lips. "The Kobalos armies have already crossed the Shanna River. As we speak, the humans are falling back in disarray. The steady advance into human territory will continue for months, right through the winter. But the triumvirate will strike ahead of the battle front swiftly and without warning, using the space between worlds. Nowhere is safe from them. And you are their first target!" Slither said, pointing at Tom. "You have slain a Shaiksa assassin and led a human army into their lands. You have also slain a member of the triumvirate. They see you as a threat that must be eliminated, and they will invade your homeland in order to finish you and your people."

Nobody spoke for a while. Alice simply reached across me to grip Tom's hand.

Then Tom said something that made my heart sink.

"Maybe I shouldn't go back to the County," he said. "That way they'll just come after me, and nobody else will get hurt."

"It is impossible to hide from the triumvirate. They will find you wherever you go. But that will not save the County; it is the home of Grimalkin, whom they also wish to destroy, and of you," he said nodding toward Alice. "They know of the power of the Pendle witches and will attack them too. They seek to conquer and rule the whole world, but the County is now their first target."

"Do you know when and how they will strike? Will they use warriors or mages?" Tom asked.

"I will try to find out," Slither replied. "If I manage to

do so, I will warn Grimalkin, and she in turn will contact you, through the little witch."

Tom had told me that witches used mirrors to contact each other across long distances. This was how Grimalkin would inform Alice when the Kobalos planned to strike. I didn't like it at all—we had witches for allies, and now this beast also seemed to be on our side. I'd known that being a spook's apprentice would have its dangers, but I hadn't foreseen anything like this!

"I'll ask you again, little humans. Do you want some stew? Otherwise it will just go to waste."

"Yes," said Tom. "I'd like some stew please."

The mage turned his back on us and rummaged in a bag, giving me my first clear view of his long tail, which was covered with short hair and curved up almost to his shoulders. It emerged from a slit in the back of his long black coat. He held out two bowls to Tom and Alice.

I returned to my dark thoughts. I had assumed that we were returning to relative safety in the County. I had almost convinced myself that Grimalkin's fears were unjustified, that the Kobalos would not defeat the human armies. I had hoped that I would now be safe and could continue my training.

But the moment Tom Ward had defeated and slain the assassin on the riverbank, he had become a target for other members of the Shaiksa brotherhood. Then he had led the attack across the Shanna River; the Kobalos mages were aware of that—especially the triumvirate.

Now I realized the horrible truth. Tom would never be safe. The war would come to us—and much sooner than anyone could have expected.

Thomas Ward

27
The Body in the Sack

WE returned to the County, and I was as happy as Jenny to be home. There was the secure feeling of being back in that old house surrounded by a garden defended by the boggart. And I'd forgotten just how good a breakfast it could make. That first morning, the bacon was perfect!

The weather was mild for late September, and the sun still held some warmth. The icy grip of Golgoth had not yet penetrated this far south.

It was good for Jenny to get back to her training, but there wasn't much time for digging boggart pits in the garden or casting a silver chain at the practice post. Even theory lessons were few and far between.

This was because we had to deal with the backlog of work that had built up in our absence. Not a day went by without the bell ringing at the withy trees crossroads.

Jenny was certainly getting plenty of experience of spook's work.

And all the time the threat was approaching like the dark clouds of a winter storm.

I would have liked to visit the farm where I used to live and see my two brothers, Jack's wife, Ellie, and their children. But I was too busy for that. My duty was first to protect people from the dark, so family concerns had to come second. However, I did send a letter to Judd at the mill north of Caster. I thanked him for keeping an eye on Chipenden and dealing with some of the spook's business while I was away. I also brought him up to date on the Kobalos.

My days were busy, and I had little time to ponder on the threat that lay ahead, but at night I found it difficult to sleep. I twisted and turned through the hours of darkness, trying to work out when and how the enemy would strike.

The only ray of light in all this was Alice. It was so good to have her back, living in the Chipenden house. Just to see her and speak to her brightened my day. I'd managed to put my doubts about her behind me. What had happened in the past was over. It was no use dwelling on it. We were happy together, and I had to look to the future.

There was still no word from Grimalkin. I'd hoped she would contact Alice, but no doubt she was in mortal danger, trying to hold back the enemy. For all I knew she might already be dead, slain as the mighty Kobalos army swept southward.

Then, one morning, a boy came with an urgent message from the small village of Wood Plumpton. Such messengers usually hated ringing the bell and meeting a spook in the gloom beneath the withy trees. Sometimes they could barely speak; sometimes they gabbled out their message so rapidly that I didn't understand a single word and had to ask them to repeat it.

When Jenny and I appeared at the crossroads, this freckle-faced boy didn't even say hello or give his name. He just held out an envelope to me. "This is from my mam!" he declared.

It was addressed to Thomas J. Ward, the Chipenden spook.

I tore open the envelope and read the message within.

Dear Mr. Ward,

I am being held on suspicion of murdering my husband. He is stone dead and I am not sorry because he was a bully and made my whole life a misery. However, I did not kill him—he was slain in a manner that speaks of dark magic. Hence I am also being accused of witch-craft. Please come to Wood Plumpton as soon as you can as they intend to burn me. You will see that I am not a witch, and your opinion as a spook trained by John Gregory will get the charges dropped. Your master was held in great esteem here.

Yours sincerely,

Annabelle Grayson

"Wait here, lad," I told the boy. "We need to go back to the house to collect a few things, but we'll set off within the hour to help your mam."

I had often accompanied my master when he dealt with similar situations. He'd even named such people as a fourth category of witch: the falsely accused. I hope I'd learned enough to sort this out. I had to think about training Jenny to cope with such circumstances.

As Jenny and I went back to the house, I handed her the letter and she began to read it.

I heard harsh cries from above and saw a flock of geese flying overhead. They were heading west, toward the sea marshes. They had migrated here from the north and would stay in the County until spring. They had arrived a month early. It was another sign that winter was approaching rapidly.

When it came, the dark, cold months would be filled with a special danger—the threat from Golgoth. If the Kobalos prevailed, this coming winter might never end, and there would be famine and death.

"Will you be able to tell whether she's a witch or not?" Jenny asked as she handed the letter back.

"I get a cold feeling when I'm near something from the dark. You get it too, don't you?" I asked.

Jenny nodded doubtfully, as if afraid to admit that she didn't. It wasn't a problem. I knew that her gifts were different than mine.

"Well, that's one way of seeing whether she's a witch," I continued. "But it isn't foolproof. I've been close to witches and not felt that warning cold at all. So we'll question her as well and try to get at the truth."

I always tried to keep an open mind. It was likely that the woman had indeed been falsely accused—though it was also possible that she really was a witch and had written that letter hoping to deceive me and save her skin.

"Do you get that cold feeling when you're close to Alice?" Jenny asked.

Her question took me by surprise. "No, I don't," I admitted. "That might be because I knew her before she became a witch. It might also be something to do with the fact that she's an earth witch."

"An earth witch? You've never mentioned that before. You're supposed to be teaching me all about things like that."

"I can't teach you about earth witches because it's all new to me. My own master never taught me about them. As far as I know, until Alice became one they simply didn't exist. All I know is that she uses the powers of the earth and works with Pan. It's not like having a familiar or using blood or bone magic."

"I don't get any bad feelings from her either," said Jenny. "Maybe she's strong enough to shield herself?"

It seemed that Jenny was trying to undermine Alice, so I didn't bother to reply.

I collected my staff and bag and some provisions for the journey. There was a note on the kitchen table from Alice. The message was brief.

Take care, Tom.

Contacted Grimalkin in the mirror. She's all right so far, but half the army is dead or wounded. They're about to fight a big battle that they can't afford to lose. She needs magical allies and wants me to talk to the witches, so I'm off to Pendle. Be back in a couple of days.

Miss you.

Alice

I folded the note into my pocket. Now I had something else to worry about. Pendle was a dangerous place. The three main witch clans often clashed, and the witches might not take kindly to Grimalkin's request for help or to Alice's presence there. They both had friends there, but enemies too. I consoled myself with the thought that Alice had powerful magic at her disposal and was well able to look after herself.

I led Jenny back to the crossroads, where the boy was waiting.

"What's your name?" I asked him.

"Josh," he replied.

"Well, Josh, I hope you can walk fast. We need to get back to where you live as quickly as we can. I'm sorry about your dad, but if we walk fast, we can help your mam. Understand?"

He nodded, and we set off toward Wood Plumpton. It was a small village just north of Priestown, hardly more than a hamlet, and I'd been there with my master a couple of times. I set a brisk pace; we had to get there before they burned the lad's mam.

✦

We arrived in the late afternoon, and Josh led us through the graveyard toward the house of the parish constable, the official who'd arrested the boy's mother.

The church was St. Anne's, and John Gregory had once been summoned here to make a decision. I pointed out a boulder beyond the rows of graves.

"See that?" I asked Jenny.

"It's over a grave!" she cried out in astonishment.

"It's a witch's grave," I explained. "She's buried head down so that if she tries to scratch her way to the surface she'll really be digging her way toward the center of the earth. The boulder is there just in case she turns round. Back in Chipenden we use bars for the same purpose, but a stone is cheaper. I came here with John Gregory to inspect that grave. They wanted to know if the witch was safely contained. My master assured the locals that it was. She's a very weak dead witch. There's no further threat at all."

"How many dead witches are strong and dangerous?" she asked.

"Perhaps one in twenty . . . most of the dead witches in Pendle are to be found in Witch Dell. They just crawl around in the dark, eating slugs, worms, and occasionally mice or rats. There are usually only a couple of really strong dead witches there, but they make that dell a very dangerous place. They can run faster than a human being, and when they catch someone, they drain the victim before ripping them to pieces."

Jenny shuddered.

"That's why the Chipenden spooks have always brought the more powerful dead witches back to the garden and used bars to keep them secure."

Soon I was knocking at the door of the constable's house.

I expected some smug, pompous oaf—in my experience, the job attracted bigots and bullies—but the man who greeted me with a friendly smile was cut from different cloth.

"Mr. Ward? I'm Constable Baxton. Mrs. Grayson is in a cell. But before you speak to her, I'd like you to see her husband's body."

"That's fine," I said, but as he turned to lead us around the side of the house, he gave a frown.

"Just you, Mr. Ward. I'm sorry, but I don't think the boy or the girl should see this. . . ."

"I agree about young Josh, Constable, but Jenny is my apprentice and needs to see it. Ours is a difficult trade, and we see some terrible sights. Part of her training is to get used to them."

He nodded grimly. "On your own head be it, but I

must warn you that this is just about one of the worst things I've ever witnessed."

Josh stayed behind, and Jenny and I followed the constable to a large shed behind the house. He lit a lantern, opened the door, and led us into the gloom. The moment we entered, I was hit by the stench of death and the buzzing of flies.

On the floor was a large burlap sack, tied at the neck with string. It was crawling with big fat bluebottles. Blood had seeped out to form a dry red puddle on the floor.

"There it is," said the constable. "Go and take a look. I put the body in the sack and got my fill of it, so I don't need a second look. After you've examined the contents, it'll be the turn of the undertaker—he's due in about an hour."

He handed me the lantern, and I passed it to my apprentice. I walked forward with Jenny and untied the string, sending the bluebottles up into a buzzing cloud that hovered over the sack. The smell was appalling and my stomach started to heave.

"Hold the lantern high, Jenny," I said, peering into the open sack.

Moments later, I was forced to turn away to be sick. The sack was brim full of fragments of flesh and bone— some no bigger than a fingernail.

28
The Promise

JENNY was sick too, so I took the lantern from her and told her to go outside. Once I'd managed to control my stomach, I looked once more at the remains, then retied the string.

I went to speak with the constable. "You were right—that was just as bad as it gets, but we both had to look. Now, could you show me where he died?" I asked.

He nodded. "It was over by the pond."

We followed him through the garden.

"It was dark magic, wasn't it?" asked the constable. "Last night it was a full moon. That's when magic's at its most powerful, isn't it? What else could have done that to a man? Nothing natural could have chopped him up into such small pieces. And those slivers of bone—how could anyone have done that? He was only missing for a few hours."

I didn't reply, for I saw that we were approaching a small pond. The grass all around it was black and dead, as were the reeds on the near bank. Everything looked scorched, and there were dead fish floating belly up on the surface of the pond.

"Is this the spot?" I asked.

He pointed down at an area close to the water. The dead grass was covered in slime—and some pieces of bone no bigger than fingernail clippings.

Jenny gazed down, her eyes wide; she looked scared.

"What was Mr. Grayson doing here?" I asked.

"He'd had a blazing row with his wife. They fought like cat and dog, morning, noon, and night. Sometimes he came here afterward to cool off. I suppose the witch had finally had enough of him—probably been storing up her magic for years to do this. I've always found her pleasant enough, but her anger got the better of her, and she blasted him to pieces!"

I shook my head. "Annabelle Grayson is almost certainly *not* a witch," I told him. "She didn't do this. I'll talk to her later, just to be sure, but something else killed her husband . . . something really powerful from the dark. It's nothing to worry about now. Everyone here is safe—it won't come back," I lied.

"What was it, a fire demon?" he asked.

I nodded. "Yes, something like that, but they're very rare. Mr. Grayson was unlucky. He just happened to be in the wrong place at the wrong time," I said, lying again.

Jenny caught my eye, and I could see her puzzlement. She was about to speak, but I gave her a quick frown, and her mouth became a hard, thin line. I didn't think there was any point in alarming the constable with the truth: that it was something far worse than a demon and could come back at any time.

None of us were safe. The whole County was in danger.

Jenny and I talked to Mrs. Grayson. I felt no warning sense of cold, and she seemed pleasant enough, if somewhat bitter. I told the constable that she wasn't a witch, and he released her.

That was the one good thing that came out of this business. Josh was reunited with his mam, and they went home together.

We couldn't get back to Chipenden before dark, so Jenny and I camped on the edge of a small wood and built a fire.

"What would you prefer," I asked Jenny, already knowing her answer, "crumbly cheese or succulent rabbit?"

She pulled a face. "I hate cheese. Give me rabbit anytime!"

So we caught a couple of rabbits and were soon cooking them over a fire. It was nearly dark, and the air was growing chilly.

"Do you think it helps, eating cheese before facing the dark?" Jenny asked.

"My master certainly believed so, but it's not the cheese itself. It's just that it's better to face the dark on an empty stomach rather than a full one—though you need a little something to keep your strength up, hence the cheese. John Gregory picked up the habit from his own master. He loved our crumbly County cheese."

"Think they're ready?" Jenny asked, nodding at the rabbits. "I'm starving!"

Soon we were tucking into our supper, the delicious juices dribbling down our chins.

"You *are* going to keep me on as your apprentice, aren't you?" Jenny asked, pausing for a moment to stare at me.

"Of course I am—just as long as you behave yourself and try not to be cheeky!"

"It's just that now that Alice is living with us, there might not be room for me."

"There's plenty of room in that big house," I told her. "We have bedrooms to spare. It's no problem."

"But it's not just that," Jenny went on. "Alice doesn't like me."

"I think you're imagining that, Jenny."

I knew it wasn't true, but somehow I had to get them to think better of each other. "She saved you from Slither, didn't she?" I pointed out.

Jenny nodded. "That makes me think a little better of her—but she would have saved anyone in that situation. . . . Will you promise me one thing, master?"

"That's the first time you've ever called me master!" I laughed. "Are you mocking me?"

"No, I'm deadly serious. I called you master because I want you to remember this moment. I want you to remember the promise you're about to make!"

I was annoyed at her tone and the way she was bossing me about, but at the same time, I could see the earnestness in her eyes. This was obviously very important to her, so I kept my feelings under control.

"Then tell me what the promise is."

"If Alice asks you to get rid of me, I want you to say no. Do you promise?"

"That's an easy promise to make," I told her. "First, Alice would never ask me to do that. Second, if she did, I would refuse. You are my apprentice, and I've a responsibility toward you. It's my duty to train you properly and turn you into a good spook. Nothing anyone could say will change that. So you can stop worrying your head. I promise!"

We continued eating in silence, and then Jenny gave me a shy smile. She looked much happier, and I was glad I'd managed to put her mind at rest.

"I didn't know there were such things as fire demons," she said suddenly.

"Oh, there certainly are. I saw quite a few in Greece when I went there with my master. But the truth is, a fire demon didn't kill Mr. Grayson. There are no fire demons in the County. The climate is too damp for them."

"So why did you lie to the constable?"

"I did it for his own good—to reassure him, and everyone else who lives in Wood Plumpton. The truth is much more frightening. But I'm a spook and you're my apprentice, so we have to face up to it, no matter how scary."

"So what did chop him into pieces and burn the grass near the pond?"

"It wasn't burned; it was subjected to an intense cold. The pond was probably frozen solid in an instant—that's what killed the fish. Mr. Grayson was slain by one of the Old Gods. He was shattered, reduced to tiny pieces by Golgoth."

29
The Butcher God

"How can you be sure that it was Golgoth?" Jenny asked.

"From what I saw in that sack, I'm almost certain. You see, toward the end of my first year with John Gregory, I came face-to-face with Golgoth in an ancient barrow up on Anglezarke Moor."

"Is that where your master had that winter house you once told me about?" Jenny interrupted.

I nodded. "That's the place. That's where I spent the first winter of my apprenticeship. Golgoth had been summoned to earth by one of John Gregory's ex-apprentices, a young man called Morgan who'd gone to the dark. Morgan wanted to become a powerful mage, so he summoned Golgoth to get dark magic from him. Someday I'll tell you the full story—or let you read my notebooks—but for now I'll just give you a brief outline.

It all went wrong for Morgan, and Golgoth blasted him with a wave of intense cold. In an instant he was frozen solid, and then shattered into thousands of pieces.

"Many people call Golgoth the Lord of Winter, but he has another name, not so well known, that's been passed down through the generations by County folk. They call him the Butcher God because of the appearance of his victims. They look like the sweepings from a butcher's floor. Golgoth wanted to stay and lay waste to the County, but he was thwarted and had to return to the dark. It took me some time to escape from the barrow; by then, Morgan's remains had started to thaw. They looked like the contents of that sack. So yes, I'm almost certain it was Golgoth."

"But why would he do that to Mr. Grayson?" Jenny asked. "Why him?"

I shrugged. "He was probably a random victim. Golgoth is now in alliance with the Kobalos god Talkus, and as Slither warned, our enemies are starting to venture into the County. They knew that, as the main County spook, I'd come to investigate. So it's a message for me, a warning of what lies ahead.

"Golgoth has reason to hate me—and the County too. It's a place where the dark has been defeated many times. The Bane, a powerful demonic entity, was destroyed in

Priestown. Morwena, the most powerful of the water witches, died north of Caster, and Siscoi, the vampire god, was slain just over the County border. The dark has suffered severe losses here. No doubt they want revenge for that."

"Could Golgoth strike us here and now?"

There was no point in disguising the grim truth. Jenny was my apprentice and deserved to hear the full facts—as far as I knew them.

"Yes, in theory he could. If he's entered the County once, he can probably do so again. The problem is, I don't know how he managed to get into our world. Morgan summoned him using a spell from a grimoire, a book of spells. Once summoned like that, he might be free to stay on earth indefinitely; he would wreak havoc, bringing a new age of ice. People would die of famine or be forced to live in caves again. But Golgoth materialized inside a pentacle from which he couldn't escape, so he had to return to the dark.

"There was only one copy of that grimoire, and it was destroyed. This means that Golgoth wasn't summoned from within the County—otherwise he'd still be here. Perhaps the Kobalos mages made a temporary visit possible? Or maybe Talkus had a hand in it? You see, I'm just speculating, just thinking aloud. Maybe Alice or

Grimalkin or Slither will be able to help. . . ." I gave a sigh, and tried to smile at Jenny. "Anyway," I concluded, "nothing can be done for now, so let's get some sleep!"

"You expect me to sleep after telling me that?" Jenny exclaimed.

Jenny Calder

30
The Night Attack

DURING the following month, Golgoth struck twice more.

The first attack was on the night of the new moon; it was almost identical to the one that had killed Mr. Grayson. A farmer was slayed while bringing in his cows at dusk. Once more we were confronted with his remains—a sack containing the same terrible fragments of flesh and bone. Golgoth was living up to his name, the Butcher God.

The second, which took place at the time of the next full moon, was different, and there was a witness to the attack, which took place in a barber's shop. The proprietor, George Smith, had just gone to fetch some hot water, leaving his customer, a man called Brown, sitting in the chair. As he came back, the barber heard a crash of glass and a terrible scream, suddenly cut off.

It was noon, but to George Smith's astonishment and terror, half of the shop was in total darkness. The large wall mirror in front of his customer had shattered, pieces of glass lying all over the floor. Brown was sitting rigid in the chair, but his head was totally white, covered in what looked like frost. Then it seemed to fragment, cascading onto the floor like shards of ice. The barber stared in horror as the man's neck began to gush with a fountain of blood. Then the darkness faded and sunlight filled the room once more.

This time, the remains only filled a small portion of a sack. Tom didn't make me look at those pieces of skull and brain, and also spared me the sight of the headless corpse. But I was there when he interviewed the barber.

"I want you to think very carefully," Tom said to the man. "Can you remember anything about that strange darkness in the shop?"

The man didn't answer right away; his hands were trembling with the terrible memories that filled his head. "There *was* something, but now I think my eyes might have been playing tricks—or maybe I just imagined it. . . ."

"Go on," Tom prompted. "Just tell me what you thought you saw."

"For a moment I saw a pair of big red eyes glaring at me out of the darkness."

The next attack happened on October thirty-first—Halloween. But this time Golgoth wasn't involved.

Alice had gone off to Pendle again, supposedly to continue negotiating for the support of the witch clans in the fight against the Kobalos. That's what Tom believed, though I had my doubts. Halloween was the most important of the witches' sabbaths, and Alice was a witch, wasn't she? Even Tom had to accept that. No doubt she was dancing around a fire with her sister witches, summoning the power of the dark.

On reflection I suppose I didn't really think that, but the idea crossed my mind. I still saw Alice as the biggest threat to my apprenticeship. She would surely want Tom all to herself in that Chipenden house. These bitter thoughts were still whirling around my head when I finally drifted off to sleep.

I was awakened by a pounding at my door. Tom was calling out my name. "Jenny! Get dressed and come downstairs now!"

I heard his boots thumping down the wooden stairs. He sounded alarmed, so I dressed quickly and followed him down. He was standing by the back door, holding his staff, the Starblade in his shoulder scabbard.

"The village is in danger—we must warn them. Pick up your staff and that lantern and follow me!"

Within minutes we were racing down the slope toward Chipenden village. I wondered how Tom knew about the danger. I suspected Alice might have used a mirror to scry the threat.

"What is it, Tom?" I asked. "Has somebody warned you of danger?"

For a moment I thought he wasn't going to reply.

"It's one of my gifts, Jenny. I can sense the Kobalos close by in the County. The village is in danger. If I'm wrong, it'll cost the villagers a night's sleep; if I'm right, it'll save their lives."

Tom went straight to the blacksmith's house and pounded on the door. The huge man was also the unofficial leader of the villagers.

"Are you trying to break down my door?" he roared, glaring down at Tom. Then he paused. "Oh, it's you, Master Ward."

"There are armed enemies coming down the valley from the east," Tom said urgently. "They'll butcher everyone in the village. We need to wake everybody and get them away!"

The Chipenden smith was the closest thing to a friend that John Gregory had ever had; he had worked on the witch pits and crafted the blades for the staffs. He'd seen Tom grow from a twelve-year-old apprentice to a young spook. Tom's warning was immediately taken seriously; the man never doubted him for a minute.

"I'll take this side of the street—you take the other!" said the smith. "Get them to assemble on the edge of the village square."

Tom nodded, and we started knocking on doors. The first was opened by a man who actually raised his fist at us. I could hear children crying upstairs, and a woman trying to soothe them.

"There's danger," Tom said. "We're evacuating the village. Get your family to the square. We're moving in ten minutes."

"Danger? What danger? What nonsense is this? I know you—you're the lad who used to work for old Mr. Gregory."

Tom pointed across the cobbled street to the burly blacksmith, head and shoulders lit by the lantern he was holding above his head.

"It's the smith's orders. Everybody must assemble now!" Tom said. "If you stay here, you could all be slain in your beds!"

Waiting no longer, we moved on while the man gaped after us.

Some villagers obeyed us without question, but if anyone argued, we just pointed to the square and moved on to the next door. There was no time to waste arguing. They soon got the message, because the square was now full of people shouting and crying in terror.

It was almost fifteen minutes before they were all gathered there. Walking back, we heard them arguing among themselves. As we approached, they turned toward us, and the smith raised his arm for silence and spoke.

"Some of you will know this young man. If you don't, he's Tom Ward, who was apprenticed to Mr. Gregory for over four years, helping to keep this village safe. Now he's the local spook and is continuing his good work. He warns of a threat from the east—enemy soldiers who intend to kill us all. So we are leaving now, heading west down the valley! Try to keep up, but we'll move at the pace of the slowest. Nobody will be left behind."

I assumed that we'd go with them, but Tom had other ideas. "We need to buy time for them to get away," he told the smith. "I intend to try and hold them off."

"I'll stay with you," said the smith. "I'm sure I can persuade a few of the lads to fight as well."

"No—it's better if you lead the others away. Take them as far as possible. If the enemy gets past me, you might have to fight anyway. Trust me on this, please. We're not just facing enemy soldiers—we're dealing with the dark here, and that's my job. But please take my apprentice with you."

I could see that the smith didn't like it, but he nodded in agreement.

"No! I want to go with you!" I protested.

"Jenny, just do as you're told. It's better that you stay safe."

"But I'm supposed to *share* the danger. That's what an apprentice does."

"Not this time. This is different. You'd only be in the way."

I was stung by this remark—but before I could protest, Tom had nodded to the blacksmith, who immediately grabbed me by the arm. Before I could object, Tom was striding off toward the east and I was being dragged in the opposite direction.

But ten minutes later, the smith had to let go of my arm, distracted by a man who'd twisted his ankle and couldn't walk. He picked the injured man up as if he was a child and slung him over his shoulder.

That was my chance. I slipped away into the darkness and ran. I went east. I had to help Tom. I couldn't let him fight alone.

It took me another ten minutes to find him. He was still some way ahead of me, skirting a small wood, holding the Starblade in both hands. Suddenly three figures emerged from the trees, heading straight for him. Judging by their size and gait, they were Kobalos warriors. I was about to call out a warning, but he had already spotted them, and changed direction to meet them head-on.

I watched as he began the dance of death, whirling and spinning, the Starblade flashing in the moonlight. Tom quickly cut down the first of his enemies, displaying all his old strength and skill. He seemed to be fully recovered at last.

Within seconds, another of the Kobalos gave a terrible high-pitched scream and was brought to his knees. Tom now seemed to be in control of the situation—but then I heard guttural shouts of command. Dozens of Kobalos warriors burst out of the trees and ran full pelt toward him.

After scything down the third warrior, Tom turned on his heel and sprinted away. I was frozen to the spot in horror, for there must have been at least forty of them streaming out of the trees. He couldn't fight so many. Had he appreciated the size of the threat? If so, why had he come here alone—to sell his life in order to buy time for the villagers to escape?

I knew that I couldn't help him, but I wasn't going to leave him to die alone. I began to run after him. The warriors hadn't seen me yet, but eventually I'd be noticed and they'd come for me too. Maybe they'd split up, but there would still be far too many of them to cope with.

Tom was now heading directly toward what the locals called the lunk stone—an ancient standing stone at the very top of a small hill. There were a lot of such stones in the area. Tom had told me that they had been there long before the first houses were built in Chipenden—maybe even before the first farms, built at a time when people were just hunters and gatherers.

He climbed the small hill and stood to the right of the stone, then turned to face his enemies, holding the sword in his right hand. Did he intend to make a stand there? The Kobalos would have to climb to reach him, so he had some sort of advantage.

I was still running toward him, but I was now converging with our enemies. At any moment one of them might glance across and see me.

It was then that Tom called out. I thought he was shouting at the Kobalos, who were closing on him fast. Then he shouted again—a single word, snatched away by the wind before I could identify it. But as I approached, I heard the word clearly.

"Kratch!"

I suddenly realized what he was attempting to do. He was next to the standing stone, which would be on a ley line. Boggarts used such hidden lines of power to travel from place to place in the twinkling of an eye. He was summoning the boggart from the garden.

Suddenly it appeared on his right. It was the cat boggart that cooked the breakfast and protected the house and garden. Most of the time it was invisible, but I'd caught occasional glimpses of it. It resembled a large tomcat with ginger fur—but now it was utterly transformed.

It was an immense entity, glowing with power; even on all fours, it came up to Tom's shoulders. Two enormous fangs curved down, their sharp points protruding below its jaw. Its ginger fur stood up on end, and its right eye glinted red like fire. Now it bounded toward its prey. Some of the Kobalos warriors tried to turn and run, but it was too fast.

It sent the first two or three flying with swipes from its gigantic paws. Another was seized in its jaws and bitten in half. Then it seemed to dissolve and became a great spinning tornado of fire and energy that smashed into the warriors. The air was filled with blood and fragments of bone, and the screams and wails of its victims.

The central mass of the attackers was destroyed in seconds. Then the vortex of fire began to pursue individual warriors as they fled back toward the trees. Not one survived.

I watched as it turned back toward us, and then my

stomach started to knot with fear. The orange vortex was heading directly for me. It thought I was an enemy; it would reduce me to fragments and absorb every last drop of my blood. I stood there terrified, frozen to the spot.

I heard Tom call out the boggart's name once more, but nothing could stop it now. It was almost upon me, a maelstrom of fire and energy—I felt its heat against my face. I closed my eyes and waited to die.

Suddenly a gust of warm air swept over me; a breath tainted with blood. Then there was only silence, and I heard the wind whistling through the trees.

I opened my eyes. The boggart was gone, and Tom was walking toward me, looking anything but pleased.

"Are you never going to learn to listen and obey?" he demanded angrily as we headed after the villagers. "When I said you'd be in the way, I meant exactly that. The boggart is dangerous—it could have killed you as well. It was full of bloodlust. You were lucky it listened to me, lucky that it recognized you at the very last moment."

We walked on in a silence that soon became uncomfortable. I asked a question to bring it to an end.

"Tell me a bit more about how you found out about the attack on the village."

"It's one of my gifts. Do you remember how I was able

to track that vartek last August, the one that was heading for Topley village? It was the same process. I woke up in the middle of the night and knew that something was wrong and where the threat was. I suppose their mages were using the space between worlds to bring warriors directly into the County. I located the copse where they were starting to assemble, but I wasn't certain about their target. Was it our Chipenden house, or the village itself? At first I wasn't sure.

"At last I decided that it had to be the village. You see, Lukrasta once showed me a terrible vision of the future. In it, I had arrived too late to help, and everybody in the village had been slaughtered. I was with the blacksmith when he died. So I planned all along to use the boggart. All I had to do was lure them to the ley line where it could reach me."

"I would have thought Slither and Grimalkin would have given us an earlier warning," I said.

"They can't find out everything," Tom replied. "And it's been a long time since we last had any contact with them. Things could be going very badly."

31
Mirrors

THE following evening Alice returned from Pendle. She and Tom were clearly glad to see each other; they hugged for a long time, talking in low voices so that I couldn't hear what they were saying. Then they went into the kitchen, and Tom beckoned me to follow.

"Alice is going to use a mirror to communicate with Grimalkin. Witches do this all the time. This is a chance for you to see it in action."

It surely wasn't right for a spook to be involved in witch practices like this, but we did need to know what was happening, and this was part of my training—something I needed to see. So I moved closer to the table, and we sat facing the kitchen fire. Outside, the weather had turned cold. Last night there'd been a heavy frost.

Alice had already set up the mirror from the room

where we washed. It was quite large—about a foot square. She placed her left palm against the glass and began to mutter under her breath. No doubt it was some sort of spell. Nothing happened, and she removed her hand from the glass and breathed on her palm before replacing it.

This time, almost immediately, the mirror began to brighten. She removed her hand again, and suddenly Grimalkin was staring out at us. Her face looked haggard and there was a smear of blood across her forehead. She kept going out of focus, the image jerky and flickering.

Alice leaned forward and breathed gently upon the mirror until it became misty, and then she began to write on it.

Golgoth is killing people in the County. How is he reaching here?

The mirror slowly cleared and the words disappeared, but then I saw Grimalkin's mouth move close to the mirror, and the image became misty again. Then she quickly began to write.

He is striking from
the Round Loaf
up on Anglezarke Moor,
Kobalos mages
are making it possible.

I couldn't make out a word of it, but Tom smiled at the puzzlement on my face.

"Grimalkin is writing normally," he said, "but the mirror is presenting her words to us backward. I've had a bit of practice, so I can read it easily enough. Grimalkin says that Golgoth is striking from the Round Loaf up on Anglezarke Moor, and that the Kobalos mages are making that possible.

"Ask Grimalkin how are they're doing it," he told Alice.

Again there was a flurry of written exchanges between Alice and Grimalkin, and I opened my mouth to ask what was being communicated. Tom held up his hand, signaling that I shouldn't interrupt. The conversation went on for a long time, and Tom didn't look at me again until the writing had stopped and Grimalkin had faded from view. Then, a grim expression on his face, he explained to me what had been communicated.

"Witches usually lip-read when using mirrors. They're skilled at it, so it's a lot faster than this. But there is some distance between Alice and Grimalkin, and the image is poor, so they've had to use writing. Still, we've learned a lot. The Kobalos mages reach the interior of the barrow by using the space between worlds. There they create a window and summon Golgoth from his domain in the dark. This happens at the time of the new moon and the full moon, when things are at their most propitious. At present he can only stay on earth for a short period of time. But at the winter solstice, they intend to employ the most powerful magic they have to bring Golgoth into the County permanently.

"The Round Loaf is the name of the barrow on the moor where Golgoth was once worshipped," he told me. "It's where, in ancient times, at the winter solstice, they sacrificed people. The Lord of Winter took their blood, became drowsy, and fell into a deep sleep. They hoped to keep him sleeping through the winter months lest he decide to plunge the County into a new age of ice.

"So it's a dangerous place, the heart of his power. If they succeed in bringing him into the County permanently, this land will belong to the Kobalos, even before their army crosses the sea to reach us. The land will freeze, crops will fail, and there'll be famine. We already saw how they were able to bring an advance guard of war-riors into the County. Once the land is devastated by cold, there'll be little opposition."

Tom turned back to face Alice. "If we got down into the barrow, could you close the portal to the dark and stop Golgoth from reaching the County?" he asked.

Alice nodded but looked far from happy. "It's possi-ble, but it's very dangerous. We'd have to be there when the mages open the portal. It has to be open before I can close it permanently. We'd have to kill the mages, and then I'd use my magic to do that. It sounds straightforward, Tom, but it's dangerous, and the timing is vital. If we don't kill the mages quickly and close the portal, then Golgoth might attack. . . . I wouldn't give much for our chances."

"Couldn't Pan help?" Tom asked.

"I can't ask him to do that. The Old Gods may be tak-ing sides, but they avoid direct confrontation with one another. They prefer mortals to fight things out on their behalf. Even the Old Gods can be destroyed."

He sighed, and then looked at her keenly. "Are you prepared to try?"

She reached across and gripped his hand. "We have no choice," she said. "We need to do this before the solstice. The closer we get to it, the stronger Golgoth will become. We need to try it at the next possible opportunity."

"Then we'll go next Thursday," Tom said. "It'll be just two days until the new moon—we'll reach Anglezarke in plenty of time. Judging by the pattern of the killings, that's when they'll most likely summon Golgoth next. It'll give Grimalkin time to get here too."

"She's on her way back?" I asked.

"Sorry," Tom said. "There was so much to tell you that I forgot to mention that. The Kobalos army has struck deep into the territory of the southern kingdoms. Two big battles have been fought, and the human armies have lost both. The second was a rout, and now, in the German forest, a third battle is imminent. As soon as it's over, win or lose, Grimalkin will return here to help defend the County. She considers it to be a priority."

We set off very early on the Thursday morning, our breath steaming in the cold air. As usual, Tom and Alice walked side by side, while I followed behind, carrying his bag. And although they held hands briefly, they seemed much more subdued on this journey; there was no giggling in the dark to keep me awake.

At first I thought they might have quarreled, but gradually I realized that it was something far worse.

"I couldn't bear to lose you," I heard Alice whisper to Tom one night as they lay close together in the dying embers of the fire. Then she began to sob.

In that moment, a chill of horror went straight through me, and I trembled from head to foot. I suddenly realized that she and Tom didn't expect to return alive from our expedition to Anglezarke Moor. I knew something else, too: If I died, I would hope to go to the light. That was where Tom would go as well, but not Alice. Now she was a fully fledged witch and destined to go to the dark.

They would be separated for all eternity.

All at once I felt really sorry for them both. The prospect of losing each other must be terrible. I didn't like Alice, but I wouldn't have wished that on anyone.

32
The Winter House

WE could see the ridge of hills and the outline of the moor ahead, but our progress was slow; we were walking through moss land, where the ground was soggy. However, as we began to climb, it became colder and the ground underfoot less treacherous.

The wind had been blowing steadily from the north, and soon the first flakes of snow were drifting into our faces. At one point we passed an abandoned farm close to a big lake surrounded by stunted willows. Tom and Alice halted and stared at it, their faces grim. I sensed that something bad had happened in this area—I could feel Alice's unhappiness.

I saw that the farm's fences were broken, the windows smashed, the front door hanging off its hinges. The barn was a ruin, with just one wall standing.

"This is what's left of Moor View Farm," Tom told

me. "Last time I came here, Alice was in the care of the farmer and his wife. They've clearly moved on."

"Good riddance to 'em!" Alice said bitterly, brushing the snow from her hair. "The Hursts were my guardians for a while. They were miserable and mean. The days I spent with them were some of the unhappiest in my life."

Then, without further explanation, she walked on, with Tom close at her heels. They'd shared a lot together. Maybe he'd tell me more one day, maybe he wouldn't. It suddenly struck me that although Alice was a witch, after spending so much time with Tom and his master, she probably knew more about being a spook than I did.

We followed the right bank of a stream until we reached a cleft in the moor, a narrow ravine. Soon sheer slopes of scree towered above us on either side; as we proceeded, the loose stones gave way to walls of rock, with the odd tussock of grass or weeds sprouting from cracks and ledges.

Soon I spotted the house directly ahead, and I didn't like the look of it one bit. It was constructed from dark stone and seemed to be built right into the cliff on our right. The windows were small, so it would be dark inside; little light would ever penetrate this narrow valley. Even the snow was struggling. The ground here just had the lightest of coverings.

The whole place made me feel uneasy; I had a strong sense of claustrophobia. I much preferred the Chipenden house, with its big garden—even if two sections contained boggarts and witches. That house was set above the village, with a view of the fells behind and a wide swathe of open sky. Here we would live like insects in a dark crack in the ground.

As we got closer, I could see that the house didn't actually touch the cliff. There was a small space behind, just enough to give access to the back door. Tom pulled a key from his pocket and dragged open the door, and I followed him inside.

I was right about the gloom. Tom asked me for his bag and produced a candle. I now saw that there was mold on the walls and spiders' webs across the windows and ceiling; there was a smell of decay and rotting food.

"We could make fires and warm up the whole house, but I really don't see the point," Tom told me. "We won't be staying long. The beds will be damp, so we'll just make one fire in the kitchen and sleep on the floor."

So that's what we did. I spent a really uncomfortable night. Despite the fire, I never got warm.

✠

Breakfast was bread toasted over the fire but without butter. I was so hungry that I even accepted a few pieces of crumbly cheese.

After we'd finished, Tom looked at me, and I knew he was going to say something bad.

"Back in Chipenden, Jenny, the boggarts and witches are kept in pits in the garden. Here there's no space for that. John Gregory had to keep them in the cellar. They are still there. It's my duty to go down and check that everything is all right. You need to come with me. It's part of your training."

I nodded but wasn't looking forward to it.

Ten minutes later, while Alice went hunting for rabbits, we were standing at the top of the stairs that led down to the cellar, holding our staffs—though I hoped we wouldn't need them. It was pitch-black below. Tom lit his candle and handed it to me.

"We'll be needing a lot of candles when we go down into the burrow tonight," he told me, "so now we'll try and manage with one. Hold it up high and keep close to my back."

We began to descend the stone steps until we turned a corner and came to an iron trellis that went right across from ceiling to floor and wall to wall. In the middle of it was an iron gate. As Tom unlocked it, a

JOSEPH DELANEY

frightening thought came to me.

"Is this to stop things from getting out of the cellar?" I asked.

We stepped through the gate, and Tom nodded as he locked it behind us. "Yes, it's the last line of defense. Even a pit can't confine a witch forever."

Beyond the gate, the steps were surprisingly wide. It seemed odd, but I soon worked out the reason. You needed a stonemason and a blacksmith to construct pits to hold witches and boggarts. They needed to get equipment and boggart stones down; those were big and heavy, hence the wide stairs.

I felt pleased to have worked that out for myself. Then there was another puzzle. As we descended, we passed several landings, and on each there were what looked like cells. Where they for keeping prisoners?

Once again, I guessed their purpose. John Gregory would have kept witches there while their pits were being prepared. They were temporary holding cells.

We were still descending; I couldn't believe how deep this cellar was. Soon I began to hear disturbing noises: faint whisperings and scratchings coming from below. Suddenly Tom stopped in front of the cellar door. The noises were coming from beyond it.

"Those sounds are nothing to be scared of, Jenny. I

334

heard the same when my master brought me down here. It's just some of the witches stirring. They get restless—they'll have heard the sound of our footsteps. They know they have visitors."

We stepped into the cellar, and immediately I realized that we should have brought a second candle. There were large areas of darkness—anything could be hiding there, getting ready to attack.

"This is big!" I exclaimed, looking up at the spiders' webs on the ceiling. It was cold and I began to shiver.

"Yes, it's much larger than the house above," Tom replied. "Come and look at this," he said, stepping closer to one of the witch pits. "There are two live witches and seven dead ones in pits down here. This is one of the live ones. Her name is Bessy."

I looked at the dark square pit with its thirteen iron bars. The corner stone bore the witch's name: BESSY HILL.

I could hear something scratching and snuffling deep in the darkness of the pit, but Tom seemed unconcerned. He knelt down and tugged at each bar in turn. He seemed satisfied and came to his feet. "We'll check the other live one next," he said, "so bring the candle."

He headed toward the far corner of the cellar and I followed close behind him, holding the candle high.

Suddenly he came to a halt and gripped his staff with

both hands, holding it across in the defensive position. I stared past him and saw two large eyes glaring at us from the darkness.

Something like a huge insect with the head of a woman scuttled toward us on all fours, claws rasping across a boggart stone. The body was covered with scales, and the four thin limbs ended in talons rather than finger- and toenails; long, greasy black hair trailed on the floor. The creature's cheeks were bloated, and blood trickled from the corner of her mouth, as if she'd just been feeding.

I knew what the creature was. I'd read about them in John Gregory's Bestiary. Lamia witches took two forms. The domestic version was identical to a human woman, except for a line of green and yellow scales that ran the length of her spine. But lamias were slow shape-shifters and could transform themselves into the ferocious feral form that now faced us, the one that John Gregory had sketched in his book.

Could Tom's mam have resembled this creature? I wondered. I shuddered, then dismissed the thought. She had married Tom's dad and brought up seven sons, she must have been a domestic. It was her blood coursing through his veins that had helped Tom recover from his terrible wound. . . .

My heart was thumping fit to burst out of my chest,

but to my surprise Tom lowered his staff and spoke to the foul, disgusting creature.

"It's good to see you, Meg. How long have you been back?"

"Almost a month," the lamia rasped. "My, my, you've certainly grown, Tom. Where's your master? Are the old fool's bones too stiff to let him come down here?"

Tom shook his head. "I'm so sorry, Meg," he said, his voice gentle, a tone that puzzled me. "But I have some bad news for you. John Gregory is dead."

To my astonishment, tears began to drip from the eyes of the lamia witch and splash onto the floor of the cellar. Why was she crying? Had she known John Gregory?

"He died bravely, fighting our enemies. But now we have new enemies from far across the sea. That's why we've come here. This is my apprentice, Jenny."

The lamia witch didn't even look at me. "Are these some of your enemies?" she asked, scuttling backward.

We followed her, and by the light of the candle, directly in front of the tunnel she must have dug to get to and from the cellar, I saw a terrible sight.

Three figures were dangling by their feet, each positioned with its head over a bucket. Two of the buckets were full of blood. The third was only half full; blood was still dripping from the corpse. All three were Kobalos warriors.

"They taste better than sheep!" rasped the lamia witch. "I would welcome more."

Before we set off for the barrow, Tom explained what had happened in that isolated old house. He told me the story of how John Gregory had been in love with Meg, the lamia witch, and how they'd spent the winters here together; how they had eventually parted when she'd left for her homeland in Greece.

I suspect that he kept certain things from me, but the most important thing, to my mind, had been revealed.

The Spook, John Gregory, had loved a witch; now history was repeating itself with Tom and Alice. Surely no good could come of it.

Thomas Ward

33
The Round Loaf

LATER, after I'd escorted Jenny back to the kitchen, I went down to talk to Meg alone. She told me that her sister Marcia had died in Greece, but she seemed unwilling to spell out the circumstances, so I didn't press her.

Feeling lonely, she had returned to the County. She'd hoped to see John Gregory one last time; in order to meet him, she'd begun the slow process of transforming back to her domestic form. For a while she had survived on the occasional sheep, roaming widely to take her prey so as not to draw attention to herself.

Then she had noticed Kobalos activity around the barrow and had started to select her prey from the invaders. I told her of our intention to confront the Old God Golgoth, and she offered her services as our ally.

I agreed readily, for I wondered whether Grimalkin would be in time to join us. I had hoped to find her already at the winter house. Who knew what opposition might face us in the barrow? We might have to manage without the witch assassin.

We needed all the help we could get.

Soon Alice returned with a brace of rabbits. While Jenny cooked our food, I told Alice about the encounter with Meg.

We set off about an hour before sunset. I wanted to walk beside Alice, but I had things I needed to tell Jenny first.

"When Alice and I go down into the barrow, I want you to keep watch outside."

"Keep watch?" Jenny asked me with a scowl. "And if I do see a threat, what on earth am I supposed to do? How will I let you know about the danger? You just don't want me to go down there with you! You don't expect to come back—you think you'll die down there. Isn't that the truth? You're trying to protect me!"

"Of course I'm trying to protect you. You're my apprentice and I'm trying to keep you safe. Look, if we don't emerge from the barrow before dawn, head back to Chipenden."

"And what would I do there alone?" Jenny said, her eyes blazing with anger.

"You could carry on your training with Judd. I'll write you a letter to give to him. I know you don't like him, but he's a good spook and he'd train you properly."

"I want you to ask yourself something." Jenny looked straight into my eyes. "When you were with John Gregory, did he always keep you safe, or did he expect you to share the danger?"

I sighed. There was no point in lying. "Mostly he expected me to share the danger," I admitted. "It's part of the training."

"Then I'll share the danger too!" she said defiantly. "Now, why don't you go and walk with Alice? I know you're dying to."

I didn't reply. I couldn't fault her logic, but I didn't like being spoken to like that by my apprentice. Angrily I went and joined Alice. We were at the far end of the clough now, at its deepest point, and I took the lead as we climbed the slippery stone steps that led up onto the moor.

We hurried toward the Round Loaf. The sun had set and soon darkness would come. The air was cold. Tonight there'd be a hard frost.

After a while Jenny came up alongside us. I thought maybe she'd come to apologize, but something else was on her mind. "There's something following us," she warned. "I just caught a glimpse of it out of the corner of my eye."

I glanced back, hoping that it was Grimalkin, but spied Meg scuttling up the slope. "It's the lamia witch. Meg's going to help us," I explained.

"Another witch!" cried Jenny in a tone of exasperation.

Alice gave her a glare and hissed angrily. I put my hand on her shoulder and smiled to calm her down.

After a few minutes, Jenny fell behind again. "Try not to get angry," I told Alice. "It's only natural that she should find it strange that I should be in alliance with witches. After all, my own master, John Gregory, felt the same way about you."

"I understand that she feels that way," Alice replied, "but there ain't no need to say things like that aloud. It's bad manners. Have a word with her, Tom, when you get the chance."

I nodded and promised to do so.

About a mile from the barrow we stopped and rested, having decided to approach once it was completely dark. It would be two hours before the new moon rose. At some time between then and midnight, the mages would appear within the barrow and open the portal for Golgoth. We needed to be in position to surprise and slay them. Then

Alice would try to close the portal.

One moment there were four of us: Alice and me, Jenny and Meg. The next, a fifth had joined us, stepping out of the gloom like a wraith. It was Grimalkin.

I came to my feet to greet her. In many ways it was the Grimalkin of old. Her skirt was split and tied to her thighs to aid movement; leather straps crisscrossed her body, the sheaths holding blades—some short throwing knives, others longer, designed for combat at close quarters.

But there was something new too. It wasn't just her gaunt face; it was the look in her eyes. She seemed utterly weary, as if she had glimpsed things that had changed her.

"What's wrong?" Alice asked.

Grimalkin opened her mouth to speak, revealing those dangerous sharpened teeth. She hesitated, as if gathering her thoughts, then uttered words that were a torrent of bad news.

"The end is approaching even faster than I feared," she told us. "The war will be lost within weeks unless we can deal with Golgoth here and now. There was one further battle after the two defeats I told you of. The formidable Germanic tribes were my greatest hope of halting the dark army of the Kobalos. They had formed alliances, uniting their strength. The mighty Kobalos still outnumbered them, but the tribes were fighting within their own vast forest; they were confident of victory. But the battle was over before it began. The Kobalos mages opened their portal to the dark and summoned Golgoth straight onto the battlefield.

"He sent a searing blast of intense cold directly into the forest, where the Germanic tribes were gathered for battle. Whatever lay in its path—flesh, wood, or bone— was instantly turned into shards of ice. I only survived because I was stationed to one side with the remnants of the Polyznian army. Thousands died, and the Kobalos cavalry galloped through, cutting our force in half and encircling the survivors.

"For now, Talkus, the new god of the Kobalos, is remaining in the background. But he is directing Golgoth against us. I see the Butcher God to be the primary threat, both at the battlefront and here in the County.

"I was lucky to escape. I came here as promised to join my strength with yours. There is one final line of defense before the Kobalos reach the northern sea that separates our land from the continent. It might hold, but not if Golgoth intervenes again. We *must* close that portal."

"That's what we come here for," Alice said. "Once we're down in the barrow, I'll use a cloaking spell to hide us.

It should work against Kobalos mages as long as we all keep perfectly still when they arrive. The moment they open the portal for Golgoth, I'll raise my right hand. That's the signal to attack and kill them. Not one must be allowed to escape. Once they're dead, I'll try to close the portal and seal it permanently."

Cautiously, under cover of darkness, we approached the barrow from the east. Soon the distinctive oval mound was just visible against the sky. There were no Kobalos guards to be seen, but this was the time of greatest risk.

I hoped we'd be in position before the new moon rose—which gave us almost an hour to get into the barrow. The secret entrance was a flat stone. Last time we'd been here, John Gregory had covered it with loose earth and stones. Now grass had grown over it. I knew its approximate position, and by jabbing into the grass with the blade of my staff, I was soon able to locate it.

It was clear that the Kobalos hadn't been using this to get into the Round Loaf. As Grimalkin had warned us, they'd been leaping right to its very heart, using the space between worlds. The Kobalos warriors slain by Meg must have been brought directly to the moor outside it.

Soon I had lifted the stone onto its edge, and with Alice's help I dragged it clear and peered down into the darkness. I looked up and saw the lamia witch staring at me.

"Could you take the lead, Meg?" I asked. "There may be blockages."

When I'd last been here, the arrival of Golgoth had caused the tunnel to collapse, and although it had been cleared by Meg's sister, Marcia, there might have been further falls since.

Without a word Meg scuttled ahead of us down the steps.

"I'll go next," I told the others. "You keep close behind me, Jenny. Alice will be behind you, and Grimalkin at the rear to guard against attack from behind. Don't light your lanterns until we are well below the surface. The barrow might be under observation, and we can't afford to show any light."

I walked carefully down the stone steps. Only when my shoulders were well below ground did I light my lantern. Now I could see the slope of the steps and a tunnel of earth waiting at the bottom. Soon the light increased as Jenny and Alice lit their lanterns behind me.

Now I was on level ground, easing myself along the earthen tunnel, which was partly supported by wooden props. Some of the timbers had collapsed, and before long they disappeared completely. There was now little to hold up the weight of earth above us; we were in real danger. Ahead I could hear Meg digging, clearing sections of blocked tunnel.

Finally I reached the large oval chamber beneath the barrow. Little had changed. The walls and ceilings were clad in stone, and the floor was an elaborate mosaic depicting fantastical creatures, from gigantic serpents to fabled creatures, half human, half beast, which my master had said did not exist.

Right at the center, the largest area of the mosaic was a pentacle, a five-pointed black star surrounded by three concentric circles. This was where Morgan had summoned Golgoth. The Old God had appeared alongside him, right at the heart of the defensive pentacle, and had frozen him solid. His body had shattered into pieces.

The thawed flesh had long since disintegrated or been devoured by rats or insects, but I could smell the faint stink of death amid the loam. His bones were still there—a mound of white and yellow fragments that filled the inside of the pentacle.

If things went badly, that would be our fate too.

34
Toppling Like a Tree

WE made ourselves as comfortable as possible, and Alice performed the cloaking spell. After that, time seemed to pass very slowly. There was nothing to be said. The chamber beneath the barrow was silent, but we were vigilant, all listening carefully for any sounds of approaching enemies, awaiting the arrival of the Kobalos mages.

I was sitting between Alice and Jenny, resting my back against the far wall of the chamber. Meg crouched by the entrance alongside Grimalkin. They were guarding the tunnel, which was our only way out. We had left the stone clear of the entrance in case we needed to make a rapid escape. We knew that someone might see it from the outside, so Meg was using her acute hearing to check for any danger from that direction.

By now the moon would be rising and the conditions for summoning Golgoth were right. If the Kobalos mages planned to strike at a target in the County tonight, they'd have to make an appearance soon.

No sooner had I thought this than there was a shimmer in the air, and four of our Kobalos enemies appeared in the middle of the pentacle. They wore body armor, with sabers at their belts, but their shaved faces marked them out as the mages we expected.

The sight of them made me nervous. They had magical abilities, so I wondered if Alice's cloaking spell would be strong enough to protect us. I held my breath, prepared for the worst, but I needn't have feared.

Oblivious to our presence, they faced one another and extended their arms until their fingertips were touching; then they began to chant in Losta. I watched Alice carefully, waiting for her signal. As soon as we moved, they would see us, but we had to act the moment the portal opened.

Alice raised her hand, and I leaped to my feet and drew the Starblade from its shoulder scabbard. But before I could take even one step toward the mages, the lamia witch had killed the first, scuttling up onto his chest and ripping out his throat with her fangs so that his blood gushed down onto Morgan's bones.

I swung at the second, the Starblade slicing deep into the armor that shielded his neck. He screamed and fell back. Out of the corner of my eye I saw Grimalkin swiftly dispatch the third mage with one of her blades.

However, a fraction of a second before I lunged at him, the fourth mage vanished. That had always been a danger—that one mage would escape.

My heart sank into my boots. Now he would attempt to counter Alice's magic from some unseen location; he'd make it difficult for her to seal the invisible gate through which Golgoth would soon emerge.

I turned to her. "Can you still close the portal?" I asked.

Alice frowned and closed her eyes, concentrating hard.

Then her eyes opened very wide and she stared at me, shaking her head. "It's too late!" she cried. "Golgoth is already approaching."

I heard Jenny give a cry of fear, and then the ground began to shake. Soon the disturbance began to intensify. Dust and small rocks fell from above, and the mosaic floor cracked in several places.

It was as if some large creature far below us was digging up through the rock to reach us—something like a vartek. I wished it *was* only one of the varteki. This was something far worse.

"The Round Loaf is on a ley line, isn't it?" Jenny asked, her voice trembling with fear.

"It's on several of those lines," I replied, already guessing what she was thinking.

"So you can summon the boggart!"

I shook my head. "The boggart would have no chance against an Old God. It would be destroyed in an instant, which would gain us nothing."

The air grew very cold and the breath began to steam in front of our faces; my heart seemed to freeze within my chest.

My mind went back to my previous encounter with Golgoth. As he'd approached, I'd witnessed similar underground disturbances, as if something huge was clawing its way to the surface, followed by the intense cold. Fortunately, as I'd told Jenny, Golgoth had been trapped within that pentacle. Despite all his threats, I had managed to resist his order to free him, and he had returned to the dark.

But there were no lit candles marking each point of the pentacle now; there was no magic circle to confine him. It was not primed to contain the Old God. And he could appear anywhere within the chamber.

The Lord of Winter had the power to bring a new age of ice to the world; he was the perfect ally for the Kobalos and their god, Talkus. He could freeze us stone dead in a second. We had no defenses against him. Even the Starblade couldn't protect me against such power. Our only hope was Alice, but she hadn't had time to seal the portal and deny Golgoth access. Now even her magic could not hope to prevail against such a mighty being.

Suddenly all the lanterns went out, and we were plunged into a terrifying darkness. Then the ground was still, and Golgoth spoke to us.

"Four fools cower before me, four fools about to die."

Grimalkin spoke up, her voice full of angry defiance. "You are the fool for choosing the wrong allies. Your time is almost over. When Talkus falls and the Kobalos city lies in ruins, you too will cease to be. You will exist only in the nightmares of children."

"Those are arrogant words, witch. In moments you will be dead. I will destroy you all!"

Suddenly the chamber was partly illuminated again. Jenny had managed to relight her lantern, and I saw that frost was creeping across the stone floor toward us. The cold was intensifying. I began to shiver, but more from fear than from cold.

"It is good to have so many of my enemies gathered together in one place. I will slay you now, one by one. You will be the last to die, Ward. Your apprentice will be the first!"

As Golgoth uttered that final word, "first," Jenny's

mousy hair suddenly became faintly dusted with frost. She screamed and dropped the lantern, but it still illuminated that terrible scene.

I knew that any attempt to intervene would result in my own death, but Golgoth was going to kill me anyway. I had to do something.

But then, reacting much faster than me, Meg scuttled out of the darkness toward the voice. Her legs were a blur, but she had barely covered half the distance before the Butcher God turned his attention away from Jenny and struck her down.

Meg was instantly covered in white ice—frozen solid. Then, with a snapping sound, her body shattered into pieces. I barely had time to take in what had happened before Alice stepped between Jenny and the voice from the darkness, protecting her from the malevolence of Golgoth.

My heart leaped in fear for her. She would be the next to die. Dressed in green and brown, with an emerald clasp holding her dark hair back from her forehead, she glowed with beauty. In seconds that lovely skin would be shriveled with cold and her bones made so brittle that they would snap like twigs. Despite her powerful magic, Alice was mortal; she could not resist the wrath of one of the Old Gods.

As I watched, I saw anger flicker across Alice's brow. Despite everything, she was determined to fight. She raised her arms and began to chant. Sparks danced at her fingertips. Then she hurled a bolt of light into the darkness, straight at our enemy, and I heard a cry of pain and anger.

I was astonished. Had Alice really hurt Golgoth? Was she that strong? Did she have a chance of winning?

But then, immediately, Golgoth retaliated. Alice fell to her knees, her whole body instantly dusted with frost. And now, out of the dark, a pair of huge, malevolent red eyes glared at her—the eyes of the Old God.

Alice was finished. What chance did she have against such ancient power? I was trembling with emotion. But what could I do? Nobody could save her now.

However, I gripped the Starblade and stepped forward. Golgoth was not using magic now. He was exerting the force of his essential being; that extreme coldness was part of him, and the Starblade offered no protection against that. I could feel the cold eating into my own bones. I wanted to run at him, but all I could do was stagger forward, realizing that it was over. We were all about to die.

The cold intensified further. I drew a breath, and the freezing air seared my nostrils and burned my throat.

Alice was now on her knees, covering her face with her hands.

"No!" cried a furious voice, and suddenly Grimalkin was running toward those baleful eyes, hurling her blades as she did so. She moved with the consummate grace of the skillful assassin that she had always been, but the courage that had helped her triumph against overwhelming odds was now surely sending her toward her death.

In an instant she was white from head to foot and halted in midstride. My heart sank into my boots as I saw her toppling like a tree. The moment her arms, head, and upper body struck the ground, she shattered into pieces. There was no blood, just white fragments of what appeared to be ice. Her flesh, blood, and bone had been frozen with such intense cold that she'd become brittle.

When Golgoth finally left this place, these fragments would thaw, just as Morgan's had. I had to acknowledge that Grimalkin was dead.

35
Boy of Tears

I gazed down in anguish. Grimalkin was a witch, but she had also been my ally and my friend. We had shared much together, and I felt a stab of loss in my heart.

It was then that I heard the music. Suddenly I was filled with hope, for it was a thin, high melody played on pipes: the music of Pan.

Suddenly Pan materialized to our right, bathed in a bright green light. He was sitting on the floor, his back against the wall, dressed in garments that were made out of leaves, grass, and bark. He was very pale, but apart from his ears, which were elongated and pointed, he looked like a human boy. Then I noticed his bare feet, with their long toenails that curled up into spirals.

Alice had told me that an Old God would not risk confrontation with one of his peers—but Pan had come to protect her.

The pipes at his lips looked like simple reeds, but the music was extraordinary. It had bewitched the animals that had materialized with him: rabbits, hares, mice, stoats, ferrets, and squirrels gamboled around him. Small birds circled his head, flapping their wings. A white dove perched on his shoulder.

Pan was smiling and looked utterly serene, happy, and confident. He was here to fight Golgoth.

But which Old God would prove to be the stronger? I wondered.

All at once I noticed the ice begin to form on Pan's feet; the animals around him were quickly coated with frost. And was I imagining it, or was the music now fainter?

Alice was crawling back toward the near wall. I saw the dove on Pan's shoulder topple forward and shatter on the mosaic floor like a glass goblet. The music died, and Pan dropped the pipes as he reached forward and touched the frozen fragments of the dead bird, his face twisted with grief. The other small birds began to drop, one by one, crunching onto the ground and exploding into pieces of white ice.

Rather than facing the glaring red eyes, Pan turned back toward us, his face full of grief and terror. Tears began to trickle down his cheeks; he looked like a child frightened of the dark.

At first I thought that Pan was looking at me, but then I realized he was staring at Alice. She had risen to her feet and had turned to face him, her whole body shaking. She was trying to speak, and I could see the terror on her face.

Slowly, as she struggled, I saw her expression change: the fear went. Now her face flamed with anger.

Suddenly she cried out to Pan. "Boy of tears—get up off your knees and fight!" she screamed. "Get up and fight! Be a man, not a boy! Shift your shape!"

In that instant I understood what Alice was attempting to do. Pan, the god of nature, had two aspects. First was the benevolent boy playing his pipes and charming the creatures of the forest. The second aspect was huge and terrible—nobody could look upon that face and live. The name Pan had given us the word "panic," the state induced in those exposed to that dread apparition.

Alice's words had the effect she intended. The boy vanished, and something huge reared up in his place.

Pan let out a great roar of anger. It was thunder; it was an avalanche racing down a mountain, destroying everything in its path; it was a giant wave obliterating a coastal town; it was the magma at the earth's core spewing forth fire; it was a blade of green grass splitting a rock.

He was now huge, towering up toward the roof of the barrow, still vaguely human in shape but somehow more than that. And the green aura that surrounded him was changing—first to orange, then to red. I could feel warmth on my face.

"Get down!" Alice screamed. "Cover your faces!"

I dropped the Starblade and threw myself down onto the rocky floor, shielding my head with my arms as best I could. But the light was so bright that I could see my bones through the flesh. It was as if the fierce fire of the sun itself was in the cavern with us. We were surely all going to burn.

Then the pain became unbearable, and I lost consciousness.

I remember very clearly the moment I awoke.

I saw Alice sitting by my bed, and for a moment I forgot all that had happened between us. I was back to the first year of my apprenticeship, looking at the beautiful girl who had been my closest friend, who had shared my life at the Spook's house in Chipenden.

Then everything came flooding back, and I sat up suddenly, grief tearing at my insides. I realized that we were back in the winter house.

"Take it easy, Tom," Alice said softly. "You've suffered

no permanent damage, but there are superficial burns to your arms, back, and shoulders. The worst trauma was in your head. Some have been driven mad when Pan is close. Once I'd brought us all back here, you were put to bed and given a sleeping draft. You've been asleep for almost two days."

"Is Jenny all right?" I asked.

"Yes. I shielded her with my body, and she came off far better than you. She's out hunting rabbits."

"Grimalkin!" I cried, remembering what had happened to her, seeing her bones shatter on the floor. "How can we manage without her? Why did she run at Golgoth like that? What a stupid waste. It was suicidal."

Alice smiled sadly and shook her head. "There was nothing stupid about it. Grimalkin knew exactly what she was doing, Tom. She didn't throw her life away needlessly. She did it to save me from Golgoth's wrath. In seconds I'd have been dead, frozen solid. She died in order to buy us all a little more time."

"I still can't believe that she's dead. It's a terrible loss. Did Pan destroy Golgoth?"

Alice shook her head. "No, but he hurt him badly and sent him back to his own domain in the dark. For now, the portal is closed and sealed, but Golgoth will eventually heal and be as strong as ever. And Pan drained a lot of his own strength to achieve that. He'll need time to recover too. The battle between them is far from over. One big danger now is that Talkus will now intervene directly."

"We'd have no defense against him then. . . ."

"Ain't quite true, Tom. He's still not reached his full strength, though if it happens soon, we'll struggle," Alice replied.

"Poor Meg," I said.

"Yes, poor Meg—but she was brave, wasn't she? Meg bought me the time I needed to begin my magic. Though I think *her* time had come, Tom. She came back to the County to find John Gregory, but he was already dead. Maybe she didn't want to live anyway. Who knows? Anyway, the Round Loaf will be her tomb, and also the tomb of Grimalkin. I replaced the stone and covered it with earth."

"The sad thing is that Meg and John Gregory won't be together after death," I said. "She's gone to the dark, while he'll have gone to the light."

Alice nodded, and I saw the sadness in her face. We both knew that the situation was similar to our own, but we let it remain unspoken. Then she came closer and put her arms around me. She was warm, and I was hungry for the heat of her body, but inside I was still cold from my memories of the Butcher God.

Two weeks have passed since the traumatic events in the chamber below the Round Loaf, and we are back at Chipenden. Slowly I'm coming to terms with the death of Grimalkin, but our future looks bleak.

Even now, a decisive battle against the Kobalos is probably being fought. If the human army is defeated, our enemies will be free to cross the Northern Sea and invade our island.

My life at the moment is bittersweet. In one respect, I've never been happier. I'm with Alice, and that's a dream come true. But with that comes the bitter pain of antici-pated loss. Alice closed the portal to keep Golgoth at bay, but our enemy's mages can still use the space between worlds to reach the County. They could come for me and Alice at any time. Talkus, the new Kobalos god, might wield power against which we have no defense.

So our happiness might well be short-lived.

I continue to train Jenny, and she is working hard and learning fast. She would make a good spook. I only hope she gets the chance to become one.

As I write, the sky is darkening to the north, and the first snowflakes of an early winter are falling toward the Chipenden garden. If the dark army of the Kobalos arrives, we will defend the County and ourselves to the best of our ability. That's all we can do.

Thomas J. Ward

The Kobalos Threat

Grimalkin's Assessment

The Threat from the Cold

As the Kobalos expand outward from Valkarky, the cold will travel with them. The climate of the earth will change, brought about by their own magic, which has been increased by Talkus.

Their god is growing in strength and is beginning to dominate a number of the Old Gods, some of which are willing to serve him. At present, the foremost of these is Golgoth, the Lord of Winter, who will be only too happy to use his powers to ensure that green fields and forests are replaced by snow and a permanent sheet of ice. There is a threat of a new age of ice.

The cold, with temperatures below freezing, is the natural element of the Kobalos. Yet some of their mages behave in a puzzling way. The high mages like to position their towers over hot springs and bathe in near-scalding water. Either they enjoy the heat, or they are demonstrating their courage and hardiness. The haizda mages, who

369

usually live far from Kobalos territory, actually hibernate through the three coldest months of the winter. So why do they retreat from the cold into sleep?

These are mysteries that need to be solved.

The Threat from Kobalos Magic

The complex hierarchy of mages poses a variety of threats. As yet, we do not even know how many distinct categories there are. We have some knowledge of high mages and haizda mages, but the others are unknown and mysterious.

Their spells too are largely unknown to us. According to the manuscript of Browne, the ancient spook, Kobalos mages can create a tulpa—a thought given physical reality in the world. Such a tulpa might only be limited by the imagination of its creator. What demons and monsters might they unleash against us?

There is also their skill with chemical and biological magic. Pendle witches have in recent years created such creatures as Tibb, a seer born of a pig. It took the combined magic of two clans, the Malkins and the Deanes, to achieve that. But this was nothing compared to the threat and power of a battle entity such as a vartek.

Lukrasta and Alice may help to counter this, and I have arranged for additional help. Using a mirror, I have already contacted some of my sister witches back in Pendle. I hope that they will soon join us and use their collective magic against the Kobalos.

The Threat from Kobalos Weapons

Unfortunately, Grimalkin did not have the chance to write this section of her report before she died. But because of our failure to seize magical artifacts from the mage's kulad, she had already decided to use a variety of weapons that she had studied in other lands during her extensive travels. The new infantry maneuvers seem like a worthwhile defensive tactic. The ice chariots also seem promising. They would cut through the Kobalos army like a knife through butter. But I have no idea if Grimalkin managed to construct any of those chariots before she returned to the County to help us in the struggle against Golgoth.

Tom Ward

The Threat from the Domains of the Dark

The Kobalos mages appear not to recognize the dark as we know it and call it by a different name, Askana—though it seems to be a different way of interpreting the same thing. In addition to the place where witches and other servants of the dark go after death, each of the Old

Gods has his or her own domain, a dwelling place within the dark.

Both Alice Deane and Tom Ward have visited the domain that seems likely to be the home of Talkus. It certainly contains many skelts, which is the shape their god assumes. When Tom Ward was on the Wardstone, it there, and the skelts continued the process that he had begun—that of destroying the Fiend. They cut up his body and carried the pieces into a boiling lake. Alice is convinced that Talkus was waiting there, newly born, and that he consumed the Fiend and absorbed his power.

Talkus is now increasing the strength of his mages— though I fear that he may leave his domain and come directly into our world. Witches summoned the Fiend to earth. The Kobalos mages might well be able to do the same with Talkus. That is my greatest concern.

Glossary of the Kobalos World

Original written by Nicholas Browne
Notes added by Tom Ward and Grimalkin

Anchiette: A burrowing mammal found in northern forests on the edge of the snow line. The Kobalos consider them a delicacy eaten raw. There is little meat on the creature, but the leg bones are chewed with relish.

Note: I tried eating the creatures (which are hardly bigger than mice) and I definitely prefer rabbit. However, they are numerous and easy to catch, and are best eaten in a stew. With the addition of the correct herbs, the meal is tolerable.—*Grimalkin*

Askana: The dwelling place of the Kobalos gods. Probably just another term for the dark.

Note: This is intriguing. Nicholas Browne could be right, but could it be that the Kobalos gods exist outside what we term the dark? Cuchulain dwelled within the

Hollow Hills, accessed from Ireland. That too was not directly within the dark.—*Tom Ward*

Baelic: The ordinary low tongue of the Kobalos people, used only in informal situations between family or to show friendship. The true language of the Kobalos is Losta, which is also spoken by humans who border their territory. For a stranger to speak to another Kobalos in Baelic implies warmth, but it is sometimes used before a "trade" is made.

Balkai: The first and most powerful of the three Kobalos high mages who formed the triumvirate after the slaying of the king, and who now rule Valkarky.

Berserkers: These are Kobalos warriors sworn to die in battle.

Bindos: Bindos is the Kobalos law that demands each citizen sell at least one purra in the slave markets every forty years. Failure to do so makes the perpetrator of the crime an outcast, shunned by his fellows.

Boska: This is the breath of a Kobalos mage, which can be used to induce sudden unconsciousness, paralysis, or terror within a human victim. The mage varies the effects of boska by altering the chemical composition of his breath. It is also sometimes used to change the mood of animals.

Note: This was used against me; it leached the strength from my body. But I was taken by surprise. It is wise to be on our guard against such a threat and not allow a haizda mage to get close. Perhaps a scarf worn across the mouth and nose would prove an effective defense. Or perhaps plugs of wax could be fitted into the nostrils.— *Tom Ward*

Bychon: This is the Kobalos name for the spirit known in the County as a boggart.

Note: It will be interesting to discover whether these boggarts fall into the same categories we have in the County or whether there are new types there.—*Tom Ward*

Chaal: A substance used by a haizda mage to control the responses of his human victim.

Cumular Mountains: A high mountain range that marks the northwestern boundary of the Southern Peninsula.

Dendar Mountains: The high mountain range about seventy leagues southwest of Valkarky. In its foothills is the large kulad known as Karpotha. More slaves are bought and sold here than in all the other fortresses put together.

Dexturai: Kobalos changelings that are born of human females. Such creatures, although totally human in appearance, are susceptible to the will of any Kobalos. They are extremely strong and hardy and have the ability to become great warriors.

Eblis: This is the foremost of the Shaiksa, the Kobalos brotherhood of assassins. He slew the last king of Valkarky using a magical lance called the Kangadon. It is believed that he is over two thousand years old, and it is certain that he has never been bested in combat. The brotherhood refer to him by two other designations: He Who Cannot Be Defeated and He Who Can Never Die.

Erestaba: The Plain of Erestaba lies just north of the Shanna River, within the territory of the Kobalos.

Fittzanda Fissure: This is also known as the Great Fissure. It is an area of earthquakes and instability that marks the southern boundary of the Kobalos territories.

Note: The Fissure is north of the Shanna River, but both have been described by Browne as boundaries between Kobalos and human lands. It is likely that the borders have changed many times over the long years of conflict.—*Grimalkin*

Galena Sea: The sea southeast of Combesarke. It lies between that kingdom and Pennade.

Gannar Glacier: The great ice floe whose source is the Cumular Mountains.

Ghanbalsam: A resinous material bled from a ghanbala tree by a haizda mage and used as a base for ointments such as chaal.

Ghanbala: The deciduous gum tree most favored as a dwelling by a Kobalos haizda mage.

Haggenbrood: A warrior entity bred from the flesh of a human female. Its function is one of ritual combat. It has three selves, which share a common mind; they are, to all intents and purposes, one creature.

Haizda: This is the territory of a haizda mage; here he

hunts and farms the human beings he owns. He takes blood from them, and occasionally their souls.

Haizda mage: A rare type of Kobalos mage who dwells in his own territory far from Valkarky and gathers wisdom from territory he has marked as his own.

Homunculus: A small creature bred from the purrai in the skleech pens. They often have several selves, which like the Haggenbrood are controlled by a single mind. However, rather than being identical, each self has a specialized function, and only one of them is capable of speaking Losta.

Note: In Valkarky, I encountered the homunculus that was a servant to Slither. The one that could speak was like a small man, and it reported directly to the mage; another took the form of a rat and was used for espionage. I found it easy to control and subvert to my will. There was a third type, which was able to fly, but I did not see it. Such a creature could be used to gather information about us at long range. The three selves of the homunculus share one mind (as did the Haggenbrood); thus, what it sees is instantly known back in Valkarky.—*Grimalkin*

Hubris: The sin of pride against the gods. The full wrath of the gods is likely to be directed against one who persists in this sin in the face of repeated warnings. The very act of becoming a mage is in itself an act of hubris, and few live to progress beyond the period of novitiate.

Hybuski: Hybuski (commonly known as hyb) are a special type of warrior created and employed in battle by the Kobalos. They are a hybrid of Kobalos and horse, but possess other attributes designed for combat. Their upper body is hairy and muscular, combining exceptional strength with speed. They are capable of ripping an opponent to pieces. Their hands are also specially adapted for fighting.

Kangadon: This is the Lance That Cannot Be Broken, also known as the King Slayer, a lance of power crafted by the Kobalos high mages—although some believe that it was forged by their blacksmith god, Olkie.

Note: Grimalkin told me that this lance was finally broken by Slither, the haizda mage with whom she formed a temporary alliance. He used one of the skelt blades, Bone Cutter, to do so.—*Tom Ward*

Karpotha: The kulad in the foothills of the Dendar Mountains that holds the largest purrai slave markets. Most are held early in the spring.

Kartuna: This kulad is beyond the Shanna River. I believe it to be the tower once visited by the haizda mage called Slither; he escaped after slaying the incumbent high mage, Nunc. I believe that the second most powerful mage in the present triumvirate has now taken up residence there, in preference to Valkarky. Many of his magical artifacts will be stored in that tower.

Kashilowa: The gatekeeper of Valkarky, who is responsible for either allowing or refusing admittance to the city. It is a huge creature with one thousand legs and was created by mage magic to carry out its function.

Kastarand: This is the word for the Kobalos Holy War. They will wage it to rid the land of the humans, who they believe to be the descendants of escaped slaves. It cannot begin until Talkus, the god of the Kobalos, is born.

Kinhos: This is the "tawny death" that comes to victims of the haggenbrood.

Kobalos anatomy: A Kobalos has two hearts. The larger one is in the same approximate position as a human one. However, the second one is smaller, perhaps a quarter of the size, and lies near the base of the throat. If decapitation is not possible, both hearts must be pierced; otherwise, a dying Kobalos warrior will still be dangerous.

Kulad: A defensive tower built by the Kobalos that marks strategic positions on the border of their territories. Others deeper within their territory are used as slave markets.

Note: A number of kulads are also controlled by high mages. They use these as dwellings; they are also used to store their magic and magical artifacts.—*Grimalkin*

League: The distance a galloping horse can cover in five minutes.

Lenklewth: The second of the three Kobalos high mages who form the triumvirate.

Losta: This is the language spoken by all who inhabit the Southern Peninsula. This includes the Kobalos,

who claim that the language was stolen and degraded
by mankind. The Kobalos version of Losta contains a
lexis almost one third larger than that used by humans,
and perhaps gives some credence to their claims. It is
certainly a linguistic anomaly that two distinct species
should share a common language.

Note: The mage that I killed near Chipenden spoke the
language of our own land, rather than Losta. Grimalkin
says that the Kobalos mages have great linguistic skill
and have made it their business to learn the languages of
more distant lands in preparation for invading them.—
Tom Ward

Mages: There are many types of human mage; the same
is also true of the Kobalos. But for an outsider they are
very difficult to describe and categorize. However, the
highest rank is nominally that of a high mage. There is
also one type, the haizda mage, that does not fit within
that hierarchy, for these are outsiders who dwell in their
own individual territories far from Valkarky. Their powers are hard to quantify.

Mandrake: Sometimes called mandragora, this is a
root that resembles the human form and is sometimes

used by a Kobalos mage to give focus to the power that dwells within his mind.

Maljann: The third of three Kobalos high mages who form the triumvirate.

Note: During my visit to Valkarky, I fought and slew Maljann in the plunder room when attempting to regain my property. I do not know who replaced him.—*Grimalkin*

Northern kingdoms: This is the collective name sometimes given to the small kingdoms, such as Pwodente and Wayaland, which lie south of the Great Fissure. More usually it refers to all the kingdoms bordering Shallotte and Serwentia.

Note: I am surprised that Nicholas Browne does not mention Polyznia, the largest and most powerful of those principalities.—*Grimalkin*

Novitiate: This is the first stage of the learning process undertaken by a haizda mage, which lasts approximately thirty years. The candidate studies under one of the older and most powerful mages. If the novitiate is completed satisfactorily, the mage must then go off alone to study and develop his craft.

Note: I believe that the haizda mage slain near Chipenden by Thomas Ward had only just begun his novitiate, which was fortunate indeed. If the haizda had been such as Slither, the one I encountered in Valkarky, he would have proved a much more deadly opponent.—*Grimalkin*

Oscher: A substance which can be used as emergency food for horses; made from oats, it has special chemical additives that can sustain a beast of burden for the duration of a long journey. Unfortunately, it results in a severe shortening of the animal's life.

Olkie: This is the god of Kobalos blacksmiths. He has four arms and teeth made of brass. It is believed that he crafted the Kangadon, the magical lance that cannot be deflected from its target.

Oussa: The elite guard that serves and defends the triumvirate; also used to guard parties of slaves taken from Valkarky to the kulads to be bought and sold.

Plunder room: This is the vault where members of the

triumvirate store the items they have confiscated, by the power of magic, force of arms, or legal process. It is the most secure place in Valkarky.

Note: In order to retrieve the property that had been stolen from me, I successfully breached the defenses of this place, which Nicholas Browne describes above as "the most secure place in Valkarky." I did not find it difficult—but this may be accounted for by the fact that my abilities, both magical and martial, were unknown to the Kobalos. I will no doubt find their defenses will be much stronger the next time I venture into that city. Additionally, the birth of their god Talkus will at least triple the magical strength of the Kobalos mages.—*Grimalkin*

Polyznia: This is the largest and most prosperous of the northern principalities that border the Kobalos lands. Their army is small but well disciplined, and their archers and cavalry are first-class. They are ruled by a brave prince called Stanislaw.

Purra (plural purrai): The term used to denote one of the female purebred stock of humans bred into slavery by the Kobalos. The term is also applicable to those females who dwell within a haizda.

Salamander: A fire dragon tulpa.

Shaiksa: This is the highest order of Kobalos assassins. If one is slain, the remainder of the brotherhood are honor bound to hunt down his killer.

Note: Grimalkin told me that at the moment of death, a Shaiksa assassin has the ability to send a thought message to his brethren, telling them of the manner of his death and who is responsible. Members of the order will then hunt down his killer.—*Tom Ward*

Shakamure: The magecraft of haizda mages, which draws its power from the taking of human blood and the borrowing of souls.

Shanna River: The Shanna marks the old border between the northern human kingdoms and the territory of the Kobalos. Now Kobalos are often to be found south of this line. The treaty that agreed on this border has long been disregarded by both sides.

Note: Before the ritualistic challenge by the Shaiksa

assassin, all bands of Kobalos warriors retreated to their own side of the river. We have yet to learn the reason for this. Much of Kobalos behavior still remains a mystery.—*Grimalkin*

Shudru: The Kobalos term for the harsh winter of the northern kingdoms.

Shaiium: The time when a haizda mage faces a dangerous softening of his predatory nature.

Shapien: A small secret group of Kobalos within Valkarky, who are opposed to the trade in purrai.

Skelt: This is a creature that lives near water and kills its victims by inserting its long snout into their bodies and draining their blood. The Kobalos believe it is the shape that their god Talkus will assume at his birth.

Shleech pens: Pens within Valkarky where the Kobalos keep human female slaves, using them for food or to breed other new species and hybrid forms to do their bidding.

Shlutch: This is a type of creature employed by the

Kobalos as servants. Its specialty is cleaning the rapidly growing fungus from the walls and ceilings of the dwellings within Valkarky.

Skoya: The material of which Valkarky is constructed. It is formed within the bodies of whoskor.

Skulka: A poisonous water snake whose bite induces instant paralysis. It is much favored by Kobalos assassins, who use it to render their victims helpless before slaying them. After death, its toxins are impossible to detect in the victim's blood.

Slandata: This is what the high mage Lenklewth called the "shameful death." Reserved for rebellious purrai, it is designed to make them weep with pain. Many cuts are made with a poisonous blade. Even the shallowest cut causes agony—as I know to my cost.

Slarinda: These are the females of the Kobalos. They have been extinct for over three thousand years. They were murdered—slain by a cult of Kobalos males who hated women. Now Kobalos males are born of purrai, human females held prisoner in the skleech pens.

Talkus: The god of the Kobalos, who is not yet born. In form he will resemble the creature known as a skelt. Talkus means the God Who Is Yet to Be. He is sometimes also referred to as the Unborn.

Tantalingi: This is a method used by Kobalos mages to see into the future. The high mage Lenklewth claimed that it is superior to both the scrying of witches and the method used by the human mage Lukrasta.

Note: When the opportunity presents itself, I will investigate this further. The future is not fixed; it changes with each decision made and each action taken. Thus all such methods of far-seeing are far less than perfect. I suspect that Lenklewth was merely being boastful.—*Grimalkin*

Therskold: A threshold upon which a word of interdiction or harming has been laid. This is potent area of haizda strength, and it is dangerous—even for a human mage—to cross such a portal.

Note: When I examined the lair of the haizda mage near Chipenden, there was no barrier in place. This was no doubt because Tom Ward had already killed the mage. So I have yet to test the strength of such a defense. Whether or not the barriers that protected the plunder room were examples of therskold or something similar, I do not know. However, they were of little hindrance.—*Grimalkin*

Trade: Although the unit of currency is the valcon, many Kobalos, particularly haizda mages, rely on what they call trade. This implies an exchange of goods or services, but it is much more than that. It is a question of honor, and each party must keep its word, even if to do so means death.

Targon: This is the name that Abuskai, the dead Kobalos mage, gave to the being that guards the doorways of fire that lead to the domain of Talkus. Jenny encountered it in the attic in the tower, and it was extremely powerful and dangerous. By using salt and iron, she bought herself time to escape. I have no idea how such an entity might be destroyed.—*Tom Ward*

Triumvirate: The ruling body of Valkarky, composed of the three most powerful high mages in the city. It was first formed after the king of Valkarky was slain by Eblis, the Shaiksa assassin. It is essentially a dictatorship that uses ruthless means to hold on to power. Others are always waiting in the wings to replace the three mages.

Tulpa: A creature created within the mind of a mage and occasionally given form in the outer world.

Note: I have traveled extensively and probed into the esoteric arts of witches and mages, but this is a magical skill that I have never encountered before. Are Kobalos mages capable of this? If so, their creatures may be limited only by the extent of their imaginations.—*Grimalkin*

Note: The winged being that spoke to the magowie and seemed to bring me back to life was a tulpa, created from the imagination of Alice.—*Tom Ward*

Ulska: A deadly but rare Kobalos poison that burns its victim from within. It is also excreted from glands at the base of the claws of the haggenbrood. It results in kir-rhos, which is known as the tawny death.

Unktus: A minor Kobalos deity worshipped only by the lowest menials of the city. He is depicted with very small horns curving backward from the crown of his head.

Valcon: A small coin, usually referred to as a valc,

accepted throughout the southern peninsula. Made of an alloy that is one-tenth silver, a valcon is the wage paid daily to a Kobalos foot soldier.

Valkarky: The chief city of the Kobalos, which lies just within the Arctic Circle. Valkarky means the City of the Petrified Tree.

Vartek (plural varteki): The vartek was the most powerful of the three types of entity that I grew from the material found within the lair of the haizda mage. The fact that it can burrow through solid rock means that it could burst up out of the ground right in the midst of a human army, so that they scatter in terror. It has three bone-tipped tentacles, the ability to spit globules of acid that could burn flesh from bone, and fearsome teeth. It also has many legs and is capable of great speed. Although it is protected by black scales, its eyes and underbelly are vulnerable to blades. It is impossible to know what size a vartek would achieve once fully grown. It could be the most daunting of the battle entities that the Kobalos may deploy against us.—*Grimalkin*

Whalakai: Known as a vision of what is, this is an instant of perception that comes to either a high mage or a haizda mage. It is an epiphany, or moment of revelation, when the totality of a situation, with all the complexities that have led to it, are known to him in a flash of insight. The Kobalos believe this is a vision given to the mage by Talkus, their God Who Is Yet to Be, its purpose being to facilitate the path to his birth.

Whoskor: This is the collective name for the creatures subservient to the Kobalos who are engaged in the never-ending task of extending the city of Valkarky. They have sixteen legs, eight of which also function as arms and are used to shape the skoya, the soft stone that they exude from their mouths.

Widdershins: A movement which is counterclockwise or against the sun. Seen as counter to the natural order of things, it is sometimes employed by a Kobalos mage to assert his will upon the cosmos. Filled with hubris, it holds within it great risk.

Zanti: These were the first of the creatures that Grimalkin studied after creating them from the samples in the haizda mage's tree lair back in Chipenden. Human in shape, they are extremely thin, with spindly scaled arms and legs. Their heads are covered in black scales rather than hair, and their eyes are positioned wide apart like those of a bird, which allows them to see ahead, to the sides, and behind them.—*Tom Ward*